D0889147

The Perfect Distance

The Perfect Distance, Volume 1

Hannah Conrad

Published by Dimension Seal Studios, 2021.

THE PERFECT DISTANCE

First edition. February 14, 2021.

ISBN: 978-1393539544

Written by Hannah Conrad.

Table of Contents

For my friends I made on the U of M Equestrian Team.

Chapter One

She always felt there was a kind of blissful insanity when moving to a new barn. Excited freshmen and transfer students were arriving to the barn to try out for the huntseat equestrian team. This barn, the Akiyama Riding Academy, belonged to the college. Kyon University prided itself on one of the best riding programs in the country of Akiyama. Students took lessons, classes involving the horses, equestrian team practice, and competed in horse shows there. The high end show barn was a quick ten minute walk across campus.

Freshman Lucy Sumner couldn't resist gasping in shock. Her eyes took in the perfectly green acres of pasture, the spotless, elegant barn, and the pristine riding arenas. The white fences practically glistened in the sun.

With how beautiful the outside was, Lucy couldn't even begin to imagine what the inside of the barn looked like.

Well, she could imagine the horses. After all, that was the whole reason she was here. Sure, this barn was definitely completely different from the small family run barn she had taken lessons at. Lucy had ridden there her whole life and had leased a Fjord gelding named Ole until his retirement. But it was a barn, and therefore nothing she couldn't handle.

Or so she thought.

"Hey, Lucy! Aren't you forgetting something?"

The voice of her best friend, fellow freshman Harley Olin, jolted Lucy out of her thoughts. She felt relieved they were attending the same school as she tried to figure out what she had forgotten.

"Oh, what could I have possibly forgotten?" Lucy pondered. "I've got everything I need for tryouts. "Riding boots, breeches, gloves, show jacket... Oh no! My riding helmet! Harley, I must have left it in my dorm room. They won't even let me ride without one!"

Lucy's hands flew to her head. Sure enough, there was no helmet covering her vibrant red hair. Her twin braids were in place, but she must have left her helmet in her room. Before heading to the barn, Lucy had debated if she should have her hair in her favorite style. Although double braids was usually only used as a style for much younger equestrians, she had grown fond of the style. She wore her hair that way most days, although she usually no longer wore the bows at the ends, out of a desire to not be viewed as immature. She must have been focused on styling her hair that she had forgotten to bring the most important part of her gear.

"Hey, it's alright," Harley said, "I'm sure they've got spare helmets here."

"At a place like this!?" Lucy dropped her voice so that the other students bustling around them wouldn't overhear, "They probably expect all boots shined and not a speck of dirt anywhere; bringing your own helmet is probably on the list of rhetorical requirements!"

At this point, Lucy didn't have enough time to run back to her dorm. And she knew Harley didn't have enough time either. Tryouts would begin soon and she would risk being late if she left.

Harley opened his mouth to say something else, but Lucy cut him off, not wanting to discuss the matter anymore, "But whatever. It's my fault for being so incredibly idiotic and disorganized."

And then she stepped forward, wanting to get on with the events of the day before they could get any worse. But before her boot had even made contact once more with the ground, her shoulder and turned head made contact with something else that nearly threw her off balance. And if it weren't for the steady hand that reached out to catch her, she would have landed in the dirt.

"You forgot to mention clumsy," Harley muttered, attempting to hold back a laugh as a goofy smile grew across his face.

"Very funny," Lucy nearly stuck her tongue out at him, but the grip that was still on her arm brought her back to reality.

"I'm so—" Lucy started, turning to face whoever it was she'd run into. But just the sight of his eyes made her feel like maybe she wasn't even sorry at all.

"Sorry," the two said at the same time.

There was a long pause, and a gaze exchanged longer than necessary...

"Uh...I'm Matt," the red haired student finally let go of Lucy's arm, and then extended his hand, which Lucy took and shook as if on autopilot.

"I'm Lucy."

"Well, I sincerely apologize for running into you with my horse here. Or, well, he's not really mine, but he was the horse I was assigned to for tryouts."

"Oh, no, really it's fine. It was totally my fault..." and then not knowing what else to say, she turned her head. In the process, her gaze shifted to the bay horse at the end of the lead rope—a tall, muscled gelding—and facing the horse completely, she said, "Hello."

And then she cringed internally while attempting to remain calm. Had she really just said hello to the horse?

But Matt only smiled.

And while Lucy thought she could get lost staring at him all day, she suddenly remembered, "Um...I need to go! The tryouts! And I forgot my helmet, and—"

"Hey, slow down," Matt chuckled, "I have to put the horse in his pasture, but if you wait for me, you can borrow mine. I'll meet you in the lounge."

Lucy was about to ask where in the world the lounge was—or rather what in the world a lounge was even doing in a barn—but as if that had settled everything, Matt gave a wave, and walked off abruptly.

And Lucy only stared after him.

"Earth to Lucy."

Lucy whipped her head around, cheeks flushing, "I, uh..." she didn't know what to say.

"You found yourself a helmet. Although if you wouldn't have walked off so quickly, I was about to offer you mine. But you've got everything you need now, so let's go."

All Lucy could do was blush as she followed her friend into the barn.

But it didn't last for long.

Her embarrassment was once again replaced by shock when she realized she didn't even know which way to look first. There were so many stalls, so many horses...and it was all so perfectly and neatly arranged. There were three wash stalls, supply and feed rooms, and two aisles of stalls that both led to an indoor arena. And there was a *second* level. Obviously, this wasn't a level that there were horses on. But there were more supply rooms, a tack room that looked like it had a very strict order to it, and, of course, the lounge.

Sure, Lucy's barn may have had a hay loft as a second level, but this barn dwarfed almost every single other barn she had ever even visited both in size and immaculate organization.

And what was even more impressive was the amount of commodities that the lounge included. It took up at least half of the second level, with a view overlooking the massive expanse of the indoor arena. There were cushioned chairs at a table, two sofas, a microwave, a sink, and even lockers for students to put their belongings. And the floor was carpeted.

"Wow," was all Lucy could say, barely able to look past the extravagance of it all to notice the twenty or so other people standing in the room with them.

"All prospective members please sign in and sign the release form," Maria called, attempting to bring order to the disarray of anxious students that Lucy was now aware of, "And please put your check for the cost of the tryouts inside this envelope."

Maria was captain of the advanced team, who Lucy had met during orientation. She had also met Sydney, the intermediate team captain, and Flynn, the novice team captain. From orientation she had learned the team divisions, and that the team captains competed with their teams even though they took lessons separately.

But letting Maria's words sink in, Lucy grimaced. Twenty dollars to try out for the team. She worked a part time job at a coffee shop, but even that was not enough to fund her equestrian...addiction...without the support of her parents. And with a barn this fancy, she only assumed that the prices would continue to skyrocket.

But it was her only chance to ride while in college, and she wasn't going to let money stand in her way.

Or the fact that there were about twenty or thirty students trying out for four competition team positions. Those who didn't make it would still be allowed to take lessons, but wouldn't be able to compete. And while all Lucy really wanted was to be able to ride, a part of her desperately wanted to make the competition team. There was one position for the advanced jumping team, one for the intermediate jumping team, and two for the novice jumping team. And Lucy, based on her experience, would be trying out for one of the novice positions.

She listened with half an ear, as she tended to do when distracted, as Maria reviewed barn conduct before Harley's tryouts for the intermediate team began. She'd hear the same spiel before her own, anyway.

When Maria was finished talking, the room erupted into conversation once more, and it seemed that Lucy was the only one who noticed the door open. It was none other than

Matt, who smiled when he saw her and made his way over to her.

"Here you go," he said, handing her his helmet, "You might need to adjust it a little."

"Thank you so much," Lucy said, and before she could say anything else, he turned to leave.

And it wasn't until she left that she realized, "Wait I don't even know where to meet him to return it!"

"You'll figure it out," Harley reassured her, "And you'll probably see him here at the barn anyway. Put it on, and I'll help you adjust it."

But when Lucy turned the helmet upside down to put it on her head, a small piece of paper floated out of it.

Confused, Lucy picked it up.

And you can return it to me on Friday afternoon maybe, at the café?

Instantly, Lucy's cheeks flushed, but she grinned, "Smooth, Matt, real smooth."

The words were followed by his number.

"Just put the helmet on already so I can go find my horse," Harley rolled his eyes. But Lucy couldn't tell if he was happy for her, or perturbed.

AN HOUR LATER, HARLEY'S tryout was complete. And Lucy's was about to begin...

As soon as she found the bridle for the chestnut mare she had been assigned to ride!

Delaney, who Lucy had taken to calling Dee, was waiting patiently in her stall while Lucy furiously searched the tack room for the bridle she was looking for.

"Harley it's not here!" she exclaimed.

Not only was she nervous about her tryout, but now she would make a horrible first impression—by being late.

"Whoa, calm down there Feisty Pants," Harley laughed, using his elementary school nickname for her that had stuck, "I found it—it's in the wrong place."

Lucy breathed a sigh of relief, and headed over to where Harley was standing.

The bridle with the name tag of "Delaney" had somehow been placed on the hook labeled for "Legacy".

"Thanks Harley."

Lucy hurried downstairs, and quickly bridled the mare, who stood calmly, flicking her tail idly at the occasional fly.

"At least you're well behaved," Lucy told the placid horse.

Maria was sitting on the bleachers at the end of the indoor arena as Lucy walked in and joined about five other students. Sydney and Flynn were seated on either side of Maria. And the trainer who would be teaching their lessons, Coach Rattenber, (who everyone referred to as Coach R, or, more commonly 'the rat', although Lucy still wasn't exactly certain why) was sitting there as well.

The arena was huge. At the moment, one side of the arena had jumps set up, and the other half was sectioned off into a dressage arena. Lucy didn't know much about dressage, but she immediately recognized the little white fence that stood less than foot high, labeled with bold black letters at certain points where the rider would be asked to transition to a different movement or gait with the horse.

In addition to the vast expanse of space inside of the arena, there were two entrances, one from each side of the stables, and a large clock was present on one of the walls. The other long wall was covered in mirrors placed at a height where Lucy could see her reflection, so she would be able to see when she needed to adjust her position and posture.

"If each of you could make your way to the mounting block, then we can begin," Maria announced, "And please make sure you have your number; without it we can't identify you."

Lucy double checked that the white paper was tied around her show jacket. Thankfully, she had actually remembered it.

When it was her turn at the mounting block, Delaney stood still. But as soon as Lucy swung into the saddle and attempted to adjust her stirrups, the mare started walking forward.

"Dee," Lucy hissed, giving the mare a small tug on the reins, "Stay put."

When she released the reins, Dee was quiet just long enough for Lucy to shorten her left stirrups, as the current length was definitely too long for her. But then another horse, a gray gelding, was maneuvered too close for Dee's liking by another nervous rider, and the mare sidestepped and gave a small kick, which almost unseated Lucy who only had one foot in the stirrup.

"Easy," Lucy warned, slightly nervous now. Sure, Dee had been well-mannered on the ground. But it seemed as though Lucy had spoken too soon...

The other student, who offered Lucy a quick apology, moved her horse far away from Dee. Lucy made sure that the mare had plenty of room away from the other horses as the captains, who had been oblivious to Dee's outburst, instructed the riders to warm up.

Trying to keep her mind from focusing on how flighty and slightly aggressive Dee seemed to be behaving, she tried to remember the basics. Heels down, shoulders back, eyes up. She avoided the scrutinizing eyes of the captains, and focused instead on the horse in front of her.

"Okay everyone, posting trot, please," Maria called.

Don't forget your diagonal, Lucy's trainer's words flooded through her mind. This was something that Lucy seldom remembered, although it was also a basic. She need to rise up and down with the movement of the trot. In order to be on the proper diagonal, Lucy needed to rise as Dee's outside leg (the one closest to the wall) moved forward.

At first when Lucy asked for the trot, Dee pinned her ears, but she listened with the slightest squeeze, eager to fly forward and chase down the horse in front of her.

"Whoa," Lucy whispered, trying to urge the mare to slow by slowing her posting instead of pulling on the reins. She was being judged on every single minute riding skill, after all.

Once she had Dee at a collected trot, she was finally able to keep the mare at a decently paced rhythm.

"Now, change directions across the diagonal," Maria's voice broke the intense silence.

Lucy followed the lead of the rider in front of her, directing Dee with her leg as much as possible before using the reins, which she was finding to be slightly difficult. Dee was certainly headstrong, and Lucy could only hope that everything would go smoothly when they started jumping.

After they crossed the diagonal—literally riding a diagonal line from one end of the arena to the other—Lucy turned Dee to the left, simultaneously changing her posting diagonal. And surprisingly, Dee was moving well. She wasn't too fast, and she wasn't pulling at the bit.

"I want the following numbers to come to the center of the arena: 244, 231, and 305. The rest of you, please transition to the canter when you're ready. Then we'll have the groups switch and perform the same exercise," Maria said.

Lucy's number was 305, but she found that she was okay with being in the second group. It would give her time to think things through—something else she also had trouble with, whether riding or not.

She played it all out in her mind; she knew exactly what to do. She'd ask for the canter, but would also make sure she gave Dee a half halt as well, in the hopes of getting the mare to understand that they needed to perform a sane and slow canter. Because somehow, she could see Dee attempting to take off with her at a gallop.

Content with her plan, Lucy was completely calm and confident watching the other riders. But then, out of the corner of her eye, she noticed something that she couldn't quite draw her gaze away from.

A white horse had suddenly appeared on the other side of the arena, led by a platinum blonde who looked to be only a little older than Lucy herself. The blonde had her hair in a single braid beneath an all-black helmet, and the contrast of the two colors made the striking platinum blonde color seem almost white. She wore tan breeches, and tucked into them with a belt was a light blue collared shirt that read "Akiyama Riding Academy". Matching the shirt, she wore blue riding gloves, and the tall boots that she wore were completely spotless.

The white horse was spotless as well—and Lucy knew how difficult it was to keep a white horse from turning random shades of brown. Or green. In fact, it was almost impossible.

But both horse and rider were as pristine as this entire barn seemed to be.

And it wasn't until she had mounted and walked the horse into the dressage arena, straight in Lucy's direction, that she noticed Lucy staring.

When Lucy met the blonde's blue eyes, she knew she should have turned away, but she couldn't. There was something so captivating about the new presence in the arena—about this rider than Lucy had never seen before.

Suddenly, the blonde's eyebrows raised, and she lifted the riding crop that she was carrying ever so slightly, as if to tap her horse on the shoulder. But instead, she left it there, so that at about a thirty degree angle from the white horse's shoulder, the end of it could be followed all the way to the side of the arena—to the rail. Which was rather perplexing to Lucy because...

Oh, shit.

The rail.

The tryouts!

Her group!

"Number 305, a left lead canter, please."

Lucy finally heard the voice that she was sure she had missed the first time. Lucy noticed the blonde's mouth contort into the slightest hint of a smirk, and her face burned as she thought, *this is so not funny.*

Heart pounding, Lucy walked Dee to the rail.

Now the last thing I need is for you to misbehave, so listen to me! Lucy thought desperately to the horse beneath her, as if Dee could read her mind.

Lucy tried to clear her mind. Really, she did.

Sit back, heels down.

But those blue eyes were watching her every move.

And Lucy couldn't focus. She really couldn't.

Instead of sitting back, she felt herself leaning forward, and so Dee, who was all too eager and knew exactly what she was 'supposed' to do, picked up the canter lead on her own.

And it was the fastest thing that Lucy had ever felt in her life.

If anything could snap her back to reality, it was Dee's hooves pounding the dirt like a storm beneath her.

"Whoa," Lucy said instinctively, giving the mare small half halts as she fought to keep her balance. But she gave Dee her head in between the half halts, knowing that holding her head back the entire time would only agitate the chestnut horse more.

After one wild trip around the arena with the insane mare keeping her head high instead of down, Dee finally slowed her canter, and eventually started trotting again.

"That's okay," Maria said, "Good job keeping her under control. Now, we'll have you all go one at a time over the three jumps that are set up. You'll do the diagonal jump first, and then circle around to the two outside jumps."

Lucy could barely keep her breathing under control as she joined the rest of the students where they had lined up on the rail, in number order, leaving Lucy last. But as she walked the mare past the middle of the arena, where the jumping portion merged into the dressage portion, she saw the blonde rider trying to hold back a laugh with one hand over her mouth.

And she wasn't doing a very good job of it.

Can this get any worse, Lucy sighed inwardly.

All she had to do was get this crazy mare over three jumps without landing in the dirt.

And it seemed simple enough when she thought about it—almost as simple as the blonde rider had made the transition from the walk to the trot look when Lucy's attention had once again strayed to the other side of the arena as she waited for her turn—but it was much harder to accomplish when said crazy mare insisted on racing full speed ahead towards the first jump.

The distance was completely off. If Dee kept barreling forward that fast they'd crash straight into it before they even got over it.

Lucy leaned back as far as she could, and finally got the mare to slow down, only giving Dee rein over the fence so that she could stretch her neck and complete the jump.

Once they landed, Lucy gave the mare a firm half halt, and circled her around to the outside line of jumps, which were two red-and-white jumps in a row. As they headed forward, Lucy could feel the difference; she had now gained Dee's attention as the mare's canter strides shortened at Lucy's request.

Dee was quiet over the jump, and didn't try to take off with Lucy upon seeing the second jump in front of her. She waited for Lucy's cues, and Lucy breathed a huge sigh of relief as they landed from the second jump. She brought Dee down to the trot, and then to the walk, and, although the mare had definitely been high strung and inane in the beginning, she gave the chestnut a pat on the neck for her efforts.

"Thank you all for taking the time to try out," Maria said once Lucy had halted, "Our decisions will be made by the next meeting, and we'll discuss divisions, shows, lessons, and dues. Let the horses walk out for a few minutes to cool down."

Lucy gave Dee slightly longer reins at the walk, but kept them short enough just in case the spirited mare decided to bolt. Or kick. Or rear. Or buck. Or do whatever it was that could pop into her mind at any given moment.

And for the first time since she had started her jumping round, Lucy allowed her attention to stray back to the blonde rider.

Her horse was nothing short of perfection. *She* was nothing short of perfection...

And now as Lucy approached the middle of the arena, she noticed the blonde rider walk her horse over to the edge of the dressage arena and halt.

Lucy was confused, but didn't think much of it, continuing to walk past. But before she was out of earshot she heard the blonde say something that made all of her embarrassment return; something that, had Lucy known about it before, may have avoided this whole situation with Dee entirely. And she said it such a way that it wasn't quite berating, yet still retained a hint of laugh:

"Delaney's supposed to wear a martingale."

Chapter Two

"Lucy, it's all right. You did the best you could," Harley tried to console her after the tryouts were over, but nothing could keep Lucy from constantly reliving what felt like the most embarrassing thirty minutes of her life.

Lucy ran her fingers through Dee's copper mane, as the untacked horse stood silently in her stall, content with the attention.

And Lucy was content to say nothing, refusing to answer her friend.

"I'm going to wait outside. Come out when you're ready to go," Harley said finally.

Lucy sighed. She had yet to take Dee's tack back up to the tack room.

And she had no excuse for being rude to Harley—snapping at him the entire time she had untacked Dee. It wasn't his fault. He was right. It was going to be all right. And she had done the best that she could.

Mentally berating herself for both her performance and her reaction, Lucy juggled the saddle and the rest of Dee's tack and carried it upstairs.

As she was distracted, the redhead clumsily burst into the room, not looking where she was going, so it was no surprise when she (very ungracefully) walked right into a person who was walking towards the door.

And of course it was none other than the blonde rider she had seen in the arena before.

For the *second* time that day, she had walked into someone. That was a record, even for Lucy.

"I'm so sorry," Lucy's words were rushed, "I wasn't looking where I was going, and I was in a hurry because my friend is waiting to take me back to campus and I spent way too long untacking, and about before, with the martingale, I didn't see it and so I didn't realize that—"

"I'm around horses all the time. If I'm not getting kicked or stepped on or walked into then something would be wrong, wouldn't it?"

The words stopped Lucy's own, halting her rambling mouth abruptly; something that she didn't know that anything, or anyone, was capable of. She'd talked right over Lucy, which, in hind sight, Lucy found herself grateful for because she probably would have just continued to make a fool out of herself—but *still*!

And Lucy didn't know what to make of the tone the words held. Was she being sarcastic? Was she joking?

But before Lucy could dwell on it further, the blonde had already begun talking again.

"And about the martingale, I actually just had to put it back in the right place. One of the freshmen must have misplaced it during the morning tryouts. I found it where Legacy's bridle is supposed be. Lower classmen can be so irresponsible."

Yeah, Lucy thought. *I'm a freshman. A very clumsy and crazy and nervous freshman, but I do my best to be responsible.*

"But I need to get back downstairs. So if you don't mind..."

And Lucy realized that the entire time, she had been standing in the doorway, completely blocking the blonde rider from leaving.

"Oh."

That was all that Lucy could manage.

Stupid, stupid mouth.

Always blabbering nonstop until she needed it to work the most.

And who was this rider, anyway? Claiming that all lower classmen were irresponsible? Lucy was in no way irresponsible. In fact, she was inanely responsible; so much so that she had practically helped run the barn where she'd leased Chip!

But a quick, "Sorry," was all she said, and she moved forward into the tack room so that the blonde would have room to leave.

"I am a complete mess. And awful at making first impressions," Lucy muttered as soon as she was alone in the room, "But apparently not so bad as others."

She quickly put the saddle on its rack, and the bridle in its *proper* place.

She'd be lucky if she would even get to ride here at all, let alone make the team. As if her actual riding hadn't gone horribly enough, she already seemed to be making enemies.

CLASSES THE NEXT DAY were exhausting.

It was only Lucy's third day, and so far, she and her room-mate Kendra only had their pre-calculus class together.

Lucy was pleased that she was getting along so well with the freshman, whose blonde hair was so long it reached the middle of her back, but she found that she didn't recognize many students from her building in any of her classes, and it was primarily the students in her co-ed dorm building who she knew the best.

Well...make that a select *few* of the students in her build-ing who she knew the best. The list included Harley, of course, and Kendra, because they were roommates. It also included Owen, an extremely enthusiastic freshman who threw himself into any and every conversation even if he didn't know who he was talking to; this antic was the only reason Lucy could say that she knew a third person on cam-pus.

And she knew Matt.

The thought made her smile.

But...other than that, I pretty much know no one, Lucy sighed, walking to her first class of the day.

Chem lab.

At 9:05 in the morning.

How she despised morning classes!

What was this life anyway, forcing her to go to college in order to be successful, extracting all of the money from her bank account—in addition to the most expensive sport known to the world—and making classes start at ungodly hours that trudged on until sunset when she would drag her-self over to the dining hall and eat food that tasted like it had been last week's left overs, spending her days running from building to building, only to find inside every single classroom the same chalkboards, strict professors, cramped desks, and—

Familiar blonde hair!?

Lucy's eyes widened as she entered the chemistry lab.

What was that rider doing here? Lucy had thought she was a trainer, maybe. Or a worker exercising the horses. Because she clearly hadn't been participating in the tryouts.

But regardless, here she was.

And she knew every humiliating little thing that had happened a mere twenty four hours ago.

The blonde hadn't seen her, so Lucy took a seat at the opposite side of the room. She occupied herself with the lab manual until the professor came in and started talking about the course, and proper sanitation, and safety procedures—

"And I have already assigned lab partners, so please come look at the roster and see who you've been paired with for the semester."

Lucy sighed. She hated assigned partners, but it looked like in the long run, it would be a good thing. She didn't know anyone in this class, and so the predetermined arrangement would save her some trouble, and of course, the embarrassment that seemed to follow her everywhere.

She waited in the line of students to find out who she had been paired with, but before she even made it to the paper, she heard her name.

"You're Lucy Sumner, right?"

She turned in the direction of the voice that belonged to none other than the blonde rider.

What had Lucy done to deserve this? Life hated her.

And how had she already known Lucy's name?

But Lucy didn't dare ask. All she did was nod her head and follow the blonde over to the lab table where she had been sitting before.

"I already read through everything. Go get a graduated cylinder and a beaker. And make sure they're clean."

Yes ma'am, Lucy rolled her eyes once she had turned her back to the blonde.

And while the entire lab followed accordingly—as horribly as it had begun—Lucy couldn't deny that she was, ever so slightly, lucky in her lab partner assignment. She may not have a lab partner who was...how should she put it...*nice*.

But she certainly had a lab partner who knew exactly what she was doing.

And that, Lucy knew as she watched the rest of the class working, was something she could be grateful for. Because after completing the lab with half an hour still left of the two-hour lab period, Lucy realized that she might actually be able to take nap before her class at noon.

But first she needed to settle one thing.

"Who are you, anyway?" Lucy demanded, turning towards the blonde the second they had left the classroom.

"My name is Elise Kyon."

And as if that explained everything, she walked out the door without looking back.

Exasperated, Lucy made her way back to her dorm room, and was greeted by her roommate with the very uplifting question of: "So, are you going to have nightmares about it tonight?"

"Ugh, Kendra, it was awful!" Lucy wailed as she collapsed face-first onto her pillow.

"Well, you know what they say. Chem lab is the stuff that horror movies are made of."

"The lab itself wasn't even that bad! It's who I have to work with for the *entire* semester!"

So much for her nap. She was going to have to vent about this for at least an hour.

"Well, who is it?" Kendra asked.

"Elise Kyon."

"Wait. Are we talking about *the* Elise Kyon?" Kendra asked.

Lucy's head shot upright, "Do you know her?"

"Not personally, no. But I've heard everything about her. She's like the talk of the school. I know we've only been here for, what, three days now? Minus orientation. But please tell me that I'm not the only one who has been hearing about her nonstop."

"Uh, as far as I know, you're the only one. Please, enlighten me so I know what I'm going to be forced to deal with for two hours of every Wednesday of my life."

"She's the daughter of the ones who own Akiyama Riding Academy and founded the city of Kyon, hence the last name. They live there. I'm surprised you didn't notice it when you went for your tryout. I've heard the house is almost like a mansion. She's a senior, a business major, and manages all of the papers and financial stuff for the team and the barn. But everyone talks about her because she's never joined the riding team. And no one ever sees her ride. And not that I know anything about horses—because I don't, it's just not my thing—but I've heard that she'll only get on and warm up when other people are watching. She'll never actually ride in front of anyone, and she never jumps when anyone else is watching, either."

"Okay. So I'll admit I feel a little stupid for not realizing the connection," Lucy grinned sheepishly, "*But* I still don't understand why it gives her the right to act like she's better than everyone else."

Kendra shrugged, "Does anyone? I mean, from what I've heard, she pretty much keeps to herself. So...good luck with all of that. This is why I try to stay out of the way of upperclassmen. Although that junior, Flynn, is extremely good-looking."

"Yeah, well, we all knew that you were after him the minute you saw he was our tour guide during orientation," Lucy rolled her eyes, "Although...I can't quite say I agree with your opinion anymore after seeing a certain someone that I ran into. Like, I *literally* ran into him."

"Oh, Lucy, details! Is he tall? Handsome? Is he an equestrian too?" Kendra fired off questions, completely ignoring Lucy's mention of her clumsiness, which, if Lucy were being honest, she was completely okay with.

"Yes, yes, and yes," Lucy answered, the picture of Matt, with his red hair and, dare she admit it, *dreamy* eyes, coming to mind.

"What's his name?"

"Matt."

"Is he a freshman?"

"Actually," Lucy frowned, "I'm not sure. But...he gave me his number yesterday, and I guess you could say we kind of have an unofficial date on Friday."

"And *when* were you going to tell me this!" Kendra grinned, "This is so exciting!"

"I was going to get around to it," Lucy waved her hand as if to dismiss it all, "Clearly I've got plenty of other things on my mind."

"Have you talked to him about it yet?"

"No. I was going to text him tonight. He wants to meet me at the café, but I work in the morning. Good thing I don't have any classes on Fridays, huh?"

"Oh, don't rub it in!" Kendra exclaimed.

"I'd never," Lucy grinned playfully, "I just think it would be the *best* thing in the world to have to wake up for an eight a.m. *biology lab* on Friday mornings."

"Well, you know what?" Kendra huffed, "Maybe Flynn will be in it."

"Flynn is a *junior*. Why would he be in an entry level biology course?" Lucy laughed.

"Hey, wait a minute," Kendra stopped, growing serious, "That actually makes no sense. Elise's a senior. Why is she in a freshman chemistry lab?"

Lucy let the thought sink in.

"You know what, that is a very good question."

THURSDAY SOON ROLLED around, and the team meeting came even more quickly than anticipated.

Lucy was nervous as she made her way to the classroom where the meeting would be held, Harley walking by her side.

"Even if you don't make the team, you can still ride," he reminded her.

"I know," she said.

"Hey, if I made the team it'll be a miracle," Harley said, trying to lighten the mood, "Everyone else is so advanced."

"Right," Lucy played along, "Because everyone else has grown up riding sophisticated horses, and you've been trying to train a reindeer how to jump."

It was a very long-standing joke that the two shared.

Blitzen, Harley's own horse, who he boarded and was currently leasing out to another rider while Harley spent the school year in college, would participate every winter in the annual holiday parade in their hometown. Blitzen would be dressed up as a reindeer with antlers and all, pulling a carriage, in order to defray the cost of boarding fees.

"You know, Lucy, one day I'm going to enter him in a show and make him wear them," Harley said.

And at the thought of this, Lucy actually laughed. Harley always knew how to bring her back down to earth; make her feel better no matter the circumstance.

Spending the entire rest of the walk debating on whether or not Blitzen would look ridiculous or endearing, Lucy barely realized that they had reached their destination until they walked into the room that was filled with anxious faces that Lucy either recognized vaguely, or didn't recognize at all.

"Good evening," Maria's voice filled the room at seven on the dot, not wasting a single second, "We have you here tonight to discuss many things—one of which being the team assignments. However, first, I want to talk to you about what your obligation to the team entails. I want to begin with lessons. If you are on the team, you are expected to lesson twice a week, with your team. If you miss more than two lesson, you will not be able to participate in the show team for the rest of the semester, which is why, as you will see on the assignment sheet, we have picked reserves.

"That being said, reserves also lesson twice a week, and it is critical that they attempt to make all of their lessons, because it isn't always known when they will be needed for shows. And for anyone who has not made the team, you are still allowed to ride, and will be considered part of our club. There is always room to improve and try out again next year to join the team.

"There is a complete show schedule, and all show team participants are expected to attend every show. Emails will be sent out to team members detailing the show schedule, the lesson schedule, and when lessons will begin. If there is a conflict Flynn, Sydney, or I need to be made aware of this as soon as possible. As far as dues go, there is a ten dollar fee per semester to be part of a club on campus, and the combined cost for membership and showing is a fifty dollar annual fee. Lessons are forty dollars each. If there is—"

Forty dollars!?

Lucy didn't even think that with her job she'd be able to afford that when she was helping her parents pay the thousands of dollars for tuition, board, books, and her meal plan.

What was she going to do—especially if she made the team? That would be forty dollars *twice* a week!

Lucy sighed inwardly, and turned her attention back to Maria, who she realized she had been tuning out for the past few seconds.

"And now, before I release the team assignments, I would like to introduce you all to someone who some of you may already know, but most of you don't. This is Elise Kyon, and she will be the one dealing with all of the paperwork and finances for the team. And I believe that she also has some points to discuss with you."

Lucy didn't even notice the blonde's presence in the room until she looked to the left of Maria, where none other than Elise was sitting by the podium, next to Flynn and Sydney.

Elise got up to speak, her hair in that perfect braid, not a crease in her clothing, and Lucy didn't even hear a word she said. All she could think of was how quickly Elise could silence the entire room.

While Maria had been talking, some students had been having side conversations, whispering or talking to one another—probably about the chances they had of making the team—or texting with their phones in their laps.

But when Elise had stepped up to that podium to speak, the room had fallen silent, and the blonde's gaze, an almost icy one, had full command and attention.

Lucy didn't register anything the blonde was saying until the very end.

"...And lastly, please do try to keep everything in order, and put anything that you use back where you found it. During the tryouts there was a misplaced bridle and martingale, which caused some..."

Lucy waited for what Elise was going to say: disorder, miscommunication, problems—

Elise looked straight at Lucy, and said, "Chaos."

Chapter Three

L ucy's riding had not been *that* bad!

Delaney had been chaos—*not* Lucy! She had managed to keep that horse under control! She had managed to get that headstrong mare over the jumps *without* the martingale that she was supposed to have! If anything, Lucy had been completely collected and composed.

Well, ignoring the fact that you spent half of the time watching Elise...

And realization hit her square in the face.

Of course Elise was out to get her now.

Lucy had spent nearly her entire tryout *staring* at the blonde rider, taking an interest in her riding when she quite obviously preferred to go unnoticed.

It all made sense, with the rumors that Kendra had told her. Clearly it was an unspoken rule that Elise's riding was not to be criticized, scrutinized, or even observed.

"So now that all of this business is settled," Maria stood at the podium once more, "Please, in an *organized* fashion, come look at the team list in the front of the room."

And of course, since Maria had said 'organized', the entire room erupted into chaos—*See, Elise, this is the real definition of chaos*—pushing and shoving to get to the front.

Instead of jumping in with the mass of students, Lucy and Harley waited patiently as their fellow classmates gave elated shouts of "Yes!" or disappointed sighs. Lucy was now too nervous—and quite truthfully, too uptight and bothered by what Elise had said—to talk to Harley. And she didn't know what to do, because watching the storm of students crowding around the stapled piece of paper meant looking in a direction that was dangerously close to Elise—and the blonde was one person she did not want to have to see.

For a long time.

So instead she turned her head to the left, to look out the window.

But instead she noticed Matt, who, upon seeing her, raised his hand and waved from where he was sitting half way across the room.

Lucy smiled and waved back at him. And then he got up and walked over to where she was sitting.

Some things are going right, she thought, and sighed happily.

"I was going to text you tonight, but I forgot I'd see you here," Lucy said.

"And you didn't bring my helmet...so I guess that means we're still on for Friday?" Matt smiled.

"Yeah," Lucy confirmed, "I work until twelve, but how does one sound?"

"That sounds perfect," Matt said, "I'll see you then."

And then he turned to leave.

"Aren't you going to check the list?" Lucy asked.

"Well, all five of my brothers were champion riders on the team, so I'm pretty much guaranteed that spot on the advanced team," Matt gave a small shrug, as if it were nothing, but then he winked before walking out the door.

And no sooner had he left than Harley said, "I don't like him."

"Hey, don't be mean," Lucy narrowed her eyes.

"He's so full of himself."

"Well, I find confidence to be a very attractive quality," Lucy crossed her arms, not quite certain why she was suddenly so defensive. But she went along with it anyway.

"People talk about him, Lucy," Harley said, "And you don't even know the first thing about him."

"Why is it that everyone seems to know everything about everyone here except for me!" Lucy exclaimed, thinking back to how Kendra had known all of those details about Elise before Lucy had even known the blonde's name.

But if Harley wanted to know what in the world she meant, he didn't ask. Instead, he jumped right back to the matter at hand, "We're talking about this when we get back to the dorms."

"Sheesh. So overprotective," Lucy rolled her eyes.

But he was her best friend. And she owed it to him to at least listen to what he had to say.

By now the commotion had died down, and Lucy decided that it was safe to look at the paper.

Careful to avoid any contact whatsoever with Elise—eye contact included—Lucy made her way over to the table at the front of the room. Holding her breath, she searched the array of names and placements, and then there, under the listing for the novice team was...

Lucy Sumner

And she didn't even bother reading the other names below hers. For a moment she forgot about everything—Elise, Matt, Harley not approving of Matt, even the money issue—and jumped up and down, shoving the paper in Harley's face.

"I did it!" She exclaimed.

Harley smiled and said, "Of course you did."

Then he turned the paper to look for the intermediate team, and in the single spot available was Harley's name.

"Good job," Lucy told him, equally as happy for her best friend as he was for her.

"See, riding a reindeer has prepared me for the insanity that is college level riding," he joked, also forgetting their little dispute for the time being.

Before Lucy could do anything else, Maria walked up to her, and to Lucy's surprise, the advanced team captain began to talk to her, "Lucy, I just wanted to commend you on your ride at the tryouts. We chose you for the team because you handled Delaney so well. The way the shows are designed, you'll be riding different horses who you've never seen before, so you need to be prepared to deal with horses of all different personalities and temperaments. And you handled Delaney's unpredictability rather outstandingly."

"Th-thanks," Lucy stammered, honored to be getting such praise from the renowned team captain.

And when Lucy turned to go, for a brief and unintended moment, she caught Elise's eye over Maria's shoulder.

And besides the fact that the gaze was now slightly less icy than it had been before, Lucy could have sworn that she had seen the senior give her a small nod...of approval?

It was perplexing, considering Elise had just told the entire team, whether they had understood or not, that Lucy's ride at the tryouts had been chaotic.

But right now, Lucy was too elated to care.

She had made the team, and that was all that mattered.

THAT NIGHT, HARLEY hadn't mentioned anything about the 'Matt issue' as he had said he would. Either he had actually forgotten in the midst of the excitement, or, more likely, he didn't want to ruin Lucy's moment of happiness. Considering she had been a complete wreck of nerves and anxiety and embarrassment for the past forty eight hours, he had probably just given her time to revel in the moment of glory.

But by the time Friday morning rolled around and they were walking to the dining hall together for a quick breakfast before Lucy biked over to the coffee shop for work, he brought up the subject again, keeping his voice low so that no one would catch wind of their conversation.

"So about what I wanted to tell you last night," Harley said, "The students on my floor talk about Matt all the time. And they don't say very nice things, either."

"Like what," Lucy challenged.

"He's...how do I put this kindly...a player."

Lucy almost laughed aloud, "I never in a million years would have thought I'd hear you say that word."

"Lucy it's not funny. You heard him. He has *five* older brothers. He needs to do something to 'impress.'"

The impact of her best friend's words really set in at this point.

"I'll take care of myself," Lucy told him, "I promise. But I need to give him a chance. Just because people talk, doesn't mean it's true."

"I just hope you know what you're getting yourself into," Harley sighed.

Lucy said nothing else as she walked through the doors and into the dining hall. Through breakfast, they turned the conversation to classes, but neither could forget the air that was left by the previous conversation about Matt, and the walk back to their dorm building was silent.

"Well, I'll see you later," Harley said.

"See you," Lucy said as she grabbed her bike from the rack in front of her dorm building.

Cutting through the parking lot and onto the sidewalk, she pedaled the distance to the the coffee shop.

And she wished she had a car.

And then she remembered that it was either a car, or college.

Or more like, a car or riding.

But...it was only ten minutes of her life. She would live. And it was all worth it in the end; save the earth, go green. Think optimistic.

Because it was going to be a good day. As opposed to Monday nights, when she worked five hours straight, she only worked two and a half hours this morning.

And she had a date this afternoon. It was something to look forward to, although she found herself not quite as excited as she had been before with a small, uneasy feeling growing in her stomach as Harley's words still swirled in her mind.

A good day, Lucy thought as she opened the door and checked herself in.

She talked briefly with the other girl on her shift—both of them took orders at the counter. Even though it was one of the smaller coffee shops of the franchise, it was definitely busy, so there were two of them taking orders at all times.

And this meant that there weren't insanely long lines, and that Lucy had a chance to breathe every now and then.

Yes. It's definitely a good day.

That was, until *she* walked in.

Was this inevitable?

It so could have been avoided. It was like she was following Lucy *everywhere*. She showed up in the most obscure of places that Lucy could be; exactly during *Lucy's* tryouts, right in the middle of Lucy's *freshman* chemistry lab, and now, right at the beginning of Lucy's work shift.

Please don't let me be the one to take her order. Please don't make me talk to her. Please, please, please, please—

If only she could have been so fortunate.

The blonde didn't even look up when she ordered, instead opening her wallet and taking out a credit card in advance, "I'll just have an iced—" but when she did look up, there was the briefest of hesitations before she said, "coffee."

"Okay. Right. Iced coffee. That'll be 1.95."

Elise handed Lucy the credit card, and Lucy momentarily forgot how in the world to use it.

But she snapped out of it, moved on autopilot, and handed the card back to Elise.

And Elise said absolutely nothing else.

Why does this always have to happen to me? And then I can't even act right. Like she'll think anything that I do is ridiculous. She already does *think that everything I do is ridiculous.*

So much for her good day.

Lucy sighed as she constructed the drink.

It just had to be her. All the time.

She put the lid on the drink, and was in the middle of handing it to Elise when...

Crap!

"Um, you know what? I think I accidentally put chocolate in here too. Just give me a minute and I'll make you a new one," Lucy said, completely and utterly annoyed at the fact that she just couldn't seem to do anything right when Elise was around.

See, this is what happens when you get distracted. You think about these things too much and you're lucky that you have half a brain that actually notices your mistakes.

And she was so busy with her internal monologue that she didn't quite register the fact that the iced coffee was no longer in her hand; the blonde had already taken it.

"That's okay. I like chocolate," Elise said, and after taking a straw from the counter, she turned to leave, Lucy staring after her.

What just even happened!?

"SO WHAT ARE YOU GOING to wear?"

Lucy was exhausted beyond belief. Who knew that her morning shift could take such a toll?

"I have absolutely no clue," Lucy groaned.

"I'd say...something sort of casual. Because it's not really a *date* date. But not something *too* casual."

"You know what, Kendra?" Lucy smiled at her roommate, "Why don't you just pick something out for me. I need fifteen minutes to chill. I should have told him two. Not an hour after my shift was over."

"I'm on it!" Kendra exclaimed, all too eager to throw together an outfit.

Lucy remained flopped on the bed, not even dragging herself to her feet until she was certain that she would agree to whatever insane combination of clothing her roommate was putting together.

"So what about this?" Kendra asked.

It was a purple top, slightly ruffled at the bottom (which had clearly come from Kendra's closet and not her own), and a pair of black leggings.

"And I was thinking that flats would like nice with it, too."

"I approve," Lucy grinned, "And plus I'm too exhausted to argue."

But only forty minutes later, all of her exhaustion had been extinguished, replaced with nothing but excitement as Lucy made her way to the café which was located on the first floor of one of the main campus buildings. She had only been there once before, passing by to get a chocolate bar on the way to one of her classes. The first week was barely over, and she'd already diminished the stash of chocolate she had in her room by at least half.

But now, here she was again, walking towards the café...and for a completely different reason. Because there in the left corner of the café, having already saved them a table, was Matt. And just his smile was enough to erase any remaining thoughts of anxiety.

"Here's your helmet," she said, offering it back to him, "You really saved me that day. I don't know what I would have done without it."

"It was no problem at all," he said, "If you know what you want, I can order for you."

Seriously, what did she have to worry about? He was such a gentleman.

"That'd be great. I'll have a sandwich."

"Any particular kind?"

"Uh..." Lucy gave it some thought and then said, "Whatever looks good. As long as it's a sandwich, I'll eat it."

"Really?" Matt laughed, "Me too."

Lucy smiled again as he got into line.

He was really nice. And she could be herself around him without feeling like an idiot—something that was not quite possible around certain unmentioned others.

When he returned, they talked about so many different things, from Matt's five brothers, to horses, to Lucy's life at home. And when they were finished, he offered to walk her back to her dorm.

He opened the door for her, even though his dorm was still a few yards further down campus.

"Thanks," Lucy said.

"Well, you know what they say..."

"What do they say?" Lucy gave him a quizzical look.

"Love...is an open door," he smiled.

Lucy laughed, "You totally just made that up."

"Maybe," he said jokingly, his radiant smile never leaving his face, "maybe not."

Chapter Four

The email with the information that had been covered at the team meeting came that night.

And in short, it meant one of two things. Either Lucy would have to get *another* part time job in order to pay for the weekly Tuesday and Friday night lessons that began in a week, or she would have to quit the team and ride as part of the club.

"Why is it so much money?" Lucy sighed.

"Well, you know I'd offer to help you out—"

"Harley, that is out of the question," Lucy told him pointedly.

She was sitting in his dorm room, where they had been watching some random TV show while talking about their classes. But then she'd gotten the email notification on her phone—which she suddenly had the urge to hurl across the room.

It just wasn't *fair*!

"Well, there's also what Maria was talking about at the meeting," Harley said, "I don't think they put it in the email."

"What do you mean?" Lucy was confused.

"They said that if anyone thought that they'd have trouble paying, to email your respective team captain and that you'd be able to work something out," Harley informed her.

Oh, right, Lucy remembered, *I stopped listening the second I heard how much the lessons were.*

"I'm going to email Flynn right now," Lucy said, "And hopefully settle everything before the first lesson."

"You've got a week," Harley reassured her, "Everything's going to work out."

And, indeed, everything did work out...just not quite in the way that Lucy had expected.

Flynn had gotten back to her two days later, offering her something that he had worked out for her that would cut the cost of each of her lessons in half; a now manageable price.

Lucy would work at Akiyama Riding Academy twice a week, on Thursdays and Sundays.

Which gave her the inevitable and much displeasing opportunity to run into Elise during her work *again*.

But she couldn't say no.

She couldn't let some stuck-up senior keep her from riding on the team. This was something that Lucy had dreamed about! The one thing that had drawn her to this college to begin with!

Her work began this Thursday, before the lessons started.

And during chemistry on Wednesday, Elise made no mention of Lucy working the following day, and didn't once acknowledge their awkward encounter at the coffee shop.

In fact, she barely talked at all, which was no surprise to Lucy. But when she *did* say something...she sure knew how to get her point across.

If the senior wanted Lucy to get her something, Lucy got it. If the she wanted Lucy to write something down, Lucy wrote it. If she wanted Lucy to get out of her way, Lucy got out of her way; this Elise never had to ask twice.

And never once did she ask Lucy to take any measurements, or perform any technical part of the experiment. Never once did she ask Lucy's opinion.

Queen's orders, Lucy rolled her eyes.

Whatever Elise said was the right answer, and if it wasn't—well, Lucy had yet to find out what would happen if it wasn't. Every calculation that the senior would write on their lab report, Lucy quickly learned, would be rewarded with nothing short of a hundred percent when it was graded.

And Lucy, although she most certainly would have helped more if asked, could only attempt to follow the precision; could only attempt to understand why the orange liquid was being mixed with the yellow liquid and forming this solid thing that was somehow transcribed into words and numbers on the paper beneath Elise's hands. Because if Lucy asked the senior to slow down and explain something to her, she feared she might end up with a predicament not much different from Delaney's episode at the tryouts.

God. I just compared her to a moody mare, Lucy's thoughts were, at this point, unable to be kept back, along with a small laugh that slipped out before she could contain it.

Elise looked up from the paper, "Is there something you find funny?" she paused for a moment, and then said pointedly, "Because there's nothing that I find amusing about the fact that while I sit here and go through every calculation *for* you, you insist on interrupting me."

It took every bit of Lucy's strength not to laugh again in astonishment.

She's worse *than a moody mare.*

Lucy's phone buzzed the next morning, just as she was leaving her building for class. The message that she saw was from Matt.

Want to meet me for dinner in the dining hall tonight?

Lucy smiled at his message, and was about to accept the offer when she remembered that she had to leave at a quarter to five and spend three hours working at the barn.

I wish I could, but I can't. I'm working at the barn now. My first shift is tonight.

Regretfully, Lucy sent the message, choosing to leave out the part about *why* she was working at the barn.

And after that, the day seemed to go downhill.

"Hey, at least you'll be around the horses," Harley told her as she grabbed her bike to head to the barn.

Yeah, but I'll be around Elise, too.

"I know," she said, "Hopefully I'll see you later."

It was a shorter bike ride than it was to the coffee shop; it only took five minutes. It was definitely a walkable distance, but she preferred her bike, however ridiculous she looked pedaling in barn boots.

Lucy left her bike outside the barn where the cars were usually parked, and then realized as she walked into the barn that she had no idea where the office was located. And she knew that she needed to find the office in order to sign in for her shift. So she walked through the barn and followed the aisle around the indoor arena in the hopes of finding the office, and there, because life answered her prayers *sometimes*, was the office, all the way down past a supply closet.

But once she reached the door, Lucy wondered if she was supposed to knock. The door was shut, but she was here to work. Surely she wouldn't want other people thinking that she expected them to do things for her—like opening the door for her.

And there you go again, analyzing everything imaginable. Just open the damn door.

Without giving it another thought, Lucy did indeed open the door, walking into the office without hesitation.

And when she did she found Elise.

Sitting at a computer.

Surrounded by so many papers that were organized in such an immaculate manner, Lucy couldn't even begin to comprehend that it was possible.

And she was on the phone.

This was not what Lucy had been expecting at *all* when she'd (finally) come to terms with the fact that she would have to see Elise for an extra six hours of her life each week.

But it all made sense.

Elise was in charge of everything that fell under 'financial'. So of course, as a 'working student', Lucy would be her responsibility. Actually, from the looks of it, it seemed as though Elise practically ran the barn herself.

And so Elise would be her...boss?

Not that the senior didn't automatically assume that role any other time they interacted, so this would be no different. No different at all.

With the exception of the fact that Elise was currently wearing barn attire, it looked like this was shaping up to be *exactly* like their chemistry lab...

"You're late," Elise said once she put down the phone, "And don't you know how to knock?"

In the entirety of the situation, Lucy was all of two minutes late. And it was *technically* due to the fact that she had to wait for Elise to finish her phone call.

"Sorry," Lucy's voice came out softer than intended.

Was she really going to let Elise push her around?

"You sign in on the clipboard on the wall when you come in and when you leave. The first thing you need to do is switch turnout. All the horses outside come in, and all the horses inside go out, unless otherwise noted. And that is extremely important. There is a chart in the feed room that has the requirements for all of the horses. If it's written on the chart that a horse is lame, sick, supposed to be in a lesson, or anything else out of the ordinary, do *not* turn that horse out.

"Second, you are responsible for picking stalls. All twenty eight of them. And I hope you know what this entails—you're not spending time cleaning them completely or replacing the bedding; that gets done in the morning. And third, you are responsible for feeding the horses. The chart in the feed room that I mentioned before has everything written out.

"You are also expected to sweep the aisle—both the top and bottom levels—before leaving. If there are any problems, you are to let me know. Do you understand?"

"Yes," Lucy said, barely even daring to breathe.

Without further instruction, Lucy walked to the clipboard and penned her name and the time she had arrived. And she was halfway out of the office, just about to leave, when she heard Elise say, "And I'd appreciate if you shut the door."

Lucy wouldn't have been able to wipe the glare off of her face if she'd tried as she shut the office door a little more forcefully than necessary.

You don't appreciate anything I do.

By seven forty five, Lucy had successfully finished nearly all of her jobs. As she swept the upper level, she listened to the sounds of the horses below her.

A huff. A whinny. The occasional grunt. The jostling of feed buckets.

In a way it was comforting; a small sense of normalcy amidst how foreign this entire barn was to a girl who was used to a small farm.

When she returned to the office after sweeping, she found that the door was closed. But she could tell that the light was off, and Elise was nowhere to be seen.

Guess my knocking would fall on deaf ears, Lucy thought as she pushed the door open, turned on the light, and made her way over to sign out. *As anything I say would, even if she were here.*

It took her all of three seconds to write her name on that paper, but it was what she saw almost hidden in a corner behind it that made her stop in her tracks.

There was an entire bookcase in the corner of that office, with boxes of papers pushed up against it. It was filled with...trophies. And ribbons. And awards of every possible shape and size. Lucy would have added 'color' to that list, but the ribbons were nearly all blue. Nothing short of first place. And right on top sat a picture that Lucy had not seen walking in the first time—a picture that captured the moment of a small white Fjord pony, frozen in time, as he trotted regally across snow-covered pasture.

"So you show up late, and I still can't get rid of you even after your shift has ended?"

Lucy cringed at the words.

Dammit, why do you always have to do things like this? You really thought you could get away with snooping around her office?

Lucy turned to face Elise. Her boss. Her lab partner. Her classmate. Or...*whatever* she was to Lucy at this point.

And at first she was just going to apologize again.

But then...she had a better idea.

She was already walking on thin ice; what more did she have to lose? And so she spoke on impulse, without really thinking.

"Is he yours?"

The question, as Lucy had suspected, caught Elise off guard, and the senior's eyes widened slightly, looking first to the picture, and then back to Lucy.

Of course Elise hadn't been expecting Lucy to ask her such a question. Lucy was entirely sure that every single person in her own place would be too intimidated to even look Elise in the eye.

Although Elise's icy composure seemed to melt the slightest bit, she covered up her shock in an instant. And the words she spoke were short and curt, "He was."

And instead of walking into the office, she turned around and left the barn.

When Lucy arrived at the barn for her first lesson, she was nearly as nervous as she had been for her tryout. And her nerves were amplified by the fact that she didn't know anyone else on the novice team. She didn't even know who she was going to be assigned to ride!

But I guess that's an answer you'll get in a matter of minutes, Lucy thought as she made her way up to the lounge.

On the table, she saw a paper where her name was written next to a horse named Titan.

"I vaguely remember turning him out yesterday," she mused aloud as she searched for an empty locker for her bag.

Then, looking back at the list, she decided to figure out who exactly her two other teammates were. They were listed by first name only. The first was Belle and the second was Owen.

Seeing Owen's name, she gave a little sigh of relief that she'd know someone before she went to go find Titan and hopefully tack him properly this time. And thankfully, he was one of those horses that only needed the usual saddle and bridle. She led Titan into the arena, where she was pleased to find that the lesson went smoothly, and definitely much more relaxed than the tryouts. Although large and somewhat speedy, Titan was content to listen to Lucy's every cue both during flatwork and jumping.

And when the lesson was over, Owen came up to her, taking off his helmet to reveal hair sticking out in every direction—including right up from the middle of his head.

"You're Lucy, right?" he said, grinning broadly.

"That's me," Lucy told him.

"I thought I remembered you."

"Well, I definitely remember you," Lucy laughed, "You were the only one to talk to me and Harley the first day of orientation."

"Yeah I guess that's right," Owen said, but then he changed topics abruptly, "But I have to go talk to Elise and I was wondering if you've seen her."

"No, sorry," Lucy said.

Thank God.

Because after what Lucy had said to her last night, she was sure that the next time the blonde saw her, she would make her pay for it.

"But she's probably in her office," she offered.

"Probably," Owen agreed, "Thanks, Lucy."

"Sure," she said, watching Owen walk down the aisle that she had so tediously swept the day before.

And as he walked away, she couldn't help but wonder if he would notice the picture in that office.

The one that Lucy just couldn't stop *thinking* about.

The little Fjord pony looked so beautiful and gentle—reminding her so much of her old lease horse, Chip.

And after the way Elise had reacted to Lucy's question, there was only one explanation that Lucy could come up with to justify the senior's actions, and it was something that Lucy also couldn't stop thinking about, no matter how hard she tried.

Elise—the same cold and seemingly indifferent Elise who had nothing but criticism and orders to direct at her ever since Lucy had arrived—had once cared very much about something.

Chapter Five

"**L**ucy, the *door*."

It was about the fifth time she had come in for work.

And she still kept forgetting to close that damn door behind her, every single time she left. She remembered to knock, but could she remember to close it?

No.

Sighing, she turned and let the door click shut behind her.

At least Elise had addressed her by name—for once.

Not bothering to dwell on it, she instead focused her mind on other things, first and foremost being her job. She brought the horses in, and turned the rest of the horses out. Then she grabbed one of the wheelbarrows from the shed, hauled a pitchfork out of the supply closet, and began going down the stalls one by one. And even though she was literally ankle deep in horse crap, she didn't care. She loved spending time with the horses; the docile, easygoing horses that let her into their stalls for a few minutes always brightened her mood.

The fact that she could be so close to such an amazing animal was always something that was unfathomable to

Lucy. Here she was, shoulder to shoulder with a creature that could crush her if it wanted to, yet instead allowed her to share the wooden box of territory that was the only thing it could call its own.

But also by now, she knew well enough which horses would run her out of their little pieces of territory in seconds—the ones who greeted her with pinned back ears, or a threatening snap of the teeth.

And Lucy worked patiently with them.

She would talk to them in a calm tone; let them examine her hands before she attempted to halter them. Usually, she would end up putting these antsy horses on the crossties, knowing that by doing so, she was most likely dodging a kick or two, or a bite on the arm. But once she was finished dealing with these horses, she could spend some extra time with the select few horses she had taken a liking to.

As she worked, she found herself actually enjoying what she was doing; it was all to be on the show team after all, and the first show was coming up in a few short weeks.

In the days leading up to those weeks, so far, her jobs were going smoothly.

Her lessons were great—a way to let out her stress; to let her focus on nothing but herself, her riding, and the horse for an entire hour, which was something that was a rarity in the midst of insane college life.

But her classes weren't too difficult, either. The resulting grades of her first exams had been on the better side, which Lucy had been pleasantly surprised about.

She had had another date with Matt that went perfectly.

Or rather, with her usual amount of optimism, she'd taken to calling it a date, since he'd asked her out again—to dinner this time. So she assumed that this meant that they were together, even though she really knew nothing at all about relationships. They hadn't kissed...yet. But as of right now she was going to call it a relationship, even if it was in its very beginning stages. And she knew that this feeling was mutual.

And so things, it seemed, were going well.

LUCY WAS ASSIGNED TO Delaney again for her eighth lesson.

"But I was told to tell you to ride without her martingale," Rattenber told her.

"Do you know why?" Lucy asked.

"It was just noted here on the horse assignments, so I wanted to make sure you that you knew."

Okay then. Round two with crazy mare.

She quickly saddled and bridled Dee, and brought her to the arena.

Not falling for any of the chestnut's crazy antics, Lucy kept a firm grip on the reins as she adjusted her stirrups, and then circled the mare so that they were far away from the other two horses in the lesson.

Dee's energetic trot, she could tell, was about to break into a canter at any moment, but Lucy sat firmly, not letting the mare get away with anything.

"Now I want you all to canter once around the ring before we start jumping, but I think it would be best to go one at a time, so that Delaney doesn't chase down the other horses."

Lucy gave her trainer a grateful look.

You don't even know how happy that just made me.

She knew that if trying to control Dee's canter alone was difficult, it would be ten times harder with two other horses in the arena for the crazy mare to go running after.

Owen, riding Titan, went first, and Belle went second.

And then it was Lucy's turn.

"Let's make this a little more organized than the first time," Lucy whispered to the mare, whose ears flicked back in Lucy's direction.

Lucy sat the chestnut's bouncy trot, and Dee needed only the slightest of cues to start cantering in the corner.

Well, calling it a 'canter' would have been an understatement. Dee shot off like a bullet beneath her, and when Lucy attempted to half halt the mare, she only tossed her head up high—an act, Lucy knew, that the martingale would have prevented. Lucy felt almost like she was riding a rodeo pony, but she followed Dee's crazy fast canter as if velcroed into the saddle; she had dealt with too many stubborn horses to let Dee get away with this.

And so Lucy did something that sounded contradictory, but knew was right.

She softened her grip on the reins, giving Dee her head.

And she let the mare get it out of her system, bolting down the long end of the arena, before she used her leg to get her to slow down.

Only after she felt Dee's strides shorten did she once again attempt to give small half halts and bring the mare down to the trot, and then to the walk.

"Well done, Miss Sumner," Rattenber praised. "Now I've set up a small course. I want you to, one at a time of course, start with the outside line, followed by the diagonal fence, and then change directions across the diagonal to the single vertical set up next to the wall.

Lucy mentally drew lines from the first jump all the way to the last, outlining the pattern, and then visualized it as Owen began the course. He and Belle both had smooth rounds with only minor missteps.

And Lucy knew that her problem with Dee would come in the beginning, getting the mare to slow in front of the second jump, and also towards the end, making sure that Dee listened to her cues to change directions. But Lucy was determined; once she set her mind to something, she knew she could accomplish anything. And after all, she *had* managed to jump Dee at the tryouts without the martingale, so she shouldn't be nervous.

Lucy circled Dee, making sure she had the mare's attention (or at least as much of it as she ever could) before asking for the canter. And her difficulties arose just where she had identified them earlier. After landing from the first jump, Dee hit the gas pedal.

Hard.

And who told you that you could do that? Lucy thought to the insane mare.

She couldn't give Dee rein like she had previously in front of the jump because their takeoff wouldn't be set up right. So Lucy was forced to pull back on the reins more than she would have liked to.

Dee tossed her head in the air before the jump, and at first Lucy thought that she would refuse, but Lucy urged her on with her heels, and the mare launched herself over the one foot vertical as if it were a mountain.

Lucy, unprepared for a jump so large, ended up leaning on Dee's neck in order to keep herself upright, and the mare, feeling how unbalanced her rider was, threw in a small buck just for spite. But Lucy stuck it out, readjusting her left foot that had come dangerously close to sliding completely out of the stirrup, and continued asking Dee to turn across the diagonal.

Luckily, the diagonal jump was only a crossrail—meaning that instead of a pole straight across like a vertical would have, the two poles formed an 'x' so that the middle of the jump was lower.

But after landing, Lucy half halted Dee again, using her leg to bend the mare through the turn, only lengthening the reins once they were going straight along the long side of the arena.

And then suddenly...Dee felt like a different horse beneath her.

After their tug-of-war battle, Dee was satisfied with the release of the reins, content with the small amount of contact that Lucy had on the bit.

Dee slowed her stride, and dropped her head, taking the full five strides that Lucy had counted to approach the fence. She took off without hesitation, and when she landed, she didn't protest to circling back down to the trot. Lucy patted the mare's neck, proud of both Dee's newfound willingness to listen, and also, of herself.

She had gained Dee's full attention—and dare she say, respect?

Lucy walked Dee to the back of the line to wait for her turn to go over the course again. She was about to lean down and give Dee another pat, when she noticed something out of the corner of her eye.

A movement of from the second level above the arena; the back of a blonde braid disappearing into the tack room.

And suddenly it all fell into place.

Dee no longer needed that martingale because Lucy may have just finally gained the respect of a certain someone else.

"LUCY, PLEASE MAKE THAT God awful noise stop or so help me the one and only day you get to sleep late I will blare music like there is no tomorrow."

Although Kendra's threat was muffled by a pillow, Lucy knew that when it came to sleeping in, her roommate took it as seriously as her life.

Well, that and her inanely long hair.

"Ugh," Lucy groaned, rolling over to slap the alarm clock, "Fine."

She was most certainly not a morning person.

It took her about half an hour to get out of bed and tame the hair that stuck out from all sides of her head, leaving her ten minutes to throw on whatever she deemed comfortable enough to traipse around campus in, grab a quick breakfast from the dining hall, and run to her chemistry lab.

She got into the classroom with a minute to spare, throwing her books onto the table noisily beside Elise's just as the professor began talking. And not even a minute had passed after the professor had finished introducing the lab to the class before Elise was already instructing her to hold the test tube, which contained a metal that was to be melted in a liquid solution over the Bunsen burner on the lab table.

"So, uh, I read the lab in advance," Lucy said, holding the solution carefully so that she wouldn't drop it. Lucy hadn't planned on really talking to Elise today, after what had happened in the office with the picture, but once again, her mouth had a mind of its own.

"Did you?" Elise asked, but it was less of a question and more of a haphazard comment.

"Yeah. I did. I wouldn't have said so if I hadn't."

Well, even for Lucy's notorious ability to speak without thinking, that had been a very...*straightforward* comment. What did Lucy think she was doing?

"I never said you were lying," Elise said levelly.

Oh, so this is what it comes down to. She needs to have the last word. Always in control. Like with everything else. But if you want to play that way, Elise, then challenge accepted.

"Well now we're just being a bit presumptuous. No one ever said anything about lying at all," Lucy said innocently.

Elise narrowed her eyes, but Lucy could have sworn she saw the beginnings of a smirk tugging at the blonde's lips.

"*You* were the one who started defending yourself, thinking I was accusing you of something."

"Oh, what's this now? You were going to *accuse* me of something?"

"I never said that," Elise was definitely not going to back down, "I only mentioned that you thought that I would."

At this point, Lucy wasn't even sure she could keep up with Elise's logic. But she had finally gotten Elise to talk to her; to hold an almost *normal* conversation with her—as normal as anything with Elise could be, anyway.

"Well, I think if that you're going to accuse me of something then you'd better do it already," Lucy challenged, looking right into Elise's blue eyes.

Let's see you take orders from me for a change.

Elise didn't look away, but she paused for a moment, before finally saying, "You're going to set our experiment on fire."

"What?"

Elise reached over Lucy's arm and turned off the burner, brushing Lucy's hand with her own in the process, which caused a rather involuntary shiver to run down Lucy's spine. But the redhead ignored it, too focused on the entirety of the situation to care.

"I accuse you of almost setting our experiment on fire," Elise repeated.

Lucy may not have been listening so intently the first time, but she had been listening enough to know that Elise had not initially prefaced her sentence with the first three words that she had added to the new one.

Elise had actually done something that *Lucy* had told her to do.

Even if it was over something so ridiculously trivial.

"But...I didn't!" Lucy said proudly in response to the senior's comment.

Elise only gave her another disapproving look, but Lucy
figured that while she had the senior's attention, she may as
well try something else. Elise had let her ride Dee without
a martingale...so did that mean she would be willing to give
Lucy more responsibility in the classroom setting as well?

Lucy couldn't help the fact that her voice came out
timidly. But regardless, it still retained a sense of authority.
She needed to say this; desperately needed to know the answer, "And so...since I'm already holding the test tube you
wouldn't mind, then, if I measured out five milliliters of the
solution like the lab manual instructs?"

And Elise looked at her.

Really looked at her.

And a million things seemed to flash in her eyes: anger,
annoyance, indignation, shock, confusion.

Her mouth opened, as if to say something, but then it
was pressed into a thin line without letting anything out.

And then those blue eyes just seemed to...soften.

"No," Elise chose her words very carefully, "I wouldn't
mind."

And Lucy had to bite her lip to fight the smile that was
threatening to grow across her face.

Never before had she been so excited to perform a step
of a chemistry experiment.

Elise had *finally* let her do something; given up control
for the first time in what seemed like forever.

Mission accomplished.

Chapter Six

"So you won't even *believe* who I talked to this morning," Kendra gushed the following Tuesday afternoon, when Lucy was trying to complete her English paper before leaving for her lesson.

"Right, because by the way you're talking, I'd *never* guess," Lucy grinned at her roommate.

Kendra narrowed her eyes playfully, crossing her arms, "Well, fine then, if you don't want to know, I'll just go tell someone else."

"No!" Lucy cried, laughing now, "Tell me what he said!"

"Well, it wasn't really anything much," Kendra grew a bit more embarrassed now.

"Is that so?" Lucy rolled over from where she had been laying across her bed with her laptop, and reached out just enough to poke Kendra in the side, "There is *so* much more to it than that."

"Okay! Fine!" Kendra said, "So I was just walking along in the dining hall, trying to find a place to sit to eat because I actually had, like, twenty minutes before my class. And naturally, there was just about *nowhere* to sit. I was about to take everything back here to the room when I heard someone say 'there's a seat open here'. And I almost didn't turn around because who would be talking to me? I'm just a freshman, and I didn't know *anyone* who was sitting in there. But I turned around anyway, just in case for some insane reason someone really *had* been talking to me, and there he was. Sitting at the table that I had just walked past, that, as he said, had one open seat.

"Of course, he was sitting with a few of his friends, and I was like 'are you sure?' and he said 'it wouldn't be a problem at all'. And so I sat down because I couldn't leave after I'd just talked to him. And then he introduced himself—even though of course I already knew who he was—but *he* didn't know that I knew who he was, obviously. And then he started telling me how much he liked my hair and—"

"Okay, if you talk any more you're going to hyperventilate," Lucy laughed, "*Breathe.*"

Kendra then made an overly dramatized scene of taking in a huge breath, and then letting it out, "So anyway, Flynn started talking about horses. And he was telling me all about this one horse that they used to have at the academy named Maximus, who absolutely *hated* him for some reason. But then the horse was sold, ironically just when he realized that all he needed to do was give the horse a few apples to get on his good side. And *then* we somehow actually ended up talking about you. Because we were talking about roommates—"

At this Lucy raised her eyebrow pointedly.

"Don't worry! All good things!" Kendra held up her hands innocently. She took another breath and seemed to settle down, Lucy being grateful that her roommate had seemingly decided to spare the rest of the details of what would have most likely turned into a half hour long conversation, "But all in all it was one of the best reasons for waking up at eight in the morning."

"That's great," Lucy said.

"And then he said that I could possibly come with him to one of the horse shows!" Kendra squealed, not able to hold it back any longer.

"Punz, that's awesome," Lucy smiled again.

"So I guess I'll see you there, too," Kendra said. "It's your home show, right?"

Lucy nodded. The home show meant that the place where the team practiced—in their case, Akiyama Riding Academy—would host the competition. All of the other competition teams for the other participating colleges would travel to Akiyama Riding Academy and ride the horses there.

Which also meant that Lucy's team would be responsible for prepping all of the horses for the show.

That was going to be a *very* long morning.

"What am I supposed to wear?" Kendra asked.

Lucy rolled her eyes, "Seriously? It's in two weeks. Do we *have* to discuss this now?"

"Maybe. No," Kendra sighed, but then, contrary to her previous subdued response, blurted, "Yes!"

"Ugh," Lucy groaned, "If we do this now, I'm going to be late for my lesson. But don't forget that you at least need to wear *boots*, okay? Don't show up there in flats or heels."

And although Lucy was joking—of course Kendra knew *that* much about what to wear in a barn—her roommate nodded her head vigorously, in tune with every single word that Lucy was saying.

DEE WAS LESS OF A NUTCASE that night. Lucy finally got the mare to carry her head properly for most of the lesson.

And also for most of the lesson...she found herself looking for Elise on that second level. But every time she looked up, she was disappointed—actually *disappointed*—to find that the senior was nowhere to be seen.

She's probably just busy, Lucy thought. *And why do you even care, anyway?*

"I don't care," Lucy told herself, as she was untacking Dee in her stall after the lesson, "I *don't* care."

"What don't you care about?"

Lucy whipped her head around to find Owen standing there.

"Huh?" Lucy asked, although she had clearly heard Owen.

"I said what don't you care about?" Owen repeated.

It seemed innocent enough when he asked it.

But Lucy didn't know how to answer him. She couldn't tell him what she had been thinking this entire time. Because even if she did, then she would have to explain to him every single little thing that had happened between the two of them from the first time she met Elise all the way up to this very day.

"Um, I was just thinking about how I don't care that...Delaney no longer has a martingale. Since she's being halfway decent and all."

"Oh, yeah, I was wondering about that! How it was you who could manage her without it, and now you're the only one who gets to ride her. I wonder if it was Elise who decided that Delaney doesn't need it anymore."

Elise had everything *to do with it.*

But she gave Owen a small shrug and said, "Maybe."

"You should ask her."

"Uh...I don't think that'd be such a good idea. She might not necessarily...*appreciate* that," Lucy said, ending her words there.

"Why not? I bet that once you get to know her she's the kindest, sweetest, nicest—oh look, here she comes! We can ask her now!"

"Owen."

He ignored her.

"*Owen.*"

Owen turned around.

"Not right now, okay?"

Owen sighed, "Okay, suit yourself."

And without another word, he walked off.

"Why is it that every time he talks to me, it's about Elise?" Lucy whispered to Dee, turning back to the mare as she finished removing the saddle.

And she didn't turn around until she was sure she heard the aisle clear of footsteps; she didn't know if Elise had heard anything that Owen had said, but she didn't know if she could talk to her at the moment even if Elise hadn't heard anything.

Chem lab was cancelled the next morning.

Lucy received the email after she had woken up and gotten dressed, just for spite.

Oh well, she thought. *More time to do homework.*

But a part of her was disappointed.

She had actually been looking forward to her lab.

Looking forward to talking to Elise again.

Almost in the way that she had been disappointed that Elise hadn't been watching her lesson; but then again, it was also for a different reason. Because there was just something about the way that Elise acted away from the barn—almost like Lucy could see a whole different side of her.

Lucy sighed, putting her books back down on her bed and sitting down beside them.

What was it about Elise that made Lucy even *want* to get to know her better?

Why had Lucy gotten so excited last week when Elise let her do something in the lab?

Why was it that Lucy wanted Elise to give up her control; her reign?

Why did Lucy *care*?

She sighed.

Some things are just...too complicated.

AND AS IT TURNED OUT, some things really *were* just too complicated.

Or idiotically simple; whichever adjective fit the events of the following day the best.

They had gone out twice! *Twice,* before the reality of Harley's statements about Matt came crashing down on Lucy as the truth.

"I should have listen*ed* to you," Lucy cried, knowing that this whole problem could have been avoided had she indeed heeded her best friend's warnings. But it didn't change the fact that what was done was done. She was completely miserable, her tear-stained face buried in her pillows, as Harley sat on the edge of her bed, "but I was so...so blinded...he was just so...*perfect.*"

"Lucy he's the *furthest* thing from perfect," Harley said bitterly. And although Lucy couldn't see his face, she imagined it contorted into a worried and angry frown, "He's the reason you're so upset, and I can't stand seeing you like this. Man, do I just want to-"

"No, Harley!" Lucy exclaimed, sitting up abruptly, while attempting to wipe her tears away, "He doesn't even know that I know!"

"Lucy, I'm not going to let you stay in this relationship, especially when you've been together less than a month and he's already cheating on you!" Harley was outraged, "If you're not going to let me deal with him, then you need to end it."

"God, Harley. I know," Lucy's voice broke.

And Harley lowered his voice, wrapping a protective arm around her, "Hey, I'm sorry. I just...I hate how upset he's made you."

Upset was an understatement.

It was a million levels of upset that she never knew she could feel.

All she could see in her mind was Matt, kissing that other girl. Right in the middle of the dining hall. He hadn't even seen Lucy—hadn't seen her walk in, and then take off running for her dorm room.

"I never want to see him again," Lucy whispered.

"I could arrange for that."

Lucy had no doubt that Harley could. And would, considering his reaction to everything.

"No, you're right," Lucy said, "I'm the one who needs to end this. I can't let him see how much he's hurt me. I need to stand up for myself."

Harley nodded, "You can't let him break you, okay? I've known you practically my entire life. You're brave. You're strong. You can face him."

"And you know what?" Lucy said, her voice growing louder as she stood, "I'm finished crying over him. He's not worth it. He's the one who's wrong, not me! I shouldn't be the one upset—he should!"

"That's more like the Lucy I know," Harley managed a small smile.

"That's right! He's going *down*!" Lucy declared.

Then she paused, and her brief moment of confidence slowly died down, "But...I don't know how to make that happen."

"You need to confront him," Harley said, "In person."

"But *when*?" Lucy said as she sat back down, "And *where*? And *what* am I even supposed to say?"

"I know I can be quite the love expert sometimes," Harley joked, trying to diffuse the tension, "but I'm afraid the breakup phase isn't my forte."

"Oh, yeah," Lucy rolled her eyes, "Some love expert indeed."

"Hey," Harley held up his hands in mock defense, "I already told you that I'd be more than happy to take care of it for you my way. But you said you didn't want me to. You need to be the one to end it. And so...if I were you, I'd march myself right up to that idiot and tell him what the hell he deserves to hear."

"Which is?"

"Everything you told me, just ten times more confidently."

"Fine," Lucy sighed, "But for now...I need to clear my mind. I can't think about this anymore."

"I'm sure that our history class that starts in ten minutes will do a very good job of that," Harley attempted to joke again.

And he succeeded; a small smile had come to Lucy's face for the first time in two hours, "It definitely will not."

"I'm all for staying here and watching mindless television shows while breaking into that stash of chocolate that I *know* you're hiding somewhere in here."

"That sounds a lot better than history class," Lucy's smile grew wider as she reached for the remote.

"Well, you know I'm only staying for the food. I wouldn't miss a lecture about world wars for *anything* else."

Lucy was actually laughing at this point.

She was so lucky to have a best friend who cared so much about her.

And so for the rest of the afternoon, Lucy was able to forget about her worries.

But by the time she had to bike over to the barn for her shift, Lucy was once again feeling upset.

She felt lethargic, dragging through her tasks.

And it was as if the horses sensed it. They would regard her with more concern and attention than they normally did when she entered their stalls, muzzles hovering the slightest second longer when Lucy's hand reached out to offer a half-hearted rub on the nose, or a scratch behind the ears.

And apparently, when it rained, it poured. Because by the time Lucy had finished her shift, after running out to bring the turned out horses in from the rain, the ground outside of the barn had turned to mud, and Lucy was a mess; her jacket was soaked through, and her boots had turned from black to a murky brown that left footprints behind her as she walked into the office.

And she was about to leave as quickly as she had arrived, when she was stopped in her tracks.

"Do you...want a ride?"

Lucy spun back around, shocked at the words she'd heard, but couldn't bring herself to give Elise an appropriate answer in a timely manner as incredulous thoughts ran through her mind.

"I just figured since it's pouring. And you biked over here. And since you also seem a little...off today."

She actually noticed? Lucy was amazed. *She actually knows that you bike here? And she actually notices that something's wrong?*

"I...uh..." Lucy trailed off before finally managing, "Yeah. That would be great."

"I'm not sure your bike will fit in my car though. You might have to leave it here."

"That's okay," Lucy said.

There was a slightly awkward silence after that as Elise continued writing on a paper on her desk. The senior hadn't looked back up at Lucy since the last time she had spoken. She merely finished writing, and was about to add the paper to a stack of identical ones on the corner of her desk when Lucy spoke up again.

She didn't know where it had come from, or what had prompted her to say it.

But it came out anyway.

"Matt is cheating on me."

Elise stopped everything that she had been doing, and looked up at Lucy, who couldn't tell if Elise was more surprised that Lucy had spoken, or what the words themselves meant.

And the second Lucy actually realized what she had said, she instantly attempted to string together an explanation, "Not that it's something you need to be concerned about. It's my own problem. I just...sorry. I shouldn't have said anything. I haven't been thinking much. At all. Clearly. But you had said that I seemed off today. So uh, yeah, that's why..." She trailed off lamely, looking to the floor.

God, Lucy, for once *could you just pull it together!? She doesn't care about your relationship problems!*

"Well," Elise said, still looking a little shocked at Lucy's sudden outburst, "I'm...sorry to hear that."

Wait, what!? First she actually notices things that you never thought she'd be considerate enough to notice, and now she's actually sorry *about what happened even though you so very ungraciously blurted it out from the middle of nowhere?*

"Really, though. I shouldn't have said anything. You have enough going on in your life as it is," Lucy still couldn't quite meet the senior's eye.

"Lucy, it's fine," Elise said as she got up from the desk, picking up her keys in the process. Then looking directly at Lucy, she added, "Sometimes we all have something we need someone else to hear."

That was probably the most sentimental thing the senior had ever said to Lucy, and it was all Lucy could think about as the two of them left the office.

"My car is parked at the house and not down here," Elise said as she reached for the jacket on the back of her chair.

"Walking for a minute in the rain is much better than biking back to campus in a downpour," Lucy said, pulling the hood of her own jacket over her head.

The two walked quickly out of the barn, where Elise led the way to a small silver car that was parked, just as the senior had said, right by the house.

When Lucy stepped inside she said, "Wow, this is a nice car."

And it was—there was no doubt about that.

Completely forgetting herself for a *second* time that evening, Lucy propped both of her feet up on the passenger side of the dashboard, saying "It's so much nicer than my old bike."

"God, Lucy, were you raised in a barn?"

Seriously, what the hell has gotten in *to you!?*

Lucy's face turned a pale shade of pink as she immediately removed her feet, visibly cringing when she saw the small streaks of dirt that her boots had left behind. And she was so busy trying to come up with a way to apologize that she barely even registered the fact that Elise was laughing.

She was *laughing*.

And then as if to prove that her comment was meant as a joke, Elise reached over and wiped the dirt away with the end of her sleeve.

Which left Lucy in complete shock.

She had just witnessed perfect, immaculate, spotless Elise clean the dashboard with her *sleeve*.

"And you thought *I* was raised in a barn?" Lucy was so amused she forgot about her own embarrassment.

"It's called being *resourceful*," Elise said as she backed the car out of its spot, "Which is the difference between being raised *next* to a barn and *in* a barn."

"I was *not* raised in a barn!" Lucy exclaimed.

"Okay, then where were you raised?"

"Maybe I was raised in a castle," Lucy shot back.

"Oh, were you now?" A smile tugged at the corner of Elise's lips, but she kept her eyes on the road, "And so were you the queen of this so-called 'castle'?"

"I was the *princess* actually," Lucy declared.

"And what did her royal highness do all that time in this castle before ending up at such an obscure little college campus?"

"Well...I talked to pictures," Lucy said matter-of-factly.

"What?"

"I had absolutely *no* one to talk to in my huge castle, so I talked to all the paintings on the walls."

"And they talked back."

"No, of course not!" Lucy exclaimed, "That'd be ridiculous!"

Elise laughed, "And you're just realizing this *now*?"

"No...I...I'm not...I don't know," Lucy suddenly grew embarrassed again.

Where had all of this come from, anyway?

"You've got quite an imagination," Elise said, turning to look at Lucy. And it was only the fact that Elise had taken her eyes off the road that made Lucy realize that they were already in the campus' main parking lot.

That had been a very quick few minutes. Even for the barn being right around the corner from the college.

Lucy only shrugged, "I guess."

"Well, I'll...see you on Sunday then?" Elise said.

"Yeah," Lucy said, as she reached for the door, "And thanks. For the ride."

Lucy expected the senior to just brush it off. Say that it was no big deal; not a problem.

But she was genuinely surprised by Elise's answer.

"Any time."

And Lucy couldn't quite keep herself from thinking that she wouldn't mind if it rained more often.

Chapter Seven

Lucy really didn't know how she was going to deal with Matt. Or when.

She wouldn't have minded avoiding it for another week.

Or two.

Or three.

But she couldn't ignore his texts for much longer without him noticing that something was wrong. And she didn't think she could survive another day with Harley constantly reminding her that she needed to deal with the situation.

Her mind was restless—conflicting emotions continued to plague her. She was still angry, first and foremost. But she was also still upset. And she was nervous because she didn't know how to face him.

And, it seemed, the only time she could actually forget about her problems was when she was around Elise.

Elise was the only one who knew about what was going on, yet didn't continue to talk about it with her like Harley or Kendra. It was as if the senior avoided any topic about emotions entirely. And she didn't strike Lucy as one of those people who constantly dwelled on everything. She just had this air about her: keep moving forward. No matter what. Just get back up and keep going.

I need to be more like that, Lucy thought to herself as she walked from the dining hall back to her dorm room, even though at this point, Lucy had successfully evaded the situation for about five days.

But, as life would have it, it would be avoidable for five days and no more.

Because there, walking directly towards her, with a large and *obviously* fake smile on his face, was Matt.

It was all Lucy could do to keep herself from visibly grimacing, or from running the other way.

Breathe, Lucy. Just breathe.

"Hey, beautiful," Matt' smile only grew wider, "I texted you last night. I thought maybe we could go out again this weekend."

Lucy felt her heart pounding.

"Matt..." She started, and then trailed off.

Confidence, Lucy. You need to just get this over and done with.

"Hey, what's wrong," he said, immediately noticing the change in Lucy's composure. He reached out to put an arm around Lucy's shoulder, and that was when something snapped inside of her.

"No," Lucy's voice grew slightly louder, "You don't get to touch me like that."

"Lucy, *what* is going on?" Matt asked, feigning innocence as he withdrew the hand that Lucy had pushed away.

"You...I-I *saw* you, Matt! You kissed that other girl. In the dining hall. You're *cheating* on me!" Lucy exclaimed.

"What are you talking about? How could you say that? I'd *never* cheat on you!"

"Matt, I *saw* you!"

"Well you *saw* wrong," Matt said, "And now here you are accusing me of something this absurd. I can't even trust you."

And now he's going to turn it around and blame it on me! Make me feel guilty when everything is his own fault!

Lucy's mind went wild as Matt continued to yell at her; continued to manipulate the situation to make it sound like *she* was in the wrong for falsely accusing him of something without any substantial proof, and how *he* was finished with *her* because of it.

Her head was spinning and his words were going in one ear and out the other, and she barely knew what was going on; could barely register Matt' angry face in front of her; couldn't even look him in the eye; could barely remember where she was...Until she turned away from Matt for a brief moment, and saw a familiar face over her shoulder.

It was a slightly surprised face.

One that didn't linger for long, not wanting to stare at the scene that was already attracting quite a few glances.

But one that lingered for a second longer than necessary, with a gaze that caught Lucy's eye.

Someone who reminded Lucy that she couldn't let Matt break her; couldn't give Matt the satisfaction of giving into his warped words.

Elise.

Lucy needed to stand her ground. She needed to show him that she wasn't afraid, even though she was quite terrified. She needed to take control of this situation; get his attention so that he was actually *listening* to her. And then make him understand what a complete—

"—*idiot* you are!"

Well now...*that* was the last straw.

"Matt, the only idiot around here is *you*!" Lucy snarled, "I *saw* you. Hell, the entire *dining hall* saw you. And you're going to act like it didn't happen? You're going to try to turn the situation around and blame *me*? Guilt me into thinking that I was wrong and that this is my fault, and that *you* don't deserve *me*? You're unbelievable, and it's disgusting. You can't talk to me about *trust*. You don't even know what trust is! And you...you are *not* allowed to dump me, Matt. *I* am dumping *you*! And I don't care that the whole school gets to witness this. I don't care that everyone gets to see this. Because now everyone gets to see what a *horrible* person you are! We're finished...even though there was really nothing much between us in the first place. But that's beside the point because we *are* finished, do you understand!?"

Matt was stunned. And while Lucy had had the urge to punch him in the face, she was fairly positive that her words had had enough of an impact.

She glared at him for a few seconds longer as the small group of staring students dispersed and went their separate ways.

But when everyone had left, and the two of them were standing there alone, Matt hissed, "I think we both have someone *else*."

And then before Lucy could say anything more, he turned away.

After all that he gets away with the last word!

She really did want to run after him and punch him in the face.

But she knew that would get her into much unwanted and unneeded trouble, and would only give Matt more satisfaction.

"Ugh!" Lucy exclaimed when Matt was out of earshot, "That good for nothing son of a—"

"Lucy!"

Lucy turned instantly to the sound of her name, seeing Harley running in her direction.

Before she could say anything to her best friend about what had happened he was already talking, "I was coming from class but I heard everything. I heard people talking and I ran right here and I just wanted to make sure you were okay..." Harley trailed off, trying to catch his breath.

"I'm fine," Lucy said, "He just *had* to have the last word. But I'm fine. It's over."

Harley wrapped his arms around Lucy, "I'm proud of you."

"I just don't understand what he said," Lucy said over her best friend's shoulder, "He tried to twist the situation and make it look like I was in the wrong. And then when he finally realized that he couldn't get away with that, he told me that I had someone else, too."

Harley pulled away, and looked directly at Lucy, "I don't want you worrying about a single thing he says. Okay? Forget about him. You weren't cheating on him. He was cheating on you."

"I *know* that," Lucy said, "But I just don't understand why he said that."

"Because he didn't want to be the only one in the wrong," Harley said, "You realized that yourself."

"And I'm not going to give it any more thought," Lucy said decidedly.

Because the effects of what had happened suddenly just seemed to settle in.

Relief hit her; it was a huge weight off of her shoulders.

She was free.

Free from Matt and all of the anxiety he had caused her.

And at the moment, there was no better feeling.

THE FOLLOWING SUNDAY, Lucy went straight to her shift at the barn.

The job had become routine enough by now; walk into that office. Sign her name on the paper.

And...close the door.

She knew well enough by now that she needed to shut that office door. As forgetful as she may be, after weeks of the same routine, she remembered.

But there was something about the way that Elise always reminded her before she left. Like Lucy was actually *needed* for something.

"The *door*, Lucy."

Now Lucy actually smiled—with her back to the senior, of course—when she shut that door behind her.

And if Elise was surprised that Lucy still 'couldn't re-member', she didn't let on about it.

Those three words...

After being ordered every Wednesday to 'get this' or 'do that'; after being instructed to 'put this horse here' or 'give this horse that'...the words weren't even commanding. Just a simple, plain reminder of a request that only Lucy and Lucy alone could accomplish.

And if Lucy were being extremely optimistic, she would even dare to say that they held a hint of amusement.

As Lucy grabbed her usual pitchfork and wheelbarrow and headed down the rows of horses, she couldn't help but feel even more relieved that Elise hadn't brought up anything about what had happened when Lucy had confronted Matt.

She just brushed it off, like always.

Pretending it hadn't even happened at all.

And Lucy was perfectly fine with that, because it gave her less to worry about.

Or rather, it gave her more time to worry about the show that was approaching in a matter of days.

And Rattenber worked them hard on Tuesday, since all lessons were cancelled on the Friday before the show so that both the horses and the students (but primarily the horses) were rested enough and prepared for the day-long show. It seemed as though the closer it came to shows, the more pressure Rattenber put on his students—and the more he seemed to live up to his nickname of 'the Rat'.

Rattenber put them through the first half hour without stirrups, but Lucy accepted the challenge.

While Titan was relaxed and calm, Lucy wouldn't quite consider him comfortable. His trot was choppy and bouncy, and his canter seemed flat. It was difficult for her to sit without leaning forward, but she fought for her balance and was grateful that they were allowed to work with stirrups for the jumping portion of the lesson.

And the riding wasn't even half as painful as Rattenber's comments—if he compared her to an animal *one* more time, Lucy could have sworn she would have just dismounted and stalked out of the arena.

"*Miss Sumner*, you're riding like a chicken with the face of a monkey! Your arms are flapping everywhere, and you need to *think* about where you're going. You need to ride more like an agile peacock—strong and confident, but *graceful*!"

Lucy didn't think she had ever heard anything so infuriating—but at the same time so downright hilarious—in her life. And she was still trying to suppress her laugher as she led Titan out of the arena.

"Well, that was rough," Owen said from where he was walking beside Lucy.

Lucy gave Owen a knowing look. Splash—a paint pony with plenty of speed and spirit—could be an interesting ride without stirrups.

"But look on the bright side—you stayed on," Lucy said.

"I'm glad about that," Owen said, "But it just reminds me of how out of shape I am! I used to avoid no stirrup work at all cost."

"Well, I guess we'd all better get used to it. Next thing you know he'll have us jumping an entire course without saddles."

Owen laughed as he turned Splash towards the opposite end of the aisle, "That'll be the day I land in the dirt."

Lucy only smiled after him and led Titan back to his stall where she removed the horse's tack and quickly brushed him down. Then, gathering everything that she needed to return to the tack room, she heard Rattenber call down the aisle, "And don't forget to sign up for the preparations for Saturday's show!"

Ugh, Lucy grimaced, *I forgot about that.*

She hurried to put away the tack and the brushes, and headed to the office. The door was closed, but she knocked as she was supposed to, and once inside, she walked over to the wall to find the sign-up sheet.

"It's not your work shift. You don't have to sign out from your lesson," Elise's comment held a bit of a laugh.

"No, I know that," Lucy said, turning around to face the senior, "Rat—uh, Rattenber said that we had to sign up for Saturday. To help out with the show."

"Oh," Elise said, "I didn't even put it up yet. But since you're already here, I guess you get first pick."

"Sounds good to me."

Elise reached into her bag which was sitting beside her desk, pulled out yet another manila folder that matched the many others that could be found *everywhere* in that office, and handed Lucy one of the papers inside.

Lucy took one glance at the list and said, "Wait, I thought we had to sign up for particular jobs."

"You sign up for a horse. It's your job to prepare the horse for the show, which includes grooming and braiding," Elise spoke to Lucy, but turned back to her computer, continuing whatever it was that she had been typing before.

"Well," Lucy said, "In that case I'll take Dee."

"Who?"

"Dee," Lucy repeated.

"I'm fairly certain that we don't have a horse named Dee."

"Oh," Lucy smiled sheepishly, "I meant Delaney. I kind of gave her a nickname."

"Okay then," Elise looked up from the computer and handed Lucy a pen, "*Dee* is all yours."

Lucy grinned, taking the pen and writing her name next to Delaney's.

"Will she wear her martingale for the show?" Lucy asked after she set the paper down on the desk.

"I think so. We wouldn't want a repeat performance from tryouts, now would we?" Elise told her, but her tone was teasing.

"Hey!" Lucy exclaimed, and then said pointedly, "I handled it very well. And thanks to all of the times I've worked her without one in lessons, she's learning to carry her head very nicely."

"So I've noticed."

You have?

"And I think you're doing a great job with her."

You do!?

"Oh...uh...thanks," Lucy managed, not used to receiving any compliments from the senior.

Elise waved it off with her hand, as if it were no big deal.

But it was a huge deal to Lucy.

Elise was so hard to please; so incredulously perfect. And yet she had just complimented Lucy.

Elise had just told Lucy that she had done something well.

✕

"I DON'T WANT TO BE here."

Lucy's groan was audible even though she had buried her face in Dee's copper mane.

It was six a.m. on Saturday morning, and Lucy couldn't help but wish that she could be back in her bed sleeping like every normal college student could on the weekend.

"You know, Dee, you're not quite as comfortable as a pillow, but you'll do," Lucy said as she yawned.

"Sleeping on the job?" Harley joked as he passed by.

"I am *not*," Lucy argued, but her head never left Dee's neck.

Harley only laughed as he turned to go.

Lucy could have sworn she had actually managed to close her eyes for a brief moment, but suddenly the chestnut mare shook her head and neck, freeing herself from the (most likely more annoying than uncomfortable) weight that was Lucy.

"I'm up this early for *you*," Lucy told the mare as she reached for a brush, "The least you can do is let me take a break."

Even though I've only been at this for ten minutes.

Lucy continued to talk to Dee as she groomed the mare, more to keep herself awake than anything else. And when she was finished grooming, she headed to the supply room. She rushed to find the string and scissors that were necessary for braiding, knowing that she had already wasted most of her time attempting to fully wake herself up. And if anything could wake her up completely, it was the commotion in the barn: students running this way and that, horses whinnying and moving and swishing their tails, and the exited, frantic, and nervous voices of her fellow teammates.

"Come on, Dee," Lucy said, leading the mare out of her stall, "Let's get you on the crossties. And hopefully you stand while I try to remember how to braid the right way."

Lucy had been taught how to braid...but she had never actually had a need to *use* the skills she had been taught because she had never really had the opportunity to show. Since this was the case, she attempted to remember what her old trainer had showed her, but everything ended up going wrong.

And she was about to give up about half an hour later. There were pieces of brown string pooled at her feet, Dee was so impatient on the crossties that she insisted on pawing the ground with her front hoof at any chance she could get, and Lucy's arms were so sore she didn't know how she'd even be able to ride when it came time to actually show.

"Having some trouble?"

Lucy whipped her head around to find Elise standing behind her, in a t-shirt...and shorts. She instantly wondered what had happened to the senior's professional appearance, but decided not to ask.

"Trouble would be an understatement," Lucy admitted, "I haven't braided in years."

"Well, we can't exactly have an unbraided horse for the show," Elise said seriously.

"I know," Lucy sighed, "I'm sorry. I should have asked for help beforehand. I didn't exactly realize how long it had been. I thought I'd be able to figure it out."

"That's okay," Elise said, "It's never too late to learn. Hand me the string. And the scissors."

Thank God, Lucy smiled as she handed over the requested items.

Maybe everything would work out after all.

Elise cut a much longer piece of string than Lucy had been working with before, and then gave both the string and scissors back to Lucy as she stepped closer to Dee, who was still shifting from side to side on the crossties.

Lucy watched intently as the senior demonstrated how to start the braid—pointing out all of the places where Lucy had gone wrong. The primary reason was that Lucy's braid hadn't been tight enough. And as Elise worked, Lucy couldn't help herself from noticing the precision of Elise's fingers. Of course, Elise had it somewhat easier, being slightly taller than Lucy. But she never missed a step, and then end product looked...well...the way it was *supposed* to look.

"You make it look so easy," Lucy complained.

"The years of experience are worth something, I guess."

Lucy didn't quite know what to make of Elise's comment, but she didn't exactly have time to analyze it. Instead, she focused on the matter at hand and said, "It makes sense now, but I don't know if I'll be able to finish in time. They need the horses completely ready in an hour and a half."

"I...guess I could help you finish," Elise offered.

"That would be *amazing*!" Lucy exclaimed.

"We'll just need to section her mane first so that she doesn't end up with a ridiculously small braid in the middle of her neck. And also, go do yourself a favor and get a stool from the supply room."

"Since when are there stools in the supply room!?"

"Since forever," Elise laughed, "Now hurry up, or we won't even finish with both of us working."

Wondering how in the world she had missed the stack of stools in the corner of the supply room (now diminished to only three with everyone braiding), Lucy grabbed one and brought it back. Then Lucy started braiding at Dee's head, and Elise at the base of Dee's neck.

Neither spoke while they worked, but Lucy found that she couldn't focus entirely on what she was doing. She kept looking over at Elise, still in awe at how quickly the senior could throw together one braid so perfectly without a single hair out of place. And she was also in awe of the fact that Elise didn't once seem to grow tired, because while she was taller than Lucy, and working at the lower part of Dee's neck, she still had her arms practically over her head.

This is the difference between having muscle and being a weakling, Lucy sighed. Her own arms were getting tired again even though she was standing on the stool. And she kept having to constantly reposition the stool as she worked her way lower down Dee's mane, while Elise, on the other hand, had to keep reaching higher in order to get the job done.

And at a certain point, Lucy couldn't help but notice that the senior's choice of clothing wasn't quite cut out for braiding. Because now every time she reached up, the hem of that t-shirt would move upwards as well.

Had Elise worn her usual polo shirt tucked into jeans or breeches, Lucy never would have seen it.

But she did, and it took everything in her not to audibly gasp in shock.

Because right above the top of those shorts Lucy saw what could be nothing but a tattoo—dark ink against Elise's pale skin.

Lucy could only see about half of it, as the other half was covered by the waistband of the shorts, but she guessed that it had to be a word. And she desperately tried to figure out what in the world is said, but before Lucy could it was covered once more, and replace by other words—*spoken* words—that turned Lucy's face from a light shade of pink to a deep crimson.

"The horse's mane is *up here*, Lucy."

And as if it weren't already embarrassing enough that Elise had noticed her staring, the senior actually sounded...*amused*.

Quickly, Lucy turned back to her half-finished braid, not once looking back at Elise until they had finished.

They hadn't quite met in the middle as planned; it was more like Elise had finished two thirds of the braids, each one the same size and shape, and then those perfect little braids met about ten or twelve large, messy, and rather unsightly ones closer to Dee's ears.

"Well," Elise said, "At least it's done."

Lucy nodded in agreement, but after checking her phone she became frantic again, "But what about her tail? And her forelock!? And she's supposed to be ready in fifteen minutes, and *I'm* supposed to be ready and I'm not even changed! I'm the second division. I have to go get my number and go tack up and—"

"Lucy," Elise interrupted the redhead's nervous string of worries, "I can finish it."

"Are you sure?" Lucy asked, not wanting to cause Elise any more trouble than she already had.

"It's fine," Elise said.

"Thank you *so* much!" Lucy exclaimed, "I'll stay later for my shift on Thursday to make up for it!"

"You don't have to do that. You're busy enough as it is."

"That's why I said *Thursday*. I'll barely be able to drag myself over here tomorrow!"

Lucy spun on her heels and left before Elise could say anything more.

HALF AN HOUR LATER, Lucy found herself atop a dun pony named Knight.

Just my luck that it's our home show and the one horse I get drawn for I've never even ridden!

At least she'd worked with him; knew his temperament on the ground from all of her rounds of turnout and stall cleaning. And thankfully, he was one of the more docile horses who didn't spook or grow angry easily.

The fourth rider in her division, Lucy was already warming up, and before she knew it, it was her turn to jump the course.

"You've got this Lucy," Harley said from where he stood by the gate, and Lucy smiled in return.

Kendra gave Lucy a thumbs up from where she sat in the stands next to Flynn, who was no doubt droning on and attempting to explain to Lucy's roommate the fine workings of the horse world (The part of the conversation Lucy had overheard was: "No, no, you've got it confused with jumpers. Hunters is judged mainly on the rider's *equitation*, that's why the courses aren't as complex!"). But Kendra didn't seem to mind; it was *who* she was talking to that mattered.

Lucy shot Kendra a small smile to acknowledge her roommate, and then without another thought, Lucy trotted Knight and transitioned to the canter.

The course wasn't anything too complicated. It consisted of about six jumps, all of them being crossrails except for the very last jump that looked to be a vertical about a foot high.

Knight took the jumps with ease, much to Lucy's relief. She didn't have to struggle with him, or fight him, or encourage him over the jumps. He was practically a push-button pony, and coming from Dee and quite a few of the other hot-tempered horses she had ridden, Knight was an angel. He kept a steady pace, not speeding up in front of the jumps, and had his own keen eye for distances.

When Lucy completed the course, she gave Knight a well-deserved pat on the neck. And when it came time for the awards later on in the afternoon, Lucy gave Knight many well-deserved carrots, because he had helped Lucy earn third place in the show, and Lucy couldn't have been any more elated.

"You're good for something, huh?" came a sneer from behind Lucy as people filed in and out of the aisle.

There were so many students from other schools heading back, talking, walking, eating, laughing...and she almost lost sight of the unwelcome commenter.

But then she saw him—the back of him anyway—already down by the doors.

Matt.

"You're horrible," Lucy seethed, eyes glaring after his retreating form.

She had known that he was here.

She had seen him take first place in his division. The perfect, wonderful, amazing champion.

"Anything *but*," Lucy muttered, "The only award you deserve is for being the biggest ass on the face of the earth."

"Is he giving you trouble again?" Harley walked up to Lucy after witnessing what had just happened.

She knew exactly the 'he' that Harley was referring to.

"More like just being annoying," Lucy said, but she brushed it off as quickly as she had let it get to her, instead turning her attention to the yellow ribbon in her hand, "But nothing's going to spoil my win!"

"Some of the team members are going out for an early dinner to celebrate," Harley said, "And I offered to drive. Want to come with?"

"Definitely!" Lucy exclaimed, giving Knight one final pat.

By the time she was finished giving the dun pony his extra attention, Harley was already half way down the barn aisle. And as she hurried to catch up with him, she nearly ran into Elise, who was coming down from the second level of the barn.

"I didn't expect you to be here still," Lucy said.

"Well, I kind of live here," Elise gave a small shrug.

"Oh, no I didn't mean it that way!" Lucy rushed to explain herself, "I just remembered people saying that you didn't stick around for the shows. I mean, not that you shouldn't. Like you said, you live here. I just thought that maybe you came down in the morning to make sure that things were running smoothly. Which...clearly they weren't with me, anyway."

"Technically I'm off today. Actually, the whole place is closed on Saturdays. Except for the weekend of the home show," Elise said. "But of course I'm never *really* off. Because guess who gets called first if something's wrong? Me. Just like every single day I'm *not* off."

That would explain the shorts and t-shirt, Lucy thought. But she didn't mention it, instead only saying, "I don't blame you for trying to get away."

It seemed as though Elise's job entailed much more than just finances and paperwork—Elise practically ran the entire business. Which was an added amount of work when said business required the care of multiple living creatures.

"It's life," Elise said, turning to go; brushing off her small moment of exasperation as if it were no big deal. As if it shouldn't be something she or anyone else should be worrying about.

But before she could leave, Lucy asked, "Why did you stay, then? Today, I mean?"

Elise only shrugged again, her back to Lucy, "Usually I don't. Sometimes I do."

Chapter Eight

"So does your offer still stand?"

"Huh?" Lucy listened with half an ear as she expertly maneuvered a snappy palomino onto the crossties before the mare had a chance to take off her arm.

"You said you'd stay later today. In exchange for helping you with braiding," Elise said, placing a hand on the halter of the palomino horse as she tried to swing her head angrily in the senior's direction despite the constraint of the crossties.

"Oh. Right," Lucy remembered, not able to tell if Elise was serious or not, "Sure."

"Only if you're not busy," Elise said, "It really isn't necessary, but I actually found something that I could use some extra assistance with."

"Well, you're in luck. My history exam was moved from tomorrow to Monday, so I'm free," Lucy joked, and then turning back to the palomino, she asked, "What's wrong with her today? She's usually so calm."

"The vet came this morning," Elise explained, "She doesn't take too kindly to needles."

"You little grump," Lucy told the mare, who pinned her ears as Lucy took her off the crossties and led her back into the stall that she had just finished cleaning.

"I'll let you finish up, then," Elise told Lucy once she had walked back out of the palomino's stall.

"Yeah. It shouldn't take me much longer," Lucy said, "Just feeding and sweeping."

And Lucy moved quickly through the rest of her work, wondering what in the world it was that Elise actually needed extra help with. She had been expecting that maybe something needed to be organized or cleaned, or a particular horse needed medication, or maybe a hay load had been delivered late...

"I was hoping that you'd be able to help me with a new horse," Elise said to her in the office about an hour later, wiping away all of Lucy's previous predictions, "He's a new training project that my parents invested in. I was hoping to work with him on the lunge line under saddle."

"Okay, so do you want me to go grab the lunge line? Where is it? In the supply room?"

"Actually..." Elise trailed off for a moment before saying, "I was going to ask you to ride."

"Oh," Lucy said—one syllable worth of shock, excitement, and nervousness.

First Elise had recognized her ability with Dee, and now the senior was trusting her with a new horse in the middle of training?

"I like to watch the horses move with someone else riding before actually working with them, and of course my parents went to see him when I was in school," Elise explained.

"That's fine with me," Lucy said, "I can go tack him up then. Which horse is it?"

"His name is Lance," Elise said, "And I know you've been working with all of the horses, but just remember to be careful around him. There's a reason he's considered a training project."

"Okay," was all Lucy could manage.

It wasn't that she was afraid of the (possibly) crazy horse. She just still couldn't believe that Elise *trusted* her to ride the crazy project horse.

Lucy walked down the aisle and found Lance's stall. And when she got there, she vaguely remembered the huge black warmblood horse with only a small white star marking below his forelock.

"You're the one who needs the chain," Lucy recalled, eyeing the same lead rope she had used to bring the horse in from turnout earlier that evening.

Lance huffed and pinned his ears when Lucy entered his stall, but Lucy spoke to him in order to calm him down, "Lance, it's okay. We're just going to go for a little ride, that's all."

The large horse's shoulder was well above Lucy's head as she led him to the crossties. The chain was merely a safety precaution; a small portion of the lead rope that ran through the rings on the halter, over the nose, that gave the handler more control and dissuaded the horse from tossing his head up and out of the handler's grasp.

Lucy briefly thought that maybe she should have gotten Lance's tack beforehand, so that she wouldn't have had to leave the clearly impatient and agitated horse on the crossties. But there was no way she was putting the horse back in his stall and going through the trouble of leading him back out and onto the crossties again.

Looks like this one's going to be a lot of work, she thought as she hurried upstairs first for her helmet and then for the tack, *Guess that's another reason Elise wants someone else to try him out first.*

But Lucy wasn't going to let the horse intimidate her. Even when Lance struck out with his back hoof when she tightened the girth, and snapped at her when she tried to bridle him, she didn't let him get away with his actions. She made sure that he was listening to her as she led him into the arena, not letting him drag her down the barn aisle.

Elise was already waiting in the arena with the lunge line, and Lucy swung into the saddle without further instruction, but after that, she waited for Elise to tell her what to do, because she had never really been in this position before. She barely dared to walk forward without being asked, and was glad when Elise finally said something (instead of staring at her with an expectant look as if Lucy should already know what she was supposed to do...).

Yes, Elise gave Lucy instruction all the time, but never while riding. And it just felt odd, being atop the horse with Elise telling her what to do. Lucy wanted to make sure that she did what she was told, but at the same time, what if Lance started acting up? What if Elise asked Lucy to do something that she couldn't do? Not that there was anything about this angry horse that scared her; she could handle him, she was sure of it. But the other strange thing was that she found herself wanting to...impress.

She had to remind herself of all of the basics, almost as if it were tryouts on repeat. She didn't want Elise to have to correct her, to tell her that her position wasn't right, or that her heel wasn't down far enough, or that she was on the wrong posting diagonal.

"You're on the wrong diagonal."

Of course, Lucy fought the urge to roll her eyes. *Just focus on the horse. Focus on Lance. Forget about everything else. Just. Lance.*

Lucy quickly fixed her mistake. And she knew that Elise had only pointed it out because Lance was a horse in training; even though it was a small mistake, anything could throw Lance off.

Lucy found it a little difficult to adjust to Lance's gait, because even though he was on the lunge line, meaning that the lunge line connected to the horse's bridle and he was moving in circles around Elise who was holding the end of the lunge line, Lance would still speed up every now and then. He would lengthen his stride, and Elise would tell her to correct him by giving him half halts; tell her to not let him get away with it even though this was just so that she could watch him move.

I could just change my position, Lucy wanted to say, *and use my leg instead of pulling on the reins.*

But she kept her mouth shut, not wanting to challenge the senior who clearly held authority. Lucy couldn't let herself forget that. This was Elise's life, Elise's job, and virtually Elise's horse. Lucy had to do as she was told...

And while she knew that this was how it had to be, Lucy found it increasingly more difficult to fight the urge to speak her opinion. Because by the time Lance was cantering, all he wanted was to take off galloping.

"Lucy, bring him back to the trot. Make him walk, and then when he's listening to you ask him to canter again."

Lucy did as Elise said, but it only earned the same response from an even more agitated Lance, and after working on the transition a few more times, Lance was starting to hold his head high, not taking kindly to the constant pressure on the bit.

"Halt him," Elise said, "He needs to understand that he can't get away with taking off like this."

Lucy fought slightly with the stubborn horse before he started trotting again, but not matter how hard Lucy tried, Lance would continue to throw in steps of the canter, until Lucy finally gave up the tug of war and just let the horse go, against Elise's request.

"Lucy, that's not halting him."

"I know, but..." Lucy paused, not knowing whether to continue. But seeing as she was the one on the horse, and the one with the most control over the horse at the moment, she decided to share her opinion with Elise, "Fighting with him isn't going to work. It'll only make him fight back harder. I think we just need to let him get it out of his system. And then get him to listen."

"So that he learns that he can take off with students and potential buyers in the future? I don't think so," Elise said, her voice firm, "He needs to learn now."

"Well, it's going to take some time, anyway. He's really green."

"That doesn't matter. The point is that he needs to learn how to behave himself before he has the chance to form these habits."

"This is only *helping* him form those habits," Lucy muttered. And she hadn't intended for the senior to hear, but clearly, Elise had.

"Lucy, I asked for your help, not your opinion. So if you don't like the way I'm handling this, then *halt the horse* and get off."

Now look what you've gotten yourself into, Lucy's mind was racing with thoughts at this point.

She was angry at herself for challenging the senior. But she was even angrier that Elise wouldn't take her opinions into consideration. Lucy felt that in this particular situation, she should most certainly be allowed to have an opinion since she, being on the horse and not on the ground, was the one who would be most affected if something were to go wrong. And clearly Elise had to respect her riding—and her ideas about riding—*somewhat* in order for her to have asked Lucy to help with Lance in the first place.

But no, she can never be wrong. And she'll never admit it, even if she knows it. Even if it's true and I'm saying it to her face.

Lance was still cantering beneath her, but her whole body seemed to be on autopilot, and while her thoughts were filled with nothing but annoyance, she wasn't entirely focused on Lance. And Lance, who had been previously trying to take advantage of a completely focused rider, jumped at the chance to take advantage of a completely *unfocused* rider.

Lance ignored all of Lucy's half halts and leg aids, but even though the horse was still cantering, he put his head back down. And in the midst of her anger, Lucy was about to breathe a sigh of relief...But she never quite got the chance. Because Lance, being the little devil that he was, suddenly gave the largest buck that Lucy had ever experienced in her life; a huge buck that succeeded in launching Lucy from the saddle, and causing her to land very ungracefully in the dirt.

Freaking ow. Tomorrow morning that's going to hurt like hell.

"That wasn't quite what I asked you to do."

Lucy's face instantly flushed as she got to her feet.

She had temporarily forgotten where she was, but there was no mistaking it now. Not only did all of her annoyance return once she remembered that only a few minutes ago she had been arguing with Elise, but embarrassment was added to the mix as well.

She had just fallen off of the horse in front of Elise.

As if Elise needed any more reason to explain why she was right and Lucy wasn't.

"At least he's walking now," Elise's words were nothing but ice.

A little concern would be nice, Lucy thought. And she really, *really* wanted to say it, but she knew she'd caused enough damage—both to herself, and, she was positively certain, all of the progress she had made with the senior.

"I can...untack him if you want," Lucy offered, in an attempt to make up for the trouble she had caused without *actually* apologizing.

She didn't think she could ever bring herself to actually apologize for what she said, because she believed wholeheartedly in those words. She believed there was a proper way that things should be done regarding horses, but that there also came a time when enough was enough, and matters needed to be dealt with differently.

"Just go, Lucy. You've done enough."

"I mean, it wouldn't be a big deal or anything—"

"I said you've done *enough*."

It was all Lucy could do to keep herself from glaring before spinning on her heels and walking out of the arena.

Why was Elise so stubborn?

So set in her own ways?

And Lucy...she was so unbelievably *angry* at herself; almost as angry with herself as she was with Elise. She *knew* that speaking her mind wouldn't end well. She *knew* that Elise wouldn't take very kindly to it. Yet...she'd let her stupid mouth get the better of her.

And because of it, she feared that she would end up as far from Elise as she had been the very first day they had met.

You get this *close to actually getting along, and then you ruin it*, Lucy thought to herself bitterly the entire bike ride back to campus. And by the time she had gotten back to her dorm room, all thoughts of completing any remaining homework had been extinguished. She was exhausted, both physically and mentally, and *dammit* she had a riding lesson tomorrow...

"*Ow*," Lucy hissed as she took the saddle off of Splash the following afternoon.

The sprightly little pony had made her work hard—and it had done quite a number on her already sore back. The best of it was when Splash had decided to start dancing in front of the tiniest little crossrail imaginable, and *right* when Lucy had figured it would be best to turn the pony around and try again, Splash launched herself over the jump from her near-stand-still prancing, throwing Lucy forward so that she had to scramble to regain her position by the time the pony cantered off upon landing.

Just breathe. Relax. It's Friday. Tomorrow you can sleep until the afternoon. Or better yet, go see a chiropractor...

Lucy, despite the unpleasant feeling of complaint from her back, brought everything upstairs with her at once, wanting to get out of the barn as quickly as possible. Because the one and only time she had crossed paths with Elise today, the senior had given her the coldest look Lucy thought she had ever seen.

Lucy raced back downstairs even more quickly than she had gone up, free of her previous trip's heavy leather items. She made her way back to Splash's stall to give the pony a carrot, and then she grabbed her bag and waited for Harley to pick her up. He had offered, since Lucy had told him all about the previous night's wonderful fall...and the rest of it as well.

"Do you think I should talk to her?" Lucy asked when the two were walking back to their building.

"I guess you could try," Harley said.

"There's no way I'm apologizing. The only one who should be apologizing is her...but somehow I don't exactly see that happening."

"I don't see that happening either," Harley laughed.

"It's not funny!" Lucy exclaimed.

"I think you should stop worrying about it so much," Harley said seriously, "She'll get over it."

"But she's *Elise*," Lucy said, "Because of my moment of stupidity, she probably won't talk to me ever again, let alone trust me to ride a horse like Lance. Oh, God, or Dee? What if I'm not allowed to ride Dee anymore—"

"Hold on there, Feisty Pants, let's not jump to conclusions."

Lucy sighed. Jumping to conclusions was a skill that she had gotten *very* good at over the past few years. She stopped what she was sure had been the beginnings of a worried rant and listened to what her friend had to say.

"Lucy, has it ever occurred to you that maybe it *wasn't* a moment of stupidity?"

"What?" Lucy was confused.

"Just what I said. Maybe it wasn't stupid of you. Maybe it was a good thing."

"And how is it good that we're no longer on speaking terms and she practically hates me again and I have to deal with her every time I go to work and every time I see her in chem lab?"

"You told her what she needs to hear," Harley said.

"Well, yeah, I know that. But it was stupid of me to choose that over...over everything else."

"You didn't choose anything. You were only trying to help."

Lucy sighed, "I mean, I *get* that, but that doesn't mean that I don't feel like what I did was wrong. Like there would have been a better way..."

"Lucy you didn't do anything wrong. Okay? And if Elise knew what was good for her, then she would listen to what other people have to say. In the business she's gotten herself into, other people's opinions matter quite a large deal. She's going to have to get used to it one way or another."

"This is true," Lucy said, knowing how the horse world really *was* full of very opinionated people, "But you're forgetting that Elise *is* one of those opinionated people."

Harley only shrugged, "I don't really know what else to say to you. Just give it time, let her cool down."

At that, Lucy laughed, "Cool down? When she sets her mind to it she can be a freaking ice queen."

"Point taken," Harley agreed.

"But you're right," Lucy told Harley when they reached her dorm room, "I always worry about these things too much."

"You mean well. That's all that matters."

"Thanks, Harley," Lucy gave him a smile.

"Hey, just remember, horses are better than people. Blitzen is the only one I can talk to who doesn't freak out at me or judge."

"*I* don't judge," Lucy laughed, as the thought of Harley's horse came to mind, reindeer antlers and all, "And what you mean is *reindeer* are better than people."

"Yes, Lucy, reindeer are *much*, better than people."

LUCY DRAGGED HERSELF to the barn on Sunday, exhausted from her shift at the coffee shop, her back still sore as she had been standing all morning.

And imagine how much better it'll feel pushing a wheelbarrow for an hour and a half, Lucy sighed as she leaned her bike against the barn entrance.

She walked down the aisle, her footsteps the only noise with the exception of the occasional huff or whinny. As the days got cooler, the pesky flies had died down, and so most of the horses were happier and friendlier with the change in the weather.

The horses get happier, and Elise gets angrier, Lucy rolled her eyes as she turned the corner.

The office door was closed as it always was, and Lucy sighed.

Did she *really* have to go in there? Was it really necessary for her to sign in? Elise would be able to see that she had come in and completed her job when all of the stalls were done and all of the horses had been fed...

Lucy bit her lip, and then knocked.

"Come in."

A curt, short response. The normal one, just more emotionless. Was that even possible? Did Elise know it was her?

Well, duh, it's the time of your shift, of course she knows it's you.

Lucy opened the door quietly, and avoided any eye contact with the senior as she quickly signed her name on the sheet. She rushed out, but before she had passed the desk,

Elise said without even looking up at her, "The railings on the second level need to be dusted today."

"I *get* it, you don't have to keep *punishing* me to remind me where my place is," Lucy muttered.

"What was that?"

Oh, you heard me.

"Nothing," Lucy said innocently.

"Shut the door."

Lucy slammed it.

LUCY WAS PRACTICALLY fuming by the time she had finished everything.

Gone were her moments of feeling bad about what she'd said.

No.

If anything, Elise needed to be put in *her* place.

She couldn't just *turn* on Lucy like this because Lucy had merely been doing what Harley had said—she had been trying to *help*.

But of course, it hadn't come off that way to Elise, who clearly thought that suggestions were an attack on her opinions.

Lucy had gotten a rag from the supply closet, and was running the fabric up and down the wooden railings of the second level, muttering under her breath the entire time, but she shut her mouth instantly when she noticed a rider enter the arena with a white horse.

She forgot I'm up here, didn't she, Lucy thought. *She forgot she asked me to do the railings.*

At first, Lucy panicked. But upon second consideration of the situation, she found a wonderful plan beginning to weave its way into her mind.

Elise hadn't looked up once.

Okay, Elise. Let's see how you ride if you don't like the way I handle a horse.

Lucy recognized Legacy, the horse that Elise had been riding when Lucy had first seen her during tryouts. And Lucy had gotten to know the horse better every time she came in for work.

Legacy was an Arabian mare, most likely seven or eight years old. She enjoyed being turned out, and disliked being cramped in her stall, although she was one of the horses who would let Lucy in and stand patiently while Lucy completed her work.

The mare wasn't actually completely white, as she had looked—and currently looked—to Lucy from a distance. She was a flea bitten gray, meaning that she had gray little flecks of color all over her (hence the analogy to 'flea bites'). Legacy's dished face, characteristic of the Arabian breed, was one that Lucy had grown to adore when the mare would stick her head over her stall door, tiny ears pricked forward, begging for extra attention or treats.

Lucy wasn't sure if Legacy actually belonged to Elise.

Technically all of these horses "belonged" to Elise. Or at least belonged to her parents, anyway. But Lucy wondered if Elise had a horse here that she could call her own, and if she had to guess, Legacy would be her first choice.

When Legacy began trotting, Lucy could only admire the way the mare moved. Her trot looked like any normal horse's trot, but when she *extended* that trot...that horse could *move*.

Legacy looked as if she were floating on air, so poised and elegant; as if each time she extended her legs she froze in a beautiful, lengthened position before she completed her next stride.

Definitely a dressage horse, Lucy thought.

She had seen the dressage saddle that Elise was using, but it was Legacy's fluid movements that convinced her of the horse's abilities.

And Elise was quiet, her grip on the reins soft, but maintaining a certain amount of contact so that Legacy carried her neck in a perfect arc, the way she was supposed to. When the senior sat that trot it was like she was one with the horse, both moving together, that platinum blond braid tossing out behind Elise like Legacy's snow white tail.

No wonder they call dressage horse dancing.

Lucy was so awestruck that she forgot about how angry she was with Elise.

Until...Legacy started cantering.

All went well for a few seconds, but then Legacy pulled a stunt like Lance had with Lucy on Thursday, speeding up and attempting to take off.

So...maybe Legacy is just another training project then?

Lucy watched as both horse and rider's moment of connection dissolved, replaced by Elise's struggle to regain control of the headstrong mare, who wasn't about to give in any time soon. Because now, Legacy reminded Lucy more of Dee, tossing her head up every time Elise tried to pull back on the reins. The harder the mare fought, the more Elise pulled.

Stop pulling! Lucy thought, knowing that with the constant pressure on the reins Legacy would only become more annoyed, which would in turn cause the mare to run even faster.

But of course the senior couldn't hear her thoughts.

Legacy was practically galloping away with her nose to the sky, and while Elise sat back and was going nowhere, it just *looked* uncomfortable.

Lucy couldn't just watch this without doing anything. She just couldn't—both for the horse's sake, and Elise's. And so she acted again, on impulse, really. She had already attempted to explain it to Elise once, so why not make her message even clearer?

"Elise, stop pulling on the reins! You're only agitating her more. You need to give her room to move; give her her head, or she's never going to listen to you. You need to *let her go!*"

Elise's attention instantaneously, yet ever so briefly, shifted to Lucy. And the split-second, wide-eyed look she gave the redhead was one of complete shock, confusion, and anger.

But in that moment, it was enough to startle the senior so much that she had stopped pulling back on the reins. And even though it was out of shock and not Elise's intention, it was enough to let Legacy lower her head slightly, which Elise took advantage of, giving the mare half halts until she came back down to the trot, and then the walk, and finally a halt.

And then Elise walked Legacy as close to the wall as she could, stared right up at Lucy with the same cold eyes from before and said, "The only one who needs to let *anything* go is *you*."

Chapter Nine

After the most awkward of chemistry labs, where Elise virtually acted like Lucy didn't even exist (with the exception of, '*Get me a beaker. No, the fifty milliliter beaker, not the hundred can't you read?*'), Lucy contemplated skipping work on Thursday.

Like, *really* contemplated it.

But looking back on her decision, she was grateful that she had had half a mind and decided to go.

Because right before Lucy started sweeping, after she had given all of the horses their nightly grain rations, Lucy noticed something wrong—with Dee. Lucy walked over to the mare's stall, and saw that Dee hadn't touched her food. And this was merely the first of the signs that Dee wasn't acting normally. Had it been any other day, the ravenous chestnut mare would have had all of the food gone before Lucy had even walked back her way. But tonight it remained untouched, with Dee holding her head low and her back to the bucket, lip curling upwards every few seconds.

"What's the matter, girl?" Lucy asked, putting the broom down next to Dee's stall to assess the problem.

As if on cue, Dee turned her entire head around and nudged at her stomach, and seconds later, she dropped to the ground and began rolling.

Crap, crap, crap! Lucy forgot about the broom completely as she ran to the office.

The door was in its usual state—closed—but Lucy didn't have time to knock.

And she didn't have time to worry about the dispute she had had with Elise.

Lucy burst into the office, and before Elise even had a chance to open her mouth, Lucy exclaimed, "I think Dee is colicking!"

Almost immediately, Elise's stiff demeanor caved—figuratively and literally, as her shoulders hunched and she put her head in her hands, "Just what I need right now."

But no more than a minute later, the senior was on her feet, heading to the filed manila folders, and saying, "I'm calling the vet. Get any food out of her stall, hay, grain, water, *anything*, and keep her standing."

Lucy nodded, "Got it."

Quickly, she made her way back to Dee's stall, job of sweeping abandoned as she removed anything that Dee could consume. She knew the consequences of colic, and how severe it could be. The insanely long equine digestive tract, crammed and folded into a tiny stomach, could become twisted or blocked very easily. The adverse results of the blockages or twists, considered colic, then led to a waiting game that could easily go either way depending on the severity of the situation. And with the changing of the weather, the horses became more sensitive, and colic more frequent.

"Why, Dee?" Lucy sighed, "You need to stay standing so that you don't cause even more damage."

She had managed to get Dee up and on her feet, but was struggling to *keep* the mare standing.

Luckily, she didn't have to wonder what to do for long. Elise showed up only a minute later, all differences and arguments set aside; this was indeed an emergency.

"The vet is an hour and a half away. So he probably won't get here for another two hours," Elise said.

"You mean he won't get here until *ten*?" Lucy asked.

"He's getting here as fast as he can. He was with another client," Elise's words were rushed, but then grew authoritative once more, "But he's still on the phone and needs to know how severe we think it is. So hold her still."

As Elise moved closer to inspect the horse, checking for whatever she knew she had to check for, Lucy couldn't quite ignore the fact that Elise had said 'we'. Or...the fact that Elise hadn't even double-checked Lucy's diagnosis—the senior had called the vet without even looking at the horse herself.

"Walk her down the aisle, and whatever you do, do *not* let her roll. You are to keep her on her feet at all times. I have to finish with her records. I'll be back in a minute," Elise instructed, already walking back to the office.

Control.

Something that Elise was insanely good at.

But...Lucy found that she didn't quite mind it as much as usual.

It was an emergency, after all.

And...was it odd that it seemed kind of...attractive?

But God, not in that *way,* Lucy's eyes grew wide when she realized the other implication of her thoughts. *It's just a respectable quality to have. Sometimes.*

Dee nearly yanked the lead rope out of Lucy's hand in another attempt to start rolling, and it was enough to snap Lucy's attention out of her odd, spontaneous thoughts, and back to the more important situation.

Lucy fought with the mare for a few moments before she got Dee walking, back and forth down the aisle like she was supposed to, and the entire time she talked to the chestnut mare, who was clearly distressed—as anyone would be in whatever amount of pain Dee was most likely in.

"How is she doing?"

It was Elise, back already from the call.

"Fighting me, clearly," Lucy said, "But I'm managing."

As Lucy circled Dee at the end of the aisle, right in front of Elise, the senior looked as if she wanted to say something, but then thought better of it. Then she looked to the ground, and then back at Lucy, and then once Lucy had completely turned around and could no longer see Elise's face, she heard a small, shaky breath before it was followed by a request, in a slightly more timid voice, "Would you mind...staying? Just until the vet comes and then you can leave. I just...hate being alone here when things like this happen."

Lucy nearly froze in place at the admitted words.

Elise wanted her to stay? After everything that had happened previously?

"No one wants to be alone when a horse colics," Lucy said, her back still to the senior, "I'll stay. And I don't mind staying when the vet comes, either."

Elise sounded slightly shocked, but mostly relieved, "That means a lot, Lucy."

Guess that's her way of thanking me?

"It's no big deal. We can take turns walking her until the vet comes, and we'll just...deal with it as it comes, I guess," Lucy said, and at this point, she had to turn around again, and walk Dee back towards Elise, and she saw Elise nod her head in agreement. And so, after Lucy had walked Dee for about ten minutes, she turned the chestnut mare over to Elise, who walked Dee silently up and down the aisle.

It was very quiet afterwards, as neither of them spoke. Lucy just found herself listening; to the horses as they drifted in and out of sleep, sighing, nickering, and swishing their tails; to the late autumn wind that blew past the slightly open barn doors; to the loud striking of Dee's hooves on the cement floor accompanied by Elise's soft footsteps.

After about forty minutes had passed, they let Dee have a short break, not wanting to exhaust the poor horse. But they knew that continuing to walk Dee was best for the mare's health—a little tiredness was nothing compared to having to undergo a surgery that wasn't guaranteed to be a success. And when two hours had passed and the vet still hadn't come, and the glow of Lucy's phone read 10:36, she wondered where in the world the vet was, and worried if he'd make it in time. Because while Dee seemed stable, Lucy knew that the proper medication needed to be administered, and that a proper examination needed to be performed in order to determine if Dee would need surgery.

"Your turn," Lucy said through a yawn, handing the lead rope over to Elise. Then she eyed the two hay bales by the doors, "You know what? I think I'm going to lay down for a few minutes. Just wake me up when it's my turn to walk her."

"Go ahead," Elise said, sounding just about as tired as Lucy felt.

Lucy yawned again as she walked over to the hay bales. She could just about fit if she curled her legs all the way up to her chest. And while it was slightly uncomfortable, and quite itchy, she found her eyes closing almost instantly.

Just a few minutes...I'll get right back up...

THE NEXT THING LUCY knew, she was waking up to—horses? And voices? And what was that awful poking in her side?

"You're really very lucky you caught it when you did. If it had been any longer she would have needed the surgery. And even then nothing would have been guaranteed."

"Actually, it wasn't me. It was Lucy who recognized what was going on. I don't know that I would have caught it in time if she hadn't been here."

"Lucy?"

"She's our student worker. Just started the beginning of this semester."

"Oh, I didn't realize you were hiring."

"She needed work in exchange for lessons."

"I see. Well, everything should be okay with Delaney now. Keep monitoring her progress, and I want an update in about twelve hours."

"Thank you so much for coming out so late."

"Not a problem."

There were footsteps.

Then a very loud, exhausted sigh.

Lucy rolled over, remembering exactly where she was, and sat up, rubbing her eyes, "I told you to wake me up."

"You were out cold," Elise's voice wasn't even the slightest bit angry—she sounded completely drained.

"So she's okay then? Dee?"

"I've never been so happy to see a pile of horse shit."

Lucy would have burst out laughing, had she had the energy. Never in a million years would she have thought she would hear Elise curse. And it was kind of endearing—in its own way that was only Elise's.

I think I need to go back to sleep, Lucy thought.

"So, I don't know about you, but it's one in the morning and I'm exhausted. And I don't think I'm in any shape to drive, let alone walk back to the house. So you're either sleeping here, or on the sofa."

"I choose the sofa," Lucy said, as she continued to pull hay off of her clothes and out of her hair, "But who's going to stay with Dee? And check on her?"

"Kai's coming. He's got it covered."

"Who?"

"Kai. He does your job every morning and evening that you don't work."

"Oh," Lucy didn't ask any more questions—she could barely keep herself awake as it was.

It took all of Lucy's energy to bring herself to her feet and follow Elise all the way up to the house, but even though she was practically sleep walking, it didn't lessen her amazement at how huge Elise's house was.

"Wow," she said, "This is incredible. It's like a castle."

Because at 1:08 in the morning, she had no filter.

"It's not really that big."

"It's big to someone who grew up in a town house."

"I thought you said that you were the one raised in a castle, anyway?"

"You remember that?"

Elise rolled her eyes, "Come on."

"Where?"

"There is no way that I am letting you sleep on my couch," Elise turned around, gestured towards Lucy's stained work clothes that now had hay practically sewn in with the fibers, "in *that*."

"Well fine then," Lucy grumbled as she followed the senior upstairs, but she was really too exhausted to actually care.

"So clearly I would have offered you a guest room," Elise said as she turned on the light in her room, "But although our house is fairly large, we don't exactly have one."

"Anything is better than a bale of hay," Lucy said, squinting at the sudden brightness.

It took her eyes a little time to adjust, but when they did and Lucy could actually see where she was, she saw that Elise's room reflected everything about Elise herself. It was primarily blue, with all white furniture, a few pictures here and there, a desk with plenty of folders and papers on it, and, of course, it was cleaner and tidier than humanly possible.

By the time Lucy was finished examining her surroundings, Elise had tossed her a pair of sweatpants and a long sleeve shirt, saying, "I hope they fit."

"Somehow I didn't picture you owning a pair of sweatpants."

"I'm a college student. If I didn't own a pair of sweatpants I'd be breaking the law."

I thought you made the law.

"Very funny," Elise said. Lucy grew slightly rigid when she realized she had spoken her thoughts aloud, but the senior continued on, not sounding annoyed at all. "Just go downstairs. I have an eight a.m. class."

"I...uh...didn't mean to say that. That happens a lot. Especially when I'm tired," Lucy sighed inwardly at her social awkwardness and her mouth's lack of an 'off' button.

"It's fine."

"No, really, I—"

"Lucy, I make the law, remember? Get out of my room so I can sleep!"

But through the senior's exasperation she thought she saw a hint of amusement.

And it gave Lucy an idea that brought a wicked grin to her face.

"I could just sleep here on the floor. And then I wouldn't even have to change."

Lucy. Filter. Now...

Oh, but it was so much *fun* to tease Elise! The look on the senior's face was priceless.

"Get out."

"Nope," Lucy plopped herself down on the floor, and stared right up into Elise's increasingly widening eyes.

"I go through all of the trouble of finding you something to wear and now you want to sleep on the floor," Elise said incredulously, shaking her head.

"What, you expect me to walk *all* the way back downstairs after all of the walking I've done all night?"

"Would it kill you?"

"Maybe."

Elise paused. And let out an audible and overly exaggerated sigh. And then said, "If I find *hay* on my floor in the morning, you're vacuuming the whole room."

Lucy was sure that the smile of a delighted toddler was present on her face, but she didn't care. Elise handed her a spare blanket and a pillow, and left the room with a change of clothes.

What the hell is wrong with you? Lucy asked herself as she pulled the blanket up to her chin and let her eyes slide shut as her head hit the pillow. *There's absolutely no reason that you had to stay here. And you can't blame your hyper mouth this time, either.*

Lucy was still trying to uncover the answer to her question when the door opened again, and Elise walked back in.

From Lucy's position on the floor, she was met with the sight of long, pale legs with clearly defined muscle, and although her mind told her not to, apparently her eyes acted on impulse the way her mouth did, and they continued to travel upwards, taking in the dark blue shorts and white tank top that were the most form-fitting articles of clothing that the senior had worn around Lucy to date, and was it just her mind going crazy or was that tank top kind of...low cut?

Yeah, it was definitely low cut. No doubt about that.

And Lucy's eyes didn't stop moving upwards until they met another rather wide set of blue ones.

Pointedly turning *away* from Lucy, Elise picked up the abandoned long sleeved shirt from the floor and pulled it over her head.

Lucy grimaced at her own actions and pulled the blanket all the way over her face.

But from somewhere in her little cocoon of darkness where she wanted to curl up and die of embarrassment, she heard a laugh.

Elise was *laughing* at her.

"Sorry," Lucy grumbled, her face burning, "That wasn't what it...I mean I...I wasn't...*God* I'm awkward. And...I'm going to stop trying to talk, now."

Lucy heard the click of the light turning off. And a small creak of the bed.

Thinking that she was safe from further judgement, she rolled over and removed the blanket from her head before she could no longer breathe. But of course, when she did so, she saw nothing but blue eyes staring down at her.

And a small smile that still looked slightly amused.

"Go to sleep, Lucy."

LUCY DIDN'T QUITE EXACTLY know *how* she had woken up.

But the sunlight that streamed obnoxiously through the room may have had something to do with it. And all she wanted was to go right back to sleep, but one look at her phone convinced her otherwise.

Had she really slept till *noon*?

What?

And...

Oh, shit.

Lucy rolled over and looked up, taking in the sight of the blonde senior still sleeping.

She had an eight a.m..

Lucy got to her feet.

And I just missed work.

"E-Elise?"

It took a few moments before the senior's eyes opened slightly, "Lucy? What the..."

Elise had one moment of confusion before everything seemed to come back to her, and her eyes shot open as she sat up, hands flying to the phone clutched in Lucy's own.

"Crap," Elise groaned and fell back onto the pillows, eyes pinched shut, "I just missed my first two classes."

"Well, I missed my shift at the coffee shop," Lucy said, "It's going to be fun trying to explain *that*."

Elise opened one eye, "Well if *someone* hadn't been so *distracting*, I was going to set an *alarm*."

Lucy's face flushed again. She had chalked her reaction up to how late it had been. And besides, it wasn't wrong to admire an appearance...was it?

There's a difference between admiring and gawking, genius, Lucy resisted the urge to face-palm.

Elise sighed, "Think you can be ready to go in a few minutes?"

"Yeah," Lucy said, all thoughts of her personal awkwardness tossed aside.

"Go wait downstairs."

This time, Lucy didn't need to be asked twice. She stepped into the hallway, and couldn't help but be slightly awed at the sight. It seemed *much* larger in the bright daylight than it had in the middle of the night. She walked down the stairs, taking in the intricately carved wood of the banister, and, in a tribute to her ever-so-childish nature, imagined herself sliding all the way down that banister instead of walking.

Now then *Elise would think you're completely crazy,* Lucy rolled her eyes, *As if she doesn't already.*

Lucy didn't exactly know where to wait, but decided on the kitchen. And luckily, she didn't have to wait for long, because only a minute later, Elise was running into the kitchen, with her backpack over one shoulder, jacket in her arms, and hands attempting to twist the ends of platinum blonde hair into the remainder of a braid.

"You already missed two classes. What's the harm in being late to another one?" Lucy's tone was joking, but if looks could kill...

"I will *not* be late to physics."

"Every action has an equal and opposite reaction," Lucy proudly recalled from her high school physics course.

"That's right. So if you don't get out the door right *now* you're going to pay for it later."

"But we didn't even eat anything," Lucy complained.

"You don't get to invade my room and my refrigerator," Elise said as she picked her keys up off of the counter, "Seriously, let's *go*."

"Okay, okay," Lucy said, "I'm coming."

Lucy followed Elise to the car, where she made a mental note to not put her feet anywhere except for the floor, and the ride to the college was short and quiet.

"Well, thanks for taking me back," Lucy told the senior as she got out of the car, "I hope you're not too late to your class."

Elise looked down to her phone before saying, "It looks like I'll just about make it."

Lucy gave a small wave before heading off—in the direction of the dining hall because *wow* was she hungry!

And of course my bike is at the barn, and I have a lesson tonight, Lucy remembered, sighing.

On top of that, she really *would* have quite the time explaining why she had missed work...

But her boss was fairly lenient, and it really *had* been an emergency. The worst that would probably happen was that she'd get a warning for next time, since nothing like this had happened before.

So she didn't really mind.

Actually, she was rather happy with the way that everything had turned out.

All awkwardness—and of course the scare of Dee's colic episode—set aside, she and Elise had been able to move past what had happened that night with Lance and work together, which made last night an overall positive in Lucy's opinion.

Because every action has an equal and opposite reaction, Lucy thought, laughing at her own joke.

No matter how much Elise tried to push Lucy away, Lucy would keep fighting to be closer.

Chapter Ten

Despite Lucy's perception of the days dragging on, the month of October, and the chill and horse blankets that accompanied it, came much more quickly than Lucy had anticipated.

"Are you ready for the show this weekend?" Harley asked, as he and Lucy walked from the latest team meeting back to their building.

"I think so," Lucy said, "I'm kind of nervous, but with Rattenber pushing us as hard as he has, I think we're all really more prepared than we think we are."

Harley laughed, "You can say that again."

The next show was indeed in only two days. They would have Friday off, as they had for the previous show, but it would still be an early morning. The show was at a barn an hour and a half away, and the team was expected to arrive by ten. So it was virtually like waking up for an eight a.m. class.

But make that an eight a.m. with a major exam.

Because the stress and anxiety that came with the pressures of showing, in addition to not knowing which horse she would end up with, really did affect Lucy.

A lot.

And more than she was letting on about with Harley.

She said a quick goodbye to her friend before heading into her room, where she was surprised to find that her roommate was still awake. And before she had even shut the door, Kendra squealed, "I have a date! I have a date!"

A grin instantly came to Lucy's face, "With Flynn?"

"Yeah," Kendra's smile never left her face, "I mean, it's technically not a *date* date..."

"I'm not buying that," Lucy said as she plopped herself down on her bed.

"He asked me to come with to your team's second show," Kendra said.

"That is *still* a date. Especially because this show isn't at our barn. I didn't even know that non-team members could go."

"Apparently so," Kendra shrugged, "But...I'm pretty excited."

"You should be," Lucy said, truly happy for her roommate.

But she had really begun to wonder that if *anyone* could go to the shows, then would...Elise go to the show?

Probably not, Lucy decided almost immediately.

Elise had pointedly said that she rarely went to the shows at her *own* barn.

But she went to this past one...

Lucy decided that she would just ask at work the next day. Elise had also said that she was off on Saturdays, after all.

"LUCY, I ALREADY *told* you, just because I'm off doesn't mean I can do whatever I want. I'm still the one who's called if something goes wrong."

"So that's a no then?" Lucy couldn't ignore the feeling of disappointment she had, even though she had been prepared for Elise's answer. And she didn't exactly understand why it bothered her, either, but she decided to focus her energy on her sweeping instead of dwelling on it.

"That's a no," Elise confirmed.

"I don't know how you do it," Lucy said.

"Do what?"

"How your life is entirely..." Lucy waved with one hand to indicate the barn and the horses, "*this*. I mean, don't get me wrong, I love being around the horses, but in the position that you're in, doesn't it ever get...I don't know..." Lucy trailed off, not exactly knowing where she was going with this, and also not entirely sure if she should *continue* to go on with this.

Because this was a topic that was usually strictly off-limits: Elise and Elise's life.

But the senior surprised her, filling in the last of Lucy's sentence with adjectives of her own, "Boring? Repetitive? Annoying? Agitating?" Elise's blue eyes were no longer on Lucy, but directed somewhere towards one of the stalls where Knight stood wrapped in a royal blue blanket, "But it's not like I have a choice. I do what my parents want. No questions asked."

Lucy felt a pang of sympathy for the senior. Lucy's own parents had told her to pursue whatever degree she wanted.

That was why she was currently undecided as far as her major.

"So...that's the only reason you're a business major."

Elise only nodded.

"But why?" Lucy asked.

"What do you mean 'why'? They want the business to stay in the family. It's profitable. And while they travel they need someone to keep it running. They need someone to pass it on to," Elise said, but somehow her words seemed more sad and distant than they had before.

Lucy wondered how much more of the senior's life had been dictated by her parents.

There is so much about you that I don't know.

Blue eyes were for the first time torn from the distance and back to Lucy, "And?"

"What?" Lucy asked, completely confused.

"You did it again, didn't you?" Elise's frown turned into a small smirk.

"*What?*" Lucy demanded.

"There *is* a lot about me that you don't know."

Lucy nearly dropped the broom as she slapped one hand over her mouth.

Oh yes, Lucy, you have *done it again*, Lucy thought as her face burned. *Stupid mouth.*

"I must say, though, you're just about the only one who's ever really cared," Elise said, and Lucy didn't know how to interpret the statement. Was Elise being sarcastic? Facetious?

"Is that...a good thing?" Lucy asked.

"I mean I don't really care either way. You can know my entire history, but that doesn't change the fact that you answer to me."

Definitely facetious.

Because...it was said in such a way that Elise was trying to hide how much it really *did* bother her. Lucy could tell because of the way that Elise was no longer looking her quite in the eye, and the way her fingers flew to her braid for a brief moment. And Lucy could only imagine what it was like, to be the daughter of highly-respected parents, expected to live up to the full potential to follow in their footsteps, and to have her life defined by others—so much so that the Elise who stood here before her could very well be someone else entirely. Someone so far removed from the Elise that could have been.

And *this* was the Elise that Lucy so desperately wanted to know. The Elise who perhaps had fears or worries; had dreams and aspirations and hopes beyond the goals her parents had set for her. The Elise who, Lucy was almost completely certain, no one else had ever seen.

"So if you don't care...then I can ask you a question," Lucy said as she picked up the broom once more.

Elise seemed to contemplate Lucy's comment for a moment before saying, "That doesn't mean I'm going to answer it."

"I'll take my chances."

Elise merely folded her arms and leaned against the nearest stall, "Then start asking. I don't have all night."

Lucy fought the elated grin that threatened to break out on her face, "So I want to know why you're in a freshman level chemistry lab."

"I'm a physics minor," Elise said, "And apparently basic chemistry is a foundational requirement for all science tracks."

"Why physics?"

"You said one question."

"Oh, come on. That's *so* unfair!" Lucy exclaimed.

Elise sighed, and scuffed the bottom of one of her perfect black leather riding boots across the ground in front of her before crossing it over her other ankle, "It would have been my major. But clearly, that wasn't happening. I convinced my parents in the beginning of my junior year that I could take it as a minor without it getting in the way of...all of *this*."

This, again, meaning the barn.

Lucy paused for a moment, and then asked, "So do you ever compete? Or show any of the horses?"

"Only in dressage. But the primary reason I show is to take the training horses to rated shows. The more experience and ribbons, the more valuable they are for sales."

Lucy nodded her head. That made sense.

Taking in the senior's appearance, this time a purple polo shirt, Lucy asked another question that had been bothering her, "So why do you always wear short sleeve polo shirts? Especially when it's so cold in here."

Elise seemed confused about the question at first; Lucy had to admit, it was kind of random. But she wanted to know and much to her surprise, the senior actually answered her, the words prefaced by a small shrug, "The cold never bothered me."

Okay. Well. It was a simple answer. Not the one that Lucy had been expecting—but then again, what kind of answer *had* she been expecting?

But no matter; Lucy had many more questions that she needed answers to.

"How did you know my name the first day of chem lab?"

"What does that have to do with anything?"

"How did you know my name?" Lucy repeated, taking note of how uncomfortable Elise suddenly seemed to look.

"I...don't even know what you're talking about."

"Ha! You hesitated!" Lucy exclaimed, crossing her arms in triumph.

"I did not."

"Answer the question."

"You're impossible."

Lucy glared.

"Fine," Elise sighed again, "I...may or may not have looked up your number from the tryouts and matched it to your paperwork."

What? Why? So she did notice me before all of this?

"Uh, you...did?"

"How else do you think you ended up being the one to ride Dee without a martingale in your lessons?" Elise said, composure completely regained.

Oh.

"Okay. Fine. Next question. Do you think you'll ever move out? Like, are you going to live with your parents for the rest of your life?"

"No!" Elise's response was so sudden and forceful that Elise herself looked a little shocked that it had come out the way it had, "I mean...*no*...I don't plan on living here for the rest of my life. I'll...just have to find some place close. Even though at the moment, I've got the house to myself. It's a rare occasion that my parents are ever home."

"Why do they travel so much?"

"They...claim it's business. They're always looking for bigger and better prospective training projects; any publicity they can bring to our business. And we're not just talking the state or the country here. We're talking *worldwide*..." Elise trailed off.

"But you don't buy it," Lucy guessed.

Elise paused, seeming to deliberate whether or not she wanted to say anything more on the subject. And much to Lucy's pleasure, the senior continued talking, "It's not that I think they're *lying* or anything. Because they're not. I just think that traveling was always their...passion. And now they want to pursue it. So they're gone more often than they're here, and while they get to do what they want, I'm stuck here."

"That is *so* not right!" Lucy was slightly surprised at how much this infuriated her, but continued ranting, "How do they have the right to do that? Like seriously, I know they're your parents, but you're an adult. They can't keep telling you what to do! They can't just expect you to—"

Elise raised her eyebrows and gave Lucy a look that clearly said 'calm yourself and stop making a scene'. Even some of the horses had stuck their heads over their stall doors to inspect the commotion.

Lucy gave a small cough, "What I meant was...that's unfortunate."

"Well, it's life."

Elise's favorite phrase.

Lucy hated it.

"I'm sure you could do *something*," Lucy said.

"That's why I have the physics minor," Elise paused for a moment, again seeming to decide how much she wanted to say before continuing, "Right now my parents have the final say on who works here. But I figured that sometime in the future when I'm running the place, I can essentially hire more employees. And then I'll have more time. It'll still be what they want—it's technically going to 'stay in the family' because I'll still be running it. And I'm hoping...to go into research, maybe. Or engineering, even though that would require more years of school..." Elise trailed off and looked to the ground, as if she thought she had said too much.

"I could totally see it," Lucy grinned.

Elise's blue eyes, now thoughtful and almost excited, once again met Lucy's own, "Really?"

"Yeah," Lucy said, "I know *I* couldn't do it. But you've got the motivation. The devotion. The *brain*."

"I don't know everything," Elise stated, rather matter-of-factly.

"Says the one who's the reason I have a hundred percent average in chem lab."

Elise only shook her head in an attempt to just brush off any mention of her academic talent. And while Lucy would have pursued it further, she let this one slide.

Because she had a much better question that she was just *dying* to know the answer to.

"So enough about school. I have one last question."

"Which is?"

A sly smile found its way to Lucy's face, "What does your tattoo say?"

One corner of the senior's mouth curved upwards. Then it grew into a smirk.

Clearly, this one was non-negotiable.

"Now *that*, I am not going to answer."

"LUCY GET *up* already! We need to leave soon!"

The excited voice of Lucy's roommate was one that was oddly out of place at six thirty in the morning. Normally, Kendra would be the one hiding under the covers, but now her roommate was practically bouncing off the walls, already dressed, including the spare pair of riding boots that Lucy had lent her (a favor in response to Kendra's nonstop complaining of how she didn't want to ruin her only pair of white sneakers that she had worn to the barn the first time).

Lucy groaned, "Fine."

She yawned, taking her time getting up, but once she looked at the clock and *understood* that it was six thirty, she began rushing around, all thoughts of tiredness gone.

"Why didn't you wake me up before!" she cried.

And thank God I had half a mind to get everything together last night.

"Well, I *tried*. But when you slept through the alarm I knew it would be torture to even get you to open your eyes."

Lucy sighed, "Go get me something to eat. I'm not going to have time for breakfast. I'll meet you back here before we go, okay?"

Her roommate didn't even seem bothered by Lucy's request—which had come out as more of an order.

"Sure," Kendra said, "But only if I can smuggle something out of there. You know how they are about that."

"Yeah, yeah, I know," Lucy said, but who could really think about food at this point, anyway? She was already nervous about the show, so the food in her stomach definitely wouldn't sit well with her later.

As soon as her roommate was out the door, Lucy scrambled to change. She threw on a pair of jeans, knowing that if she left in her show breeches they would get destroyed before she even got to the barn. She did, however, put on her white show shirt, placed the navy blue show jacket in her bag with the breeches, and threw an old, normal, zip-up jacket over the show shirt.

Then she pulled on her tall show boots and double checked her bag to make sure she had everything—forgetting things had become commonplace for Lucy, and she didn't want a repeat of the tryouts when she had left her helmet in her dorm room.

Especially because it led me straight to Matt, Lucy was instantly repulsed at the thought.

As if her stomach need something else to churn over.

And she didn't know why she got so anxious about these shows, either. She was a good rider. Not the absolute best, but good enough to have proven herself worthy to be a part of the team. So why did she continue to doubt herself?

In the same way that you almost let Matt talk down to you.

The thought, although Lucy had tried to banish it, resurfaced against her will.

But she shoved it away again, not wanting to dwell any more on Matt. Even though she would see him today (since they were on the same *team*, as much as that disgusted her as well) she hoped that they wouldn't exactly cross each other's paths. And transportation was only going to help her in this regard; the college provided a bus, but team members could drive if the distance was within two hours away. Naturally, Harley had offered Lucy a ride, who had passed the offer along to Kendra. However, as Lucy had assumed, she would be taking the bus with Flynn, as team captains were required to travel with the team.

Not a minute after Lucy had closed her bag, Kendra burst through the room and tossed Lucy a bagel before saying, "I need to go catch the bus. And Harley was at the dining hall and told me to tell you to meet him in the main parking lot."

"Thank you *so* much," Lucy said, "And I guess I'll see you there, then."

Kendra gave a small wave before heading down the hallway, leaving Lucy to shut the light and close the door.

Bag over her shoulder, Lucy hurried to the parking lot, where Harley was already waiting in his car. And before she could even get in he said, "So I think I left my helmet at the barn."

"Oh," Lucy said, resisting the urge to laugh, "And you tell me that *I* forget things."

"Yeah, well," Harley mumbled, "Hopefully we won't be late, now."

"I doubt it," Lucy said as they headed off campus and turned down the road towards the barn.

It only took three minutes this morning; there was barely any traffic at all. It certainly didn't provide Lucy with enough time to put her hair into her two signature braids as she had planned to. And so by the time they arrived, Lucy had one braid half completed, and had to continue it while she followed Harley into the barn and up to the lounge, where Harley was certain that he had left the helmet in one of the lockers.

But when they walked in, Lucy was surprised to find Elise there. And the senior's slightly widened eyes made Lucy realize that Elise was equally as surprised to see them.

"I thought you had a show today," Elise said.

"We do, but Harley left his helmet here."

"Oh," Elise said, "Actually I think I might have it in the office. I had to clean everything out of here yesterday, and came across a helmet."

And it wasn't until the two of them turned to follow Elise down to the office that Lucy suddenly realized how ridiculous she must look; what with her old, worn jacket half zipped, the hood probably inside out and flopped somewhere over her shoulder in her rush to put it on, her show shirt buttoned all the way up to the collar, her torn jeans paired with tall show boots, and only one completed braid with the rest of her hair loose down the left side of her face, she was sure she was making quite a fashion statement. She might work in old clothes, but the fact that she was at this *particular* barn looking the way she was, especially with the half-done hair...it made her a little self-conscious. And her desperate scrambling to start her other braid, while simultaneously attempting to fully zipper her jacket, didn't go unnoticed by Harley.

"You look fine."

"What are you talking about?" Lucy said, trying to brush it off.

Harley gave her a look that told her that she knew exactly what he was talking about. But she only rolled her eyes, too tired to argue with him.

And Elise, if she caught any of the conversation, chose to ignore it, simply walking into the office and returning with the helmet that she had found, "Is this it?"

"Yeah," Harley said, "Thanks for holding onto it."

"Not a problem," Elise said, "Good luck at the show."

Harley said a brief thank you, and Lucy echoed his response, her attention focused on finishing her braid. And by the time she had wrapped the last of the elastic around it and muttered a quick, "There. That's better," she found that Harley had already turned to go. And she was about to turn on her heels and follow him when she heard something that kept her rooted in place.

"I thought it looked nice," Elise's eyes were soft; she wasn't joking, or making light of the situation, "You should wear it down more often."

"O-oh," Lucy said, genuinely surprised, as compliments from Elise were rare, "Thanks."

The senior gave her a small smile before heading back into the office and closing the door.

"Lucy, come on!"

Harley's call drew her out of her stunned state, and it was an abrupt enough distraction to keep her from trying to analyze why her face now seemed to be burning.

OKAY, LUCY. DEEP BREATHS. It's all going to be okay.

The barn was a rush of commotion everywhere she looked, and the petite pinto horse that Lucy had been assigned to ride was shifting nervously beneath her. As if Lucy needed anything more to worry about, now the *horse* seemed nervous. Lucy could feel the worry radiating through the saddle, and saw nervous ears flicking back and forth.

The arena was smaller than the one they all practiced in, but that didn't make the large strangeness of it any less intimidating as Lucy walked the pinto horse, Patriot, into the arena. She couldn't even pick out the face of her roommate or any of her teammates in the crowd.

Focus on the horse. Just the horse.

The course consisted of all vertical jumps this time, but their heights were fairly low. The majority of them were set to the minimum height requirement for her division with the exception of the last two.

As she prepared to canter, she could feel Patriot already pulling at the bit.

I'm always stuck with the troublemakers, Lucy sighed.

She had to ask twice for the gelding to pick up the canter lead, and Lucy breathed a sigh of relief when he picked up the correct one.

When she directed Patriot at the first jump, he took it with ease, but jerked his head up when he landed, and Lucy knew that he was going to try to move faster towards the next jump. To prevent this, she leaned back and put a little more pressure on the reins, but still gave Patriot room to move. Her efforts paid off, enabling them to get over the next three jumps without a problem.

They were moving at a steady pace, heading towards the second to last jump. And Lucy was sure that everything would go smoothly from there on out. But, as if she hadn't already had enough trouble, 'smoothly' was far cry from the word she would have used to describe what happened next.

Lucy had looked for the distance; saw that they were ideally two strides away. When suddenly...Patriot decided that the bright yellow coloring on the poles of the jump was terrifying. And instead of going over the jump, he skidded to a stop, throwing Lucy slightly off balance.

Why? Lucy groaned internally.

The refusal would count against her. And she would only get two more attempts at the jump; three refusals counted as a disqualification.

Lucy turned Patriot in a circle to face the jump again, and this time, she tapped Patriot with her heels on the approach. But then she felt the sudden jolt of a second refusal, this time tossing her forward onto the gelding's neck.

At this point, the entire crowd had gone silent, much to Lucy's displeasure. But she let all thoughts leave her mind except for those of Patriot.

And how he'd better listen *this time...*

Lucy circled Patriot once more. And, after having gone through it twice already, Lucy could feel exactly when Patriot became unsure and was about to stop. And so she did something that she normally tried to avoid at all costs. Sometimes it was inevitable, like it was in this moment. And it wasn't that it was a *bad* thing either. The horse needed to learn to respect the rider, and often needed a little extra encouragement.

Lucy resorted to the riding crop that she carried in her right hand, and reached behind her to tap the horse behind the girth.

But when she did this, she was *not* expecting such a reaction from an experienced school horse.

Patriot pinned his ears and bucked.

Forget about getting over the jump; now all Lucy wanted was to stay in the saddle. Which she managed, thankfully. The buck was nothing compared to the one than had thrown her off of Lance, but it still caught her off guard. And the realization that she was now disqualified didn't even hit her until Patriot was once again calm and walking.

Lucy sighed, walking the horse out of the arena and tuning out the commentary of the announcer.

If only someone didn't think that the color yellow was life threatening.

"IT WAS *awful*," Lucy complained at work the next day.

She and Elise had actually struck up a conversation before Lucy's shift began, which was something that didn't normally happen.

"I'm sure it wasn't that bad," Elise said, "What happened?"

"The horse refused twice. And then instead of just refusing the second time, he had to go ahead and buck like a maniac. So I was disqualified," Lucy recalled the information, even though, somehow when she said it, it didn't seem as dramatic as it had felt in the moment.

"Did you stay on this time at least?" Elise asked—no doubt remembering the crazy experience that Lucy had had with Lance.

"Yes," Lucy said, very matter-of-factly, "Yes I did."

"Then it wasn't awful. It just could have been better."

Lucy contemplated the senior's comment. Somehow Elise didn't always strike her as optimistic, but it was moments like this that sometimes caused her to change her mind.

Lucy shrugged, "I guess."

"And you placed third at the last show."

She remembers that?

"I did," Lucy said.

"Then you shouldn't worry about it."

"But it was the last show before break," Lucy sighed.

"Lighten up," Elise said—and the words seemed extremely out of place coming from the senior.

"Well, maybe I could if there was something to look forward to in the near future besides a million exams and studying and work and riding in the freezing cold—" Lucy stopped there, realizing that everything she had just stated was something that she hadn't really meant to say aloud at all.

And although Lucy sounded frustrated and was full of complaints, Elise didn't seem to mind, instead giving the redhead something else to think about, "You can look forward to the party."

"Huh?" Lucy asked, "What party?"

"Your team insists on having a party before winter break," Elise said, and from her tone, Lucy couldn't tell if the senior approved of this or not.

"Since when? And where?" Lucy was still slightly confused.

"Since as long as I can remember," Elise said, "And as far as *where*...my parents offer the house."

"*What*!?" Lucy exclaimed incredulously.

"Well, they're gone nearly all the time. So what would it matter, anyway?"

That was a point that Lucy couldn't argue with. And also one that she didn't know quite how to respond to. So...she decided to ask a question that had suddenly formed in her mind and was in no way going to stop bothering her until she asked it: "So do you ever, uh, go to one of these parties?"

"No, I usually don't."

Okay. Well, really, there was no surprise there.

But still, Lucy couldn't help the incredulous smile that came to her face, "So you mean to tell me that a whole group of insane college students is allowed to just invade your *house* and have a *party* without supervision?"

"My parents have someone stay at the barn just in case, although everyone I know who's stayed has ended up falling asleep on the job. And the team captains attend the party. They're technically the supervisors..." Elise looked down at one of the papers on her desk, "But I'm fairly certain that many things have happened that they haven't yet been inclined to share with me."

"But why do you let it continue, then? Why don't you do anything about it?" Lucy asked.

It didn't seem like Elise at all, always in control and maintaining order, to allow the crazy members of the team to wreak havoc in her own house.

Elise only shrugged, "It's a way for them to celebrate the first half of the show season, I guess. It only happens once, before the semester is over."

But here was Elise again, avoiding the question. Diverting it from herself. Holding something back.

And although it frustrated Lucy beyond belief that they'd come so far, and Elise still refused to open up, Lucy didn't want to push her.

If she did, they'd have to start over from the beginning, like when Lucy had critiqued Elise's riding.

And while all had worked out afterwards, Lucy didn't want to ruin anything.

She didn't think she could handle it if Elise shut her out completely.

"*Lucy*, the door."

Lucy froze in place on Thursday evening.

Something about Elise's comment had caught her off guard.

Instead of placing emphasis on 'the door', as she usually did, Elise had pointedly placed emphasis on Lucy's *name*.

Elise—who strung her sentences together so precisely; who chose her words so carefully, with some inconspicuous intended meaning behind each phrase that Lucy was always determined to uncover—had said something in a way that Lucy never thought she would.

You're being crazy. Thinking way too much into it, Lucy told herself as she closed the door. *It means nothing...*

But did it? Did it mean *something*?

The thought plagued Lucy's mind as she worked.

Why was Elise so hard to understand? How could she seem like she was opening up to Lucy, but then ever so subtly revert back to hiding again? Answering Lucy's questions, and avoiding others? Sometimes opening up, yet most times hiding behind such rigid, emotionless features that Lucy could barely read them. It was the presence that Elise put on in front of others; the one that Lucy had gotten past quite a few times...but had never completely gotten *through* to.

Lucy could picture the senior clearly in her mind, even though Elise was nowhere to be seen; not a hair in that platinum blonde braid out of place. And those perfect ice blue eyes that Lucy could only *sometimes* get to actually *see*.

Only *sometimes* would they soften; looking at Lucy as...as what?

Her equal? Her friend?

And then sometimes Lucy could get her to smile.

That wonderful little smile that was Elise's and Elise's alone—not bright and radiant, but a small tug at the corner of one side of her mouth.

A smile that Lucy completely adored...

Wait, what?

Lucy stopped short.

It...was a smile that Lucy enjoyed bringing to Elise's face. And that laugh that would sometimes come with it...

What? What? What!?

'*Lucy the door.*'

She wanted Elise to need her for something.

To *want* her for something.

"Oh my God," Lucy breathed.

She had to place a hand on Dee, from where she was standing in the mare's stall, to steady herself.

'*Lucy, the* door.'

She wanted Elise to need *her* for something.

'Lucy, *the door.*'

'*Lucy.*'

'Lucy.'

How had she been so blind?

The way she felt the need to look presentable. The way she reveled in every compliment. The way she sought approval. Her desperate and ceaseless longing to be *closer*...

Lucy had been so caught up in trying to get through to Elise that she hadn't even begun to understand *herself.*

She liked Elise.

Lucy *liked* Elise.

"Oh God, Dee," Lucy whispered, her words heard only by ever attentive ears of the chestnut mare, "I like Elise."

Chapter Eleven

For the rest of the week, Lucy couldn't exactly think. It was more like she moved on autopilot, her mind consumed by only one thing—this strange realization.

Lucy had no other way to describe it.

She had never felt this way before, and spent many hours trying to logically talk herself out of it. There had to be *some* other reason to explain it; some other answer for her strange attraction besides the one that had so suddenly dawned on her.

But there just...wasn't.

She *liked* Elise.

And eventually she just accepted it.

She had never been in any relationships in the past. Actually, Matt had been her first official date (minus the prom date her high school friends had found for her; he was definitely not someone that Lucy would have found on her own). And she had thrown herself at the chance to go on a date with Matt without even really considering...*anything*.

"My life is complicated enough already," Lucy sighed, putting her head in her hands.

Even the pre-calculus problem that she was currently attempting to solve seemed simpler when it took her half an hour to get the right answer.

And the one thought that plagued her mind the most was that if she herself had just realized this *now*, did anyone else know?

Did *Elise* know?

And did she...*could she*...feel the same way?

No, Lucy thought, almost immediately. *How could you even think like that? She just barely started to have normal conversations with you. And you don't even know anything about her...in that regard, anyway.*

And Lucy apparently barely knew anything about *herself*, so how could she jump to conclusions about someone else?

Lucy took in a sharp breath and let it out slowly.

She could deal with this.

She could live with this.

She just...wasn't quite sure *how*.

MAYBE WHAT LUCY HAD overlooked *most* in her careful deliberation on the matter was just how natural talking to Elise and getting to know her better really seemed to be.

Lucy had worried that, after this, she would let her thoughts get the better of her; making her even more self-conscious in the presence of the senior with her newfound realization. But everything just seemed to remain, well, *normal*, the next time Lucy showed up for work.

And maybe...that was what mattered most.

No, it was *definitely* what mattered most.

It wasn't something that she had to *deal* with.

Because if it was normal, then it was something that just *was*.

And Lucy wasn't going to ignore it.

Or apologize for it.

Or make excuses for it.

She liked Elise.

And while she wasn't certain that the senior felt the same way, Lucy was *almost* positive that she was single.

But of course, there you go again, jumping to conclusions, Lucy reminded herself as she worked her way down the rows of stalls. If there was one thing that was good about being assigned to stall work, it was that it gave her plenty of time to think. And she spent a good portion of the next Sunday's shift wondering if the idea was too good to be true.

She had never seen Elise with anyone; had never heard her *mention* anything about anyone. So it was a fair assumption.

Just not one that can be proven entirely true.

Such complications.

Lucy sighed, deciding that she had thought about it enough for one night. She finished with the stalls and went to feed the horses, and when she did so, she made sure to double check the list to make sure that none of the horses' feed requirements had changed. But when she looked at the paper, while there were no notes about dietary adjustments, Lucy noticed something on her list of assignments that she had missed. She had been so caught up in her own thoughts that she hadn't really read the list; just assumed that everything was the same as it always was. Because not once yet had she actually been asked to do anything different written on the piece of paper.

But there, in Elise's handwriting next to the normal typed list of jobs, was 'finish unloading hay delivery'.

My favorite thing in the world, Lucy groaned.

She checked her phone, seeing that it was nearly seven fifteen. Had Lucy paid attention, it would have been the first thing that she would have done. But...at least it said 'finish'. So, that had to mean it had to be at least half done, right?

Guess you'll just have to go and check.

Lucy knew that, at her old barn, unloading hay was quite a tedious job. It came stacked on the truck about four or five bales high, and however many bales deep...and each one weighed about fifty pounds. The bales would all have to be taken off of the truck, and then stacked once more in the hay barn, which needed to be done very carefully and precisely because if one was out of place or slightly off balance, the entire stack could topple over within a few seconds.

And when Lucy walked outside, she saw the pile of hay bales still sitting in the back of a black truck that she had just so happened to miss while bringing horses in and turning them out.

There were still about thirty or so left.

Great. And she expects me to do all of this by myself?

Thankfully, because it had indeed been started before she had arrived, the hay bales were only stacked three high on the truck. So while she would have to actually climb up onto the truck and toss the top ones down, she would be able to reach the rest of them from the ground afterwards.

Why? Lucy groaned again, tossing her head all the way back and staring up at the sky, in a single moment of allowing herself to feel bad for her current predicament.

But when she did that, she noticed that even though it was nighttime and everything was growing darker, the clouds seemed to have lost their white hue and turned gray...

Dammit.

Well, now she had royally screwed up.

Now it was going to rain, and all these hay bales couldn't get wet because being soaked by rain, and then stacked in a humid environment to dry could cause them to catch fire *very* easily.

And I can't do it all by myself that quickly!

So she had two options.

She could *try* to get it all done before it started to rain. Or...she could go admit to Elise that she hadn't been paying attention (although she didn't need to know *why*) and ask her for help. But if she tried to get it all done, she knew that whatever she didn't get inside would be wasted, essentially. And she knew that Elise would probably be more upset with her if that happened, because hay wasn't cheap. So quickly she hurried to the office and knocked, hoping that Elise wasn't busy or on the phone. And luckily, she wasn't.

"What's up?" Elise asked.

"So...I kind of didn't *completely* read the list of what I had to do. And I just saw that note about unloading the hay now. And it looks like it's going to rain, and I know that they can't stay out there. But I don't think I can do it all by myself. I mean, I *could* do it by myself if I had more time, but I don't think I *do* have that much time because of the rain. And I didn't exactly know what to do and I'm sorry because I should have paid more attention, but I was just so used to the normal routine and I know it's no excuse but—"

"Lucy, calm down."

Lucy felt her face burn slightly when she realized she'd been rambling, "Sorry," she apologized again.

"I should have told you before you started," Elise said.

And that was the last thing Lucy had expected to hear from the senior. Elise wasn't blaming Lucy for being unaware (well, more like being insanely lost in certain thoughts). She was....saying that it wasn't entirely Lucy's fault.

"You shouldn't have to tell me. It was written there. I should have seen it," Lucy said.

"Well, what's done is done. So why don't we stop talking and go finish as much of it as we can, okay?"

We?

Did that mean...

Elise typed something else on her computer, and then stood from the desk, "Come on. Let's not waste any more time."

Yes!

Lucy grinned. Now she wouldn't have to do it all by herself.

She turned and followed the senior back to where she had left the untouched stack of hay bales.

"So if I toss down the hay bales from the top can you just bring them inside and we'll stack them all later?" Elise asked.

"That's fine with me," Lucy said, perfectly happy to stay on the ground.

And the view's not too bad either, Lucy thought, as she watched the senior effortlessly climbed into the back of the truck and started lifting those hay bales like they were five pounds instead of fifty.

But don't get distracted, Lucy reprimanded herself, *that's the whole reason that you're in this predicament to begin with.*

But somehow...the word 'predicament' didn't seem to fit the situation any more.

Because she really enjoyed working with Elise.

In a way, it was almost like working without anyone else; the senior didn't really talk at all. She was completely focused on the task at hand.

And *that* was what Lucy like the most. She could be in Elise's presence without feeling the need to actually say anything at all.

With the two of them working together, the hay bales were under cover just before the rain began. And it wasn't just a light rain either—it was a *downpour*. The pastures were definitely going to turn to mud and...

Oh crap.

"The horses are still out," Lucy said, and followed it with a sigh.

She looked to the ground in the hay barn, where the bales of hay were tossed here and there, in an extremely unorganized disarray around her feet, and remembered that she still had to feed the horses, and sweep the whole barn, and *now* she would have to bring in all of the horses in turnout...

"I'll get them."

"What? No, you don't have to do that," Lucy said. Elise had already helped her with the hay bales, after all.

"You need to finish stacking these," Elise was already turning to go.

"But it's pouring and you don't even have a jacket."

"It's just rain," Elise said, and before Lucy could say anything more, she stepped outside.

You could have given her your *jacket*, Lucy thought only seconds later.

But she didn't dwell on it.

In the words of the senior, what was done, was done.

And so, Lucy began stacking the hay bales one by one. But because she was starting a new pile, most of the hay bales just needed to be moved around to make a stable base, which left only a few remaining hay bales to actually be lifted on top of the others. So while it felt like it had taken her forever, Lucy found that it had only taken her about ten minutes.

And now all she needed to do was finish feeding the horses and sweep without her arms falling off.

She pulled her hood all the way over her head and ran to the main barn, attempting to avoid the massive puddles that had pooled in various spots along the path, but inevitably ended up misjudging most of them.

When she was once again inside, she unzipped her jacket, and while attempting to shake off as much of the excess rain water as possible, made her way to the feed room. On her way there, she saw Elise walking back from the opposite end of the barn; no doubt having just brought in the last of the horses. But what Lucy noticed as Elise came closer was that, because of the senior's lack of a jacket, her entire shirt was soaked through, making the material cling to her in such a way that Lucy had to force herself to look away from it. And when she had managed to do that, she noticed something else. Elise had her hair all the way over to one side, completely wringing it out. And when she let go of it, Lucy saw that it wasn't in a braid; instead it fell loosely around the senior's face, slightly wavy, and...

Really pretty.

"I think there's something that I definitely need to look into," Elise said, and it took Lucy a moment to realize that the blonde was now only a few feet away from her and actually talking to her.

Like wearing your *hair down more often?*

"And...what would that be?" Lucy managed to string together a response.

"Getting run-in sheds for the pastures. Then we could actually leave the horses out there because they'd have somewhere to go."

Lucy nodded slowly, "Yeah. That...would be a good idea."

And it would be a good idea to stop staring...

"Well I think I'm going to change," Elise said, after a few moments, when Lucy couldn't exactly seem to pull herself together, "And with everything you have left to do, I'm sure I'll be back by the time you're finished and I can drive you back to campus."

Seriously. Lucy. Focus.

"Right," Lucy said, "Yeah. I have to finish. Feeding. And sweeping. And a ride back would be great."

Lucy's face burned again as soon as the senior had left.

I'm a mess.

But the thought that refused to leave Lucy's mind was the fact that...Elise didn't seem to mind.

THE CHILL IN THE AIR was definitely present when Lucy biked to the barn the following Sunday, and she instantly regretted not wearing something warmer. But there was nothing she was going to be able to do about it now. Instead of focusing on how cold she was, she left her bike leaning against the barn doors and walked to the office to sign in. But when she rounded the corner, she was met with a sight that made her eyes grow wide.

The office door was...*open.*

But why?

Maybe she's expecting someone else, Lucy thought.

But that couldn't be right. Because it was only Lucy who worked on Sundays, and by now, she knew that the lesson schedule on Sundays both began and ended early, meaning that all of the Sunday lessons ended before Lucy's shift.

Lucy didn't know what to think.

Except for one thought that came briefly to her mind, however twisted and obnoxious and annoying the person who had spoken those words to her was...

Love is an open door.

And her face burned slightly when she recalled that phrase in this particular scenario.

God, stop thinking so much about this! She just left the freaking door open, that's all. Now go walk in there like a normal person and sign in.

Forcing her legs to work once more, Lucy walked the rest of the distance from where she was standing to the door, and, since it was open, she didn't bother knocking. Instead, she just walked inside, and Elise didn't even look up from her computer.

This was just too *weird*.

And when she put the pen down from signing her name and headed back to the door to leave, no annoyed, sarcastic, or amused request to shut the door followed, and Lucy actually had to *remind* herself to leave the door open.

It was definitely strange.

But in a way, it was kind of pleasant.

I could get used to this, Lucy thought, smiling as she went to work. Every time she walked in and out of the barn with the horses, she could turn her head towards the office and glance inside. Sometimes all she would be able to see was the top of platinum blonde hair over the computer. Other times, she saw two blue eyes staring back at her, which would make Lucy slightly self-conscious—enough to cause her to blush slightly and look away. But not before she could catch the senior's small smile out of the corner of her eye. And it wasn't just a genuine smile—it was the one Elise had when she was none other than amused at the redhead, which only made Lucy's blush deepen.

She was kind of thankful that when she moved on to stall work, she would be all the way down the aisle, which would keep her both out of Elise's sight, and from having to resist the urge to look at the senior. If she was being honest with herself, she rather enjoyed watching Elise work as much as she enjoyed working *with* Elise. When the senior was focused and in her element, it seemed as though nothing could keep her from completing the task at hand.

Except when she catches you looking at her, Lucy blushed again at the thought.

These feelings of hers...they were really going to get the better of her, weren't they?

Lucy sighed, shaking her head, and willing her thoughts to stop flying frantically through her mind. And it worked for a while, as she allowed herself to be distracted by all of the horses and their unique personalities.

Dee was always her favorite. She had taken a clear liking to the mare from the start, and it seemed as though Dee had done the same with Lucy. She was the only horse who would not only let Lucy come into her stall, but—as this had become one of Lucy's bad habits at her old barn—encroach upon her personal space; running her fingers through Dee's copper mane, ducking under Dee's neck if she had to get to something on the other side, throwing her arms around her when she needed a hug.

Dee had really become like a best friend. Lucy felt almost as close to this mare as she had felt to Chip, and in a way, it was comforting. While she knew that Chip would always have a special place in her heart, this headstrong yet sweet little mare was a close second, if not vying for first.

Giving Dee one final pat, Lucy worked her way down the rest of the stalls.

The only other horse who tolerated Lucy's clinginess *almost* as much as Dee was, surprisingly, Legacy. The fleabitten Arabian mare, while Lucy had first expected her to be somewhat unfriendly or even aggressive, seemed to fit none of the 'mare-ish' stereotypes. *With* the exception of being insanely possessive of her food.

It didn't matter how long Legacy had known Lucy; it didn't matter how much Legacy associated Lucy with *brining* the mare her food every Thursday and Sunday; if Lucy was physically in the stall with that mare when she was eating, she would be given the honor of receiving a death glare, complete with pinned back ears, and a snapping of teeth that would come within inches of Lucy's own personal space.

Whether actually biting her, or just threatening her, was the intention, Lucy vowed that she would never find out. So instead of going *into* the stall to give the Legacy her food, she would stand outside and pour it through the bars of the stall and into the feed bucket.

But she took advantage of the mare's calm demeanor whenever food wasn't present, twisting the mare's the white mane and forelock around her fingers, patting her on the shoulder, or scratching her behind the ears—which was something, Lucy had discovered recently, that the mare enjoyed quite a bit. The way Legacy would sigh contently, lowering her head slightly, tail swishing idly, her eyes sometimes closing, never failed to bring a smile to Lucy's face. And it made Lucy wonder how much quality time Elise ever spent with her horses.

If Legacy was even hers.

When Lucy had leased Chip, she was at the barn every single day, even if it wasn't to ride. She was content hand walking him, grooming him, standing in the stall with him, turning him loose in the arena, taking him on trail rides,

watching him graze and play in the field with the other horses...

And Elise was either in that office, or riding. And she
wasn't even riding for fun, either. She was riding to work.

Work. Work. Work.

That was all it ever was.

But she already told you that she doesn't enjoy it, Lucy remembered. *So maybe it's not that she doesn't* want *to. It's that
she can't. She doesn't have the time.*

And while Lucy felt another pang of sympathy for the
senior, she knew that, at the moment, there was nothing that
she herself, or even Elise, could really do about it. Sighing,
Lucy went to the supply room to grab a broom and finish her
work for the night.

But of course, on her way back to return the broom, before she could enter the supply room that was so conveniently located right across from the office, Lucy couldn't help but
let her attention stray as the senior, who had obviously just
finished something that had to have taken her a long time
to complete, closed her eyes, leaned back in her chair, and
stretched her arms over her head.

And it wasn't even the actual movement that had caught
Lucy's attention.

It was what that green polo shirt did.

Why had Elise picked today of all days to leave that shirt
untucked?

And Lucy's attention was solely on the hem of that shirt,
her eyes unblinking as it moved upwards, ever so slightly, re-
vealing the top of that tattoo. But not even the tattoo was
her main focus. With a mind of their own, her eyes seem to

have an ulterior motive, hijacking what was probably her one and only chance to find out what in the world that tattoo said by *continuing* to follow the path of that shirt hem until they were focused on the sight of abs the likes of which Lucy swore she had never seen in her life.

Or just the likes of which you have never been so drawn *to in your life*, Lucy thought as her face burned.

And Lucy had thought that maybe her brain had processed her awkward gawking reaction in enough time...but oh, if she could have only been so fortunate.

In the time it took for Lucy to realize the implications of her behavior, the senior had already opened her eyes, and Lucy was once again met with a look that wasn't too far from the one she had been given the last time she had been caught staring.

Quickly, Lucy turned and busied herself with putting the broom away, knowing that she couldn't walk herself into the office and sign out until she could keep herself from blushing furiously.

Okay, just chill. You can do this. Pretend it never even happened, Lucy instructed herself.

She walked past the blonde without looking at her, signed out faster than she ever had before, and almost celebrated the fact that Elise had chosen to ignore her until...

"If I had known it was going to be such a distraction, I would have just told you to close the door."

Okay, well. It was pretty hard to pretend that it had never happened when Elise insisted on teasing her about it.

Lucy turned around, positive she had turned a shade of red that matched her hair, "I...um...about that. Yeah. Sorry. It, uh...it won't happen again."

When she saw the senior smirk, Lucy could have face-palmed right then and there. She had just screwed up even more embarrassingly than before—she hadn't denied that 'it' had been a distraction! Of course, Lucy would only have been denying it because she didn't necessarily *want* Elise to know. But then again, how much more obvious could she be? She had totally messed this up. And Elise was in no way going to let this one slide.

"So you no longer feel the need to stare as I slave away at the computer. I don't know whether to be relieved or deeply offended."

And although Lucy knew the senior was only joking, she felt the need to attempt to explain herself, which, of course, *really* did her in. Because while her mouth *thought* it could fix things, it only had this unfailing tendency to make every-thing worse, "No, it's not that at all! I mean, I won't, if you don't want me to. Because I could. But that'd be weird. Be-cause I'm just insanely awkward...and you're gorgeous. Wait, what!?"

Lucy's hand, instead of face-palming, slapped itself over her mouth.

She knew that her mouth had a mind of its own, but *re-ally*? Even she hadn't been expecting to say something *that* crazy! It wasn't like it wasn't true—God, it was *definitely* true. But she didn't have to actually *say* it!

And apparently, she wasn't the only one who was unpre-pared for such a comment—Elise herself now looked a little flushed, which was a sight that Lucy had never seen before. While she stood there dumbfounded, all she could do was stare back at the senior who had, for once, been effectively rendered speechless. And that was perhaps the scariest realization of all.

Elise *always* had a response.

But she didn't have time to think about it further, because a knock from behind her startled both of them. Elise's eyes snapped from Lucy's own to somewhere above Lucy's shoulder (by the senior's immediate reaction, Lucy had no doubt that Elise was grateful for the excuse to do so), and Lucy turned her head. But dread filled her at the sight of the person who had been standing there for who knew how long as the whole awkward moment had transpired.

"I'm sorry to interrupt this very *enlightening* moment, but I have paperwork to drop off for the team," Matt' words were said in such a way that Lucy couldn't decode the hidden meaning she was *certain* they held. Because while his words were meant for Elise, his attention had been directed towards Lucy.

She glared at his back as he brushed past her and dropped a folder onto the desk in front of Elise. He couldn't just come in here and talk to Elise in such a berating manner—even if he was speaking in Lucy's direction.

"You don't have to be so rude about it," Lucy said angrily, before Elise could even speak.

Matt feigned complete innocence, "Like I said. I didn't want to interrupt. And it seems like you two have plenty to discuss, so I'll be on my way."

With that, he gave a small shrug, a horrible smile, and left.

"I hate him," Lucy seethed, not really caring whether he had gone far enough to be out of earshot or not.

"I'm not exactly a fan of his, either," Elise said, speaking for the first time since Matt' arrival (and, quite frankly, the first time since Lucy's awkward outburst).

"What'd he do to you?" Lucy joked, in an attempt to change the topic and put her previous awkwardness behind them.

Elise shrugged, "Nothing really. But he doesn't really strike me as someone nice. I mean, half the time he doesn't even treat the horses with any respect. And...he didn't treat you very nicely. My opinion of him kind of went downhill after that."

The senior left it at that, but Lucy was slightly shocked. Did it really bother Elise that much that Matt had been so nasty to her?

"Well in a way it was kind of my fault, for seeing him for something he wasn't," Lucy mused aloud, "I didn't listen to Harley's warnings. I should have."

"Hey," Elise said, and the fact that her tone was so serious caught Lucy slightly off guard, "You can't blame yourself for anything. He was *wrong*. Wrong to treat you that way. No one deserves that. *You* didn't deserve that."

Now Lucy was even more shocked at Elise's words. She sounded almost...defensive. And when Elise herself realized this, she looked down at the desk, obviously somewhat uncomfortable, but said, "It's true, though."

"Thanks," Lucy said, and she smiled.

Elise gave her a somewhat quizzical look, "For what?"

"Sometimes I just need to be reminded, that's all. About what's reality and what's not. I let myself get carried away too much with what I'm thinking. I twist the truth around. Make it something it's not. Because I worry about everything," Lucy finished with a shrug.

Elise was silent for a moment, but then she said, "It's okay to worry. I know it sounds kind of contradictory, but it can be a good thing sometimes. It puts everything into perspective—shows you what's most important to you."

Well, Lucy knew that Elise was certainly book-smart. But she found these words of wisdom to hold far more meaning than anything Elise had ever said to her before. Maybe it was because the senior had said it so seriously. Maybe it was because it was *Elise*, and Elise just didn't say things like that—to anyone.

Or maybe...it was because it was true.

Because there was one thing that Lucy had done an awful lot of worrying over lately.

Elise.

And Lucy was almost entirely positive that she knew what was most important to her.

Chapter Twelve

"So my midterm grade was actually decent. But it went downhill from there. And now I only have, like, four weeks to get it back up."

The comment from Lucy's roommate—who was currently flopped across her bed with her legs propped up against the wall and her long hair spilling off onto the floor—was punctuated with a melodramatic sigh.

"Hey, no one said pre-calc was easy," Lucy answered, rolling her eyes, "My midterm grade wasn't that great. And it *still* managed to go downhill."

"Maybe we should check out tutoring," Kendra sighed again, "Although I'd really hate to give up even more of my free time. But the final will be right around the corner before we know it. And our last exam, too."

Lucy gave a small shrug, "I barely have time for everything as it is."

"Yeah, well, you're at the barn all the time. It's too bad horses can't teach math," Kendra laughed.

"No. But I bet Elise could," Lucy hadn't even thought before the sentence popped out of her mouth.

She had been avoiding bringing up the topic of the senior with her friends as of late, and now she grimaced for letting it slip. She didn't want anything *else* to slip as well, considering she had only just recently been able to come to terms with her...how had she put it before?

Oh, right.

Feelings.

Certainly not crazy possessing thoughts that made her stare like an insane person and say things that only made her sound like more of an idiot than she already felt.

"That's true. She's a senior. She had to have taken the course already. Plus she's like, *really* smart," Kendra agreed, "You should ask her to tutor you."

"What?" Lucy exclaimed, "No way!"

Elise had *way* too much to do as it was. Or really, it was more like Elise had way too much to think about. The last thing the senior needed was Lucy coming to her with her problems. Not that she could share all of that with her roommate. That was information that Elise clearly didn't want the entire school knowing.

"Hey, you mentioned it," Kendra said, "Why the sudden defense?"

"No reason," Lucy shrugged, trying trying to brush it off. But inevitably, as always, she just made the situation worse, "I mean, no. You're right. She is really smart. Like, genius smart. And talented. And she knows just about everything there is to know about chemistry. Which means she's probably good at calculus, too. Plus she knows everything about horses. And she's strong..." Lucy's eyes widened when she realized she had said the last sentence aloud, courtesy of the fact that her mind had so spontaneously selected this *very* moment to replay the image of the senior lifting those hay bales. Quickly shoving the memory aside, Lucy added, "With numbers. I'm sure she's strong in any subject that requires...calculations."

Even in her roommate's upside-down position, Lucy could see a smile spread across Kendra's face, "Anything *else* you'd like to add?"

Although Kendra was only joking, Lucy felt the blush that was now present on her face, "I don't think so," Lucy said, in her most nonchalant voice ever.

Kendra only laughed, "Okay. Well, the way you were headed there I wouldn't have been surprised if you'd ended with 'gorgeous.'"

Lucy's face reddened even more. There was no way that Kendra had heard about that...was there?

"I...no. I wouldn't. Why would you think—"

Lucy stopped mid-sentence when she realized Kendra was now laughing harder, "*God*, Lucy I was joking. But by the way you're reacting, you'd never know."

Lucy narrowed her eyes at her roommate, concluding that Kendra's teasing was only genuine. But that still didn't change the fact that Lucy was insanely embarrassed and had no feasible way of getting herself out of this mess. She glanced down at her phone and almost sighed with relief when she saw what time it was, and, in a voice that was a *little* too cheerful, she exclaimed, "Oh, look! Gotta run, or I'll be late for work!"

Quickly, she grabbed her jacket, and headed out the door. But before she could close it, she heard, "Yeah. Wouldn't want to be late to see Elise, huh?"

"Is it *really* that obvious?" Lucy grumbled as she walked down two flights of stairs before heading out the door.

But it didn't matter, really.

Her friends were bound to find out eventually, weren't they?

Stop worrying about it, Lucy reminded herself, as she took off for the barn. *There's only one thing that you're allowed to worry about. One thing worth worrying about. And it doesn't involve being concerned with who else might know.*

Lucy found herself wondering whether the office door would be open again before she even got to the barn. All throughout the week, when she had been at the barn for her lessons, she noticed that they door had definitely been closed. As it always had been before. Meaning that it had only been open when...Lucy had come for her shift. And to Lucy's surprise, the door was once again open, and she couldn't help but smile at the sight.

Guess she doesn't think it's too much of a distraction, then, Lucy thought as she walked towards the office.

Although she was sure that Elise had seen her, the blonde didn't acknowledge Lucy until she had walked through the door, but Lucy didn't mind at all.

"Hey," Lucy said when she passed the desk.

It was the first time she had actually greeted Elise without waiting for the senior to speak to her, but hey, there was a first time for everything, wasn't there?

"Hi," Elise looked up from her computer. If she was surprised that Lucy had spoken first, she didn't show it, "You're early today."

Yeah, well. That's what happens when you have to bail yourself out of awkward situations, Lucy thought. But all she said was, "Guess it took less time to get over here today," before heading back towards the door.

And while Elise didn't answer her—not that Lucy's comment had really warranted an answer—the senior surprised her by not only getting up from her desk, but following Lucy out of the office. And of course, Lucy's curiosity got the better of her, as it always did, "Don't you have all that paperwork to do?"

"I finished most of it," Elise said, continuing to walk as she spoke, which meant that Lucy had to follow in order to listen to the rest of what the senior was saying, "But I need to get Legacy ready for a show this Friday, so that's kind of a top priority on my to-do list right now."

"Oh," Lucy said, walking with the senior all the way to Legacy's stall. It was a Sunday, which meant that there really wasn't much time until said show would be happening, "I assume it's a dressage show?"

"Yeah. It's in the morning too, which means I have to miss class, but it is what it is," Elise answered, reaching over Lucy's shoulder to grab Legacy's halter off the door before leading the mare onto the crossties, "It's her first rated show. I've got high hopes for her. But we'll see," Elise shrugged, "She doesn't like to listen at the canter."

Lucy knew this all too well. After all, it had been Lucy herself who had very bluntly told Elise that she was going about it all wrong. She wondered if the senior had recalled that little episode when she'd added that last comment about Legacy's behavior. Actually, Lucy wondered if Elise had only mentioned it so that *Lucy* wouldn't bring it up. It was a touchy subject for both of them, solely because they had clashing opinions. So instead of staying on the topic, Lucy asked a question that she'd had for a while now, "So is Legacy your horse?"

By this point, Elise was already taking the royal blue blanket off of the Arabian mare, but, unlike Lucy, the senior had the ability to talk as she worked without breaking her concentration, "I wouldn't necessarily call her mine. She's mine as far as training purposes. And so is Lance. But none of the horses here are actually...*mine*."

Lucy gave Elise the most confused look in the world, and seeing the redhead's expression, Elise sighed, but continued on with an explanation—most likely because she knew she would be interrogated further if she didn't elaborate, "I already told you that my parents see this as a profitable business. And so...that's exactly what it is. A business. They don't see horses as pets. Or friends. Or whatever you'd like to call them. My parents see them as monetary objects. They think that getting attached to a particular horse is a frivolous waste of time and money. So every horse that I have ever seen or worked with has eventually been leased. Or sold."

The senior kept her eyes away from Lucy's ever softening gaze, preferring to focus her attention on brushing Legacy's coat extra thoroughly as a means of distraction.

"I didn't realize," Lucy said after a moment.

"How could you have?" Elise said, finally turning towards Lucy with blue eyes that were somewhat hard, "Besides, it doesn't matter."

It does matter! Lucy wanted to say.

Clearly it did, because the situation seemed to affect Elise more than she was letting on—which was how it always was. But Lucy didn't quite know how to say that to Elise without the senior getting defensive. So instead Lucy gave a small shrug, and voiced the phrase that she was surprised Elise hadn't already, "Hey, it's life, right?"

Elise gave a small nod of agreement, and nothing more. And Lucy knew that she should probably have taken it as her cue to leave, but she also knew that she wanted to ask one more question that would hopefully distract Elise from the sudden downhill trail their conversation had taken, "So what's her show name?"

Lucy's only major showing experience had been with the team, but even before that she'd known that all show horses were given 'show names' to be registered with, and then 'barn names' to be called by on a daily basis.

"What, Legacy's?" Elise asked.

"Yeah."

"It's a long one," Elise said, "She's registered as 'Queen of the North Mountain.'"

Lucy mulled the name over in her mind before concluding, "It suits her. She seems kind of regal to me."

"Hence why I've taken to calling her Legacy."

Lucy smiled, "Royalty to be remembered for generations."

Elise rolled her eyes, "Let's hope."

"She's definitely got potential. Because her extended trot—now *that* is something," Lucy said in all seriousness, remembering the fluid movements of the Arabian mare.

"The goal is to eventually work with her on more advanced movements. A lot of the training horses I've worked with in the past have actually sold before I could work with them on a higher level. I think it would be fun to teach her the pirouette or passage or piaffe. Something tells me she'll have no problem with the counter canter, but flying lead changes are going to be a nightmare."

Lucy found that she loved when Elise talked about all of the technical terms of dressage, even though she had only heard of two—the counter canter and the flying lead change, to be precise. The other three that Lucy couldn't even pronounce...well, she wouldn't be able to recognize them if she *heard* them again, let alone saw them in motion.

But that was beside the point, because Legacy was still fairly green, and still needed foundational work. So that much Lucy understood. But the rest of it went right over her head, and so she only nodded in agreement, savoring the sound of the French terms that rolled so easily off the blonde's tongue.

"Do you even have any idea what I'm talking about?" Elise asked with a laugh, taking in the redhead's blank expression, although Lucy was trying really hard to make it look like she had understood.

"Nope," Lucy grinned widely, "But it sounds complicated."

"Complicated to speak, teach, and perform, but making it all look effortless...that's the world of dressage for you," Elise said.

"Dressage kind of suits her, then, if you think about it," Lucy said, "Being a queen and regal, she moves with poise and grace."

"Whatever you say," Elise's comment held a hint of a laugh.

"It definitely doesn't seem like something I'd be particularly good at. Jumping takes balance, but I'm better at throwing myself over a hurdle than I am at making the bounciest trot in the world look like floating."

"Is that supposed to be a compliment?"

"Maybe."

"Legacy's got a rather smooth trot."

"It doesn't make you look any less graceful," Lucy said, but when the words were out, Lucy panicked slightly. Why in the world did her mouth never know when to stop? Would Elise take the more straightforward compliment as it was, or think that Lucy was making light of the crazy canter situation that Elise had been struggling with?

"It's Legacy who does all the work," Elise mumbled, but both of them knew that this was far from true. No matter what the discipline, while the horse had to do a lot of work, the rider had to work equally as hard to direct, guide, and balance a thousand pound (and sometimes even larger) animal. And the rider's work was twice as hard with an untrained horse.

"Whatever you say," Lucy teased, using the senior's words from before.

"Shouldn't you be getting to work, anyway?" Elise asked.

"I got here early, so it's all good," Lucy paused to check her phone, and she turned the screen so that Elise could see it, "Technically my shift is starting now. So I'm right on time."

But before Lucy could put her phone away, she was slightly confused when Elise's fingers suddenly wrapped around the screen for a brief second, as if to reposition the phone so she could see it better. And when she let go, she asked, "Is that your horse?"

Lucy turned the phone back around, taking in one of her very favorite pictures of Chip; his little dun head peering out from his stall, tiny ears alert, and his signature Fjord mane curved with his neck in the direction of the phone. And even though she saw him every time she looked at her phone, looking at the picture never failed to make her smile.

"I leased him until he retired," Lucy explained, "He taught me just about everything I know. I got to jumping small crossrails with him the year before he retired. His name is Chip. But...I like to call him Chocolate Chip," Lucy added sheepishly, "Chocolate and horses...life doesn't get much better than that."

To Lucy's surprise, Elise smiled, "Chocolate, huh?"

"Literally my two addictions," Lucy said, "Although one of them is *significantly* more expensive than the other."

"Which is the reason you're supposed to be working," Elise joked, turning the phone back around so that she could see it, "And now you've gone from on time to three minutes late."

"I'm going, I'm going. Sheesh," Lucy rolled her eyes, pocketed her phone, and headed back down the aisle to bring the horses in from turnout.

But as she did so, she couldn't help but wonder if Elise's interest in Chip had had anything to do with the picture of the snow-white Fjord horse that sat on the bookcase in Elise's office.

IT WAS GETTING LATE, and Lucy had actually finished early, despite starting three minutes late.

And when she walked upstairs to sweep, she wasn't surprised to find that Elise was still working Legacy in the arena.

Okay, so maybe I'll watch for a bit, Lucy thought.

And even though watching had only gotten her into trouble time and time again, she couldn't help but let her eyes stray to the pair in the arena. There was no doubt that they worked well together when Legacy wasn't fighting. The mare would still lengthen the trot when asked—a sight that never failed to amaze Lucy. And Legacy's circles were nothing short of impeccable.

But the real test was the canter, and Lucy was completely awe-struck when Legacy not only *listened* to Elise's cues, but *continued* to listen all throughout the transition.

Legacy wasn't pulling back, and her head was down. And Elise...was barely putting pressure on the reins at all.

Because...

No, it couldn't be.

But...

Oh my God, it is. It's a freaking Pelham bit.

Lucy's eyes narrowed in on the white horse's muzzle, noticing for the first time that the metal contraption in the horse's mouth wasn't just a simple snaffle bit.

No.

It was *definitely* a Pelham bit, and Lucy didn't know how she hadn't realized it sooner. Everything she saw was characteristic of the Pelham bit—from the bulkier appearance, to the curb chain that ran under Legacy's chin, to the double set of reins that ran from the bit to Elise's gloved hands.

And those hands certainly didn't need to pull as hard because *much* more pressure was being exerted on the horse's mouth, and also the top of the horse's head, which would explain why Legacy wasn't fighting, and why Legacy was more inclined to keep her head down.

And while Lucy knew that the bit could only inflict pain if used incorrectly (Elise was *not* using it incorrectly), she still hated to see *any* horse be put into a "correction" bit, even if it was for a training aid.

"Elise, *why*?" Lucy found herself saying, before she knew what was even coming out of her mouth, "She doesn't deserve that."

The entire barn was so quiet that she could have heard a pin drop. And because of this, even though Lucy had barely raised her voice, she had said it loud enough for Elise to hear. And when the blonde looked up at her with slightly narrowing eyes, Lucy couldn't help but think, *Oh, crap. Here we go again.*

"What?"

"I said..." Lucy's heart was pounding. Was it worth it? It wasn't like Elise was abusing the horse, for God's sake. It was perfectly humane. But..."I said, she doesn't deserve that. The bit. The Pelham."

Elise's eyes narrowed further.

Stupid mouth.

"It's a training aid, Lucy. It's legal. And I know how to use it."

Don't say it. Don't say it. Don't—

"You barely even gave her a chance with the snaffle."

"And *you* don't know how long I've even been working with her to even make that decision."

"But it's not *right*."

"It's only wrong if it's *used* wrong. And I'm not using it wrong. So that makes it right."

"No, it doesn't."

"The horse is not in pain, Lucy."

"I know that, but it doesn't mean it's not uncomfortable."

"Once she learns to carry her head the right way, then it won't be needed."

"She can learn another way," Lucy argued.

"How, by letting her run in circles without showing her that she can't be the one in control? No!"

"But how long do you think you're going to need it for? And then you'll go back to the snaffle and she'll do the same thing! And you have the show coming up..." realization hit Lucy square in the face when she said those words, "Oh my God."

"Lucy—"

"You're going to use that on her at the show, aren't you?"

"*Lucy*—"

Lucy cut the senior off again, "Okay, you know what?"

But those slightly threat-tinged words were where Lucy stopped abruptly. Because at this point, she didn't know what else to say, even though she had so many mixed emotions going through her head. And Elise was waiting, having been spoken over twice already, with one hand her hip, and her mouth pressed into a thin line.

And as Lucy stared back, she realized that she couldn't continue this.

Not if she wanted to have to start all over with Elise *again*. And this bit...it *wasn't* cruel. It was just Lucy's perception. She had grown up with these opinions because of those who had taught her—people who wouldn't resort to these types of training aids until every other option had been exhausted. And Elise was right, how did Lucy know that every other option hadn't already been explored. How did Lucy know how long Elise had been working with Legacy? Maybe Elise had been working with the mare for months? Or a year?

And while the bit may be uncomfortable, it wasn't inhumane.

Elise was experienced—certainly more experienced than Lucy. And Legacy, just as Elise had said, wasn't in pain.

And so Lucy bit her bottom lip, swallowed her pride, opened her mouth, and said, "You're right. She's your training project. You have to handle her however you feel is necessary. You're much more experienced than I am, and I don't have the authority to make those kinds of decisions. So, whatever. Use the bit. Take her to the show with it. It's your call, not mine."

Elise looked a little surprised, but all she said was, "Well, I appreciate you finally realizing this, but I still don't think you completely understand."

If the senior was going to say more, Lucy didn't really want to hear it. She was already annoyed beyond belief that she was practically apologizing for something that she fully believed in, and she'd certainly done plenty of interrupting earlier in their conversation (if she could even label it as such), so it definitely wasn't a problem for her to interrupt again, "I'm pretty sure I understand. Okay? And it doesn't matter. It's not my concern. I shouldn't have gotten involved."

And with that, Lucy left before Elise could say anything else.

She didn't know if what she had done was right. But she knew that the last thing she wanted was for Elise to be upset with her.

And if that meant letting her use Pelham on Legacy...

Then let her use the dumb bit.

THE DOOR WAS STILL open on Thursday when Lucy showed up for work, so she took that as a good sign.

"Hey," Lucy said when she walked into the office, hoping not to discuss anything about their dispute on Sunday, or the show.

They hadn't spoken about it during chem lab on Wednesday, but then again, they had had something else to keep them preoccupied. And now...not so much.

And Lucy couldn't have even said that she was surprised when the first thing out of Elise's mouth was, "Look, I never fully got a chance to explain myself on Sunday," without even acknowledging Lucy's greeting.

"Elise, it's fine," Lucy said, "You don't need to explain yourself."

And she didn't know what else she could or couldn't keep herself from saying, so she walked out of the office without saying anything else, and without waiting for Elise's response.

And she tried to forget about it while she worked—tried to forget about it when she cleaned the stalls.

But when she walked into Legacy's stall and saw that the mare hadn't touched her hay from earlier in the day, she instantly grew concerned for the amount of pressure Legacy had been put through. If that bit was hurting Legacy enough not to eat...

She's going to be fine. She's not your horse. Get over it.

Before she left the stall, she gave Legacy a pat on the shoulder, and told the mare that it was all going to be okay.

I hope.

Lucy didn't know what to think anymore.

This didn't change *anything* that she felt towards Elise...in *that* regard, anyway...but it certainly frustrated her that because she wanted to salvage what she had with the senior, she was being forced to put her beliefs aside.

But maybe that's just it. The closer you can get to her, the more you can help her understand.

Lucy wanted nothing more than to show Elise that there were other ways to get a horse to listen instead of force and control. Sure, the senior probably knew this already. But it was all too easy to fully understand something, yet doubt its practicality, and Lucy was almost completely positive that that was what had compelled the senior to jump to such an extreme method of training. Morality was one thing, but Lucy knew firsthand that it could take a back seat when faced with frustration—especially now, since she'd thrown her arguments for Legacy's sake out the window in order to preserve her friendship with the senior.

And while she could have worried about the entire time she spent feeding the horses, Lucy ended up running into someone who not only let her forget, but gave her something else to focus on altogether...

"What are *you* doing here again!?" Lucy exclaimed, noticing those obnoxious sideburns from yards away.

"Oh, I thought I'd drop by," Matt gave Lucy a smile that disgusted her.

"And why would you do that? During my shift, yet?"

"Why not? I can't spend quality time with the horses?"

Lucy couldn't handle it.

She just couldn't handle it at this point.

First the whole thing with Elise and now...now *Matt*?

Life absolutely hated her.

But she couldn't let Matt know that he was bothering her. That would give him way too much satisfaction—and she was certain that was his main intention.

"Then go ahead. Spend *quality time* with the horses," Lucy said, brushing past him.

She had Legacy's dinner ration in her hands, and was about to pour the grain it into the feed bucket when Matt said, "I can do it."

"*What*?"

She didn't even understand what was happening. Was Matt doing this to be nice? To spite her?

Matt gave Lucy another smile.

Oh, it was definitely to spite her.

And she would *not* give him the satisfaction of scream-
ing at him.

"Okay," she said, in her most nonchalant voice possible,
"Go ahead."

*And when Legacy rips your face off for being in there with
her when she eats, it'll be* karma.

Lucy handed over the container to a very confused looking Matt (no doubt because Lucy hadn't even put up a fight),
and she smirked when her back was to him.

*And you know what, I don't think I want to be around to
witness the blood.*

By the time she had gone back into the feed room and
come out with the next horse's grain rations, Matt was once
again standing outside of Legacy's stall.

And unharmed, too, Lucy thought, slightly disappointed.

"So Legacy's going to be taken to a show tomorrow?"
Matt said, and it was more of a statement than a question.

Lucy's back was to him once more as she entered the
stall opposite of Legacy's, and through gritted teeth she answered, "Yes," when all she really wanted to do was slap him.

"It's too bad she doesn't stand a chance," Matt taunted,
and when Lucy turned around he had a wicked grin on his
face.

"Well, what's that supposed to mean!" Lucy exclaimed,
completely forgetting about her plans to stay calm and jumping right to Legacy's—and Elise's—defense, "Have you even
seen that horse move!? She's a natural. And Elise's got plenty
of experience—more experience than you *ever* will!"

"Defensive, defensive, aren't we?" Matt mocked.

"Does it *matter*?" Lucy shot back hotly.

"Some things matter a lot more than others," Matt gave another wicked smile and tossed an object that was thin and green upwards from his hand, but he caught it before Lucy was able to see exactly what it was. And with that, he walked off, leaving Lucy slightly confused, but mostly disgusted.

"What the *hell* was all of that about?"

ON SUNDAY, LUCY KNEW that the first thing she wanted to ask Elise was how the show had gone. Because on Friday night, when Lucy had shown up for her lesson, she couldn't find the senior anywhere, and had chalked it up to the fact that Elise had most likely been tired and had headed to the house instead of staying at the barn.

And so Lucy was all set to head to the office and ask, when she noticed something.

The door was closed.

Okay, Lucy thought.

Open for a few days...and then shut again.

Odd, but that didn't mean it meant anything.

Maybe Elise was on the phone?

Yeah, that has to be it. She's on the phone.

But as much as Lucy wanted to believe those words, something told her that wasn't the case.

Hesitantly, she brought one hand up to the door, and knocked.

"Come in."

Why did the words seem so...*cold*?

Lucy turned the handle, opened the door, and stepped inside.

"Hey," she said. But when she didn't get much of a response she asked tentatively, "How...was the show?"

Elise didn't even look at Lucy when she answered, "I guess you could say...it didn't exactly go as planned."

"What?" Lucy was confused, "I don't understand."

"Really?"

"Uh, I'm sorry. But no, I don't."

"Well, let me explain what happened then," Elise said, and Lucy didn't know quite what to make of the blonde's tone, "In the morning, Legacy was acting rather...how should we put it...out of sorts? Somewhat lethargic? I had asked Kai to come help me trailer her to the show, and he thought that maybe something was wrong, but she wasn't really exhibiting any signs of sickness, so we trailered her to the show anyway. Only because it was twenty minutes away. If it had been a longer trip, we wouldn't have chanced it. But because it was so close, we did. When we got there, she was acting *slightly* more normal. But when I put her through her warm-up, something felt off. And apparently, other people noticed it, too. Now, you understand that this was a rated show, yes?"

Elise waited deliberately for Lucy's response and Lucy, still confused, confirmed, "Yes."

"At rated shows, the rules are much more strict. And therefore *enforcing* the rules becomes something that is much more often encountered as far as drug testing goes. And when I was approached saying that they had chosen to test the horses for this particular show, it wasn't like I could tell them that they *couldn't*. I was slightly concerned, because we couldn't particularly pinpoint *why* Legacy was behaving in the way she was, but then again, we had *nothing* to hide. So we waited for the blood samples to be drawn, and by the time we had gotten back into the arena, Legacy was acting more like herself. Kai and I decided that it was just the unusual surroundings that had caused her to act abnormally, and that the change of environment during the drug test had actually helped to calm her before we got back into the arena. She was listening better, and she was much more alert.

"And so, as you can imagine, once we were certain that she was fine, we were confident in the fact that she would be able to handle showing in her division. And when the time came for our class, she put forth one of her best efforts yet. Sure, she still tossed her head slightly, but she wasn't fighting me nearly as much as she had before. And we placed sixth, out of fifteen."

"Did it *occur* to you that she wasn't fighting because of the *bit*?" Lucy asked.

"Did it ever *occur* to you that when I had wanted to *explain* myself to you that there may have very well been a good reason for it? I was trying to tell you, Pelham bits are illegal to use in dressage competitions. I could only compete with her in the snaffle."

Lucy's mouth slowly formed an 'o' shape before she said, "Oh," feeling like the biggest idiot on the planet. But...Elise wasn't smiling. And in fact, she still looked downright *mad*. And Lucy was confused, because hadn't Elise said that they'd placed sixth?

"But once again, you didn't let me finish," Elise contin- ued, "That night I got a call from the coordinators of the show, telling me that we had been disqualified."

"What!?" Lucy exclaimed.

"You heard me," Elise said, tone once again icy, "We had been disqualified. Because somehow, Legacy's drug test came back as *positive* for a *tranquilizer*."

"*What*?" Lucy repeated, narrowing her eyes, "That couldn't be possible. You and Kai were the last ones to be around her. And the only one who was near her before that was..."

Lucy stopped mid-sentence, realization hitting her like a punch in the stomach.

Oh, God, she wouldn't really think that—

"*You* were the last one near her. *You* were the only one left in the barn on Thursday night," Elise's words were abrupt, cold as ice.

"You have *no* right to think that I did that!" Lucy ex- claimed defensively.

"Well, it seems fairly obvious to me—how you were so adamant about me not using that bit! If she'd been any more out of sorts, we wouldn't have taken her to the show and there, problem solved. Simple as that."

"Elise, I would *never* endanger a horse like that! Whoev- er did that must have given her one hell of a dose, because for it to only be *wearing off* that late in the morning...You should just be lucky she's okay!" Lucy was fuming, and she could barely finish one sentence before she began another, "I would never purposely *drug* a horse. And especially not over something as trivial as a *bit*. Okay? Yes, I was annoyed that you were using it, but would it drive me to such extremes? *No*!"

"And what proof do you have?" Elise asked—clearly in no mood to see anyone else's perspective on the matter.

"What proof do *you* have!?" Lucy shot back.

"Much more than you, at the moment," Elise said levelly.

At this point, Lucy was highly aggravated, her mind barely able to wrap itself around just exactly *what* was happening. But through her anger, she fought to remain calm, knowing that it was the only way she was going to be able to handle this. She took a breath and said, "Look, Elise. I *know* you're angry right now. And I *know* that, unfortunately, every sign at the moment points to me. But you're wrong. You're wrong, and somewhere, somehow, I *know* that you know it. You don't want to believe me because you need someone to blame. But I care about these horses just as much as you do, and I know how much Legacy means to you, even if you don't want to show it. And I want you to understand that I would never do something like that. You *know* that I would never do something like that. Hell, I was the one who didn't want you to use the bit that I thought was *uncomfortable*, and you're telling me that I was the one who *drugged* the horse? There's something a little backwards about that, don't you think? Just...*please*, Elise. Please, *please* trust me."

"I really don't know who I can trust anymore," Elise said coldly.

Forget calm.

Lucy glared, "You know what? I try to be reasonable with you! I try to be calm about it! I...I can't *do* this! I can't just *stand* here and *take* this when I know I haven't done anything!"

"Then *leave*."

Lucy's glare narrowed, but she wasn't so sure now if it was for show, or if it was to hold back the tears that she suddenly felt.

This could *not* be happening.

After everything she had done—every single precaution she had taken to make sure that this friendship that they had stayed intact...

It was all for nothing.

She was so incredibly mad at Elise for not believing her.

How in the world could Elise accuse her of an act that could possibly harm a horse?

Lucy *knew* that Elise knew that she would never do such a thing.

You know what, I'll show her how much these horses mean to me. I'm not going to leave. I'm going to stay here and take care of them, because they deserve it even if she doesn't deserve my help.

And Lucy's only consolation was Dee. She spent nearly half an hour in Dee's stall, trying to calm herself down with her arms wrapped tightly around the mare's sturdy neck. Dee would occasionally twist her head around, positioning it just so that it was next to Lucy's own and leaving it there for a few seconds. The mare's soft breaths were actually quite comforting against Lucy's tear-stained face.

'It's okay' Dee seemed to be saying *'It's all going to be okay.'*

But if Lucy was certain of one thing, it was that everything was most certainly *not* okay...

She didn't sweep the barn that night.

And she never went to sign out; Elise would know that she had stayed once she saw that everything had been taken care of.

And then you'll see. You'll see how much I really do care. You'll see that I'm right.

When she stepped outside, she found that it had started snowing.

And Elise, most certainly, did not offer her a ride back to campus.

"LUCY, PLEASE STOP CRYING."

It was all Lucy could do to calm down enough to tell Harley what had happened on Sunday.

She had kept it to herself for an entire day, but by the time Tuesday night had come around, and Lucy realized that she would have to see Elise in chem lab on Wednesday, Lucy knew that she needed to tell someone. She had two of the most conflicting emotions regarding the situation, and she knew that if she didn't talk it out, it might just drive her past the point of insanity.

"I'm *trying*," Lucy said. She was sitting cross-legged at the foot of the bed in her friend's room, not even able to look at him when she talked, "It's just...I'm so incredibly *mad* at her for ever thinking that I'd do something like that. But at the same time, it...it *hurts* me more than it makes me mad because..." Lucy trailed off, not knowing whether to admit it or not. But this was Harley. Her best friend, "Because...I *care* about what we had and—"

"Well, that was fairly obvious."

"What?" Lucy was so startled by Harley's response that she momentarily forgot what she had been going to say.

Harley sighed, "I'm certain that if it were any other one of your friends accusing you of this you'd probably be more inclined to yell at them than cry over it."

Friends.

Lucy almost laughed at how casually he said the word. But she put it behind her (along with her almost-confession), and took a moment to contemplate Harley's blatant reasoning, "I definitely yelled at her."

Harley gave her a *look*.

"Okay," Lucy sighed, "Okay, fine. I know. You're right. I just can't stand the fact that she pushed me away for so long, and then she opened up, and now...now it's right back to where we started, but *worse*. It's like...she was *looking* for a reason to push me away again."

"I don't think I'd go that far with it. But you need to see it from her perspective, too," Harley said, "You really *were* the last one in the barn that night."

Lucy narrowed her eyes, "I *know* that."

Harley held up his hands, "Hey, I'm not blaming you for anything. I'm just saying, she has a point. I know you'd never do that."

"No, what I mean is I *know* that. I stood there and *told* her that I can see it the way she sees it. That I *was* the last person in the barn that night...*wait*," Lucy narrowed her eyes even further, thinking back to the vague memories she had of that Thursday, "Harley, just because I was the *last* person in the barn that night doesn't mean that I was the *only* person in the barn that night!"

"What?" Harley asked, sounding slightly confused.

How had Lucy not seen it before? It was so glaringly obvious—she had just been too blinded by what she had been feeling to really take into account what *had* happened that Thursday night!

"I *wasn't* the only person there on Thursday night," Lucy said slowly as the reality of the situation hit her.

"*Matt* was there."

Chapter Thirteen

"*What*?" Harley asked, concern written all over his face.

"Matt was there the night that Legacy was drugged," Lucy repeated, though she was fairly certain that Harley's question had functioned more as an outlet of surprise rather than as a request for clarification.

"He showed up during my shift," Lucy continued, remembering everything that she'd been too blind to see before, "He showed up right when I had to start feeding the horses. Right when I was about to feed *Legacy*. I thought he was there to annoy me, because he had shown up so conveniently to drop off papers for the team during my shift only a few days before...and he said that he'd give Legacy her food. And I didn't want to say no to him, because I didn't want to give him the satisfaction of *arguing* with him...and that *must* have been it. Because for the tranquilizer to have shown on the drug test, and then to have been mostly wearing off by the time they arrived at the show...it only makes sense that she had to be drugged the night before the show. And he said...what was it now? *Dammit* why can't I remember? He said...it was something about...about Legacy being taken to the show, and how she wasn't going to stand a chance, and that green thing—he had that green thing in his hand! Why didn't I realize all of this sooner! God, I'm an idiot. It makes me want to just march right up to him and—"

"Whoa, whoa, okay," Harley said, and Lucy could tell that he was trying very hard to keep up with her rushed talking—which was evidently an effort of little success as far as actually understanding Lucy's words, "Slow down, and tell me again exactly what happened."

Lucy took a breath, attempted to calm herself, and started over, "Okay. So Matt showed up at the barn *right* when I was about to feed Legacy. And he said he'd go in and give the horse her dinner. And *I* just figured he'd come to spite me; that he was looking for an argument. And I didn't want to give him the satisfaction, so I told him he could. I went back into the feed room after that because I *know* how Legacy gets if you're in there when she has her food, and I was fairly certain that things were about to go downhill. But when I walked out of the feed room, Matt was standing outside of Legacy's stall, and everything was fine.

"But then he *stayed* there, said that thing about Legacy 'not having a chance' at the show, and he had this little green thing in his hand. And I was so unbearably mad at him for saying that about Legacy that I couldn't even tell what it was, but it *must* have been the cap to the syringe he used. I *know* he was the one who did it. There was no one else there!"

Harley looked thoughtful for a moment, and then he said, "Okay. I believe you. I did before, and now you have the evidence. But...why would he do that? He's certainly not the nicest person in the world, but what would make him want to drug a horse? What does he have against Legacy? Against Elise?"

Lucy contemplated Harley's questions.

What *did* Matt have against Legacy and Elise?

It wasn't like he was competing in the show. And Elise wasn't on the team, so he wasn't competing with Elise for *anything*.

Unless...

"Oh my *God*. He did not!" Lucy exclaimed, eyes widening in shock.

"What am I missing now?" Harley asked, his tone light, but by the way his eyes narrowed slightly, Lucy knew that her friend was mainly concerned.

Matt hadn't been competing with Elise for anything except...

Lucy.

He knew.

He'd known from the very beginning how much Elise meant to Lucy.

From the moment he'd said that Lucy had had 'someone else', to the moment he'd walked in on Lucy's awkward confession the night he had dropped of the paperwork...

Matt hadn't done this to get to Elise.

He'd done it to get back at *Lucy*.

Because he knew—he *knew* that Elise would jump to conclusions. He *knew* that Elise would blame her because she was 'the only one around'. And he *knew* how much it would hurt Lucy.

He knew, before *Lucy* had even know.

How twisted and disgusting he was, planning this whole thing out, wrecking Elise's chances at the competition, and *endangering* a horse! And in a way, maybe it *was* Lucy's fault. Because this entire situation had happened over *Lucy*.

"Lucy?" Harley prompted, "What is it?"

"He *knew*, Harley," Lucy whispered, but she could say no more.

Harley waited, but when Lucy still refused to speak, he asked, "What does Matt know?"

"He...he knows how much Elise means to me," Lucy's voice was barely audible, and she closed her eyes as she spoke, "He knew Elise would blame me. He set me up. Because he knew it would break me."

Harley opened his mouth to say something, but then clamped it shut again, realization passing through his eyes, "Lucy, are we talking...*more* than just friendship here?"

And while Harley hadn't actually spoken a name aloud, the message was clear.

"Maybe," Lucy said, hugging her knees to her chest, "I'm really mad at her right now. But...yes."

Everything was just *so* screwed up right now.

"Okay," Harley said slowly, "Well, I'll admit I didn't exactly see that coming."

His words only made Lucy want to curl into herself further and disappear, but when she felt Harley's arm around her, she let her head find its way to his shoulder, tears burning at the back of her eyes once more.

"But there's nothing wrong with that," Harley said, "The only thing that's wrong is what Matt did. And you can't blame yourself either. Because I know you, and I know you're jumping to your own conclusions in that crazy mind of yours. But it's not your fault."

It took Lucy a few more minutes to calm down to the point where she could talk. But when she could form her own words again, she said, "Thank you. I don't think I tell you often enough how lucky I am to have you. You're the only one who I can actually talk to."

"Hey," Harley said, "That's what I'm here for."

"Well, now you know. Now you know that part of me wants to march down to the barn and knock some sense into her, but the other part of me...is just devastated," Lucy sighed.

"You have every right to be mad at her, Lucy. And she had no right to blame you as quickly as she had. But now you have an idea of what really did happen, so I think that what you need to do is tell her that. Tell her what you know. And...let her come around to seeing that you're right. Because there isn't anything else that you can do," Harley reasoned.

Lucy nodded against her best friend's shoulder, "You're right. You always are."

"Well, I wouldn't say *always*."

"Okay, fine," Lucy said, smiling for the first time in hours, "Maybe not always. But most of the time. And that's good enough for me."

Lucy really wanted to skip the lab the following day.

But she couldn't.

If she did that, her grades would suffer, and she couldn't let the entire situation spiral out of control like that.

So she forced herself to go, and of course, the experiment that they had to perform was a titration.

And Lucy really wasn't any chemistry expert, but she knew enough (although primarily through the rumors that had spread from the students who had performed the experiment in the beginning of the week) to know that titrations were some of the longest experiments to complete. And even better yet, if they went one drop over the point of equilibrium, the entire experiment would have to be done *again*.

Well, if she's good for anything right now, it's that we're almost guaranteed to not *have to suffer through this twice...*

It was so unbearably frustrating, working with Elise and knowing that they couldn't discuss what had happened between them during the lab. Being in the classroom instead of the barn, it was like a whole different world—a whole different world where their little 'altercation' wasn't completely disregarded but, perhaps, placed on the back burner to deal with sometime later. Elise was completely focused on the lab, pretty much ignoring the redhead except for when she would occasionally hold out a piece of lab equipment with an expectant look on her face.

"You could just *ask* me to take it from you," Lucy mumbled.

And while she knew the senior had heard her, the lack of response showed that Elise just blatantly refused to answer. Because the one thing that still hung over the both of them was that, even if they weren't *talking* about what had happened, it didn't mean that it *hadn't* happened.

Sighing, she took the beaker full of a liquid that she identified as the base—in essence, the opposite of an acid. Both solutions were colorless, but Lucy knew it was the base because that was what they had to start with. And as she looked from the clear liquid in the beaker and then back up to the table in front of her, she watched Elise work. She watched the senior set everything up precisely, knowing that, especially now, Elise wouldn't trust her to connect a power cable to an outlet.

Or even be near her damn horse, she scowled as her thoughts drifted elsewhere once more. Because no matter how Elise may act towards her in the lab, she knew that once they walked out the door, everything would be different; or, rather, the same as it had been the night that she first accused Lucy of being the one to drug Legacy.

Hot and cold.

That's what it always was with the senior.

Though more recently, she'd been seeing a little too much of the so called 'Ice Queen' side than she'd ever bargained for.

Why was it that she just had to have the world's biggest crush on the world's most *stubborn* person? Because really, no matter how many times the senior adorably bit her bottom lip in concentration, Elise was definition going to get a piece of her mind once they were finished with this lab...

"*Lucy.*"

The word, stern in tone and abrupt in length, pulled the redhead once more out of her thoughts.

"Sorry, what was that?"

"I said I need the beaker," Elise repeated the words that had gone completely over Lucy's head before.

Lucy narrowed her eyes, determined to get the senior to let her do something in the lab today besides having the role of the holder of all equipment, "I know where it goes. Move over."

Elise's eyes seemed to pierce into her own for a second longer than necessary, but the senior was the one who broke their staring contest first, with a loud sigh and a curt, "Fine."

All too pleased with herself, Lucy placed the liquid from the beaker into a flask, and then put the flask on the ring stand, which held the buret—a device that would slowly add another liquid into the flask.

"See," Lucy said, proudly and just a little too smugly.

Elise only sighed again, stepping back towards the counter to fill the space that Lucy had so graciously vacated.

So that you can have full rein of the rest of the experiment, Lucy rolled her eyes.

Oh, how she couldn't wait until the rest of this lab was over...

THE MINUTE THE TITRATION was finished and all of the supplies had been cleaned and put away, Lucy wasn't even sure who ran for the door the fastest. Though of course, as always, it was Elise who had managed to slip out the door before her, and Lucy hurried down the steps to keep up with the senior's pace. But once they had reached the main level of the building, before Elise had a chance to get even a foot away from her, Lucy grabbed the back of the blonde's backpack, and didn't let go until Elise had turned around to face her.

"What?" Elise asked, crossing her arms. She knew just as well as Lucy did that there was no way she was getting out of this one.

And to Lucy's surprise, the word didn't sound as cold as it normally would have been...just impatient.

Lucy took a breath and said, "I just wanted to say again that it *wasn't* me. You've had plenty of time to think it over. And so have I. And yesterday, I remembered something. I was too caught up in my anger to realize it before. I was *not* the only one in the barn on Thursday night. Matt was there. And I think he's the one who drugged Legacy."

Elise seemed as though she considered Lucy's words for a moment, before asking a question not unlike the one that Harley had asked only a day earlier, "And why would he do that?"

But somehow, when the question came from the senior herself, it struck a chord inside of Lucy that it hadn't with her best friend, and she suddenly found herself glaring, "So within seconds you're wondering why *he* would do something as horrible as that, and you decide in only a day that I *would* do it? You're *incredible*."

Because at this point, Lucy had had enough.

Lab had been bearable...but *this*?

She just couldn't deal with it anymore.

Because she cared.

She cared so damn much about Elise; so much about making Elise understand what had happened, and who the real culprit was, and how never in her life would she ever even *think* of putting a horse in danger.

But she was so incredibly mad, and right now, her anger was taking a stronger hold than anything else she was feeling. And so before she could do or say anything else that would make the situation worse, she pushed past Elise and ran outside, the cold air hitting her hard in the face.

THE NEXT TEST, LUCY knew, was work.

The snow still remained a heavy coating on the ground, nowhere near budging with the crazy drop in temperatures they'd been experiencing lately. And so Lucy asked Harley to drive her to the barn with the arrangement for him to pick her up when her shift was over, as the forecast for the mid-November Thursday called for nothing but more snow.

"Just stay calm," Harley told her, knowing all too well, just as Lucy herself did, what could sometimes happen when she let her anger get the best of her.

"I'll try," Lucy sighed.

"Call me when you're done. I'll be free to get you any time."

Lucy nodded to let him know that she had heard him, but she didn't exactly want to continue talking. Worry had settled once more in the pit of her stomach, and she didn't think that she could force herself to say anything else.

Lucy stopped at Dee's stall before she headed to the office, the mare's soft muzzle against her hand enough of a comfort, for the time being, for her to face whatever was to come. Giving the mare a final pat, she stepped away from Dee's stall and turned the corner...and was met with the sight of the office door not entire closed, but slightly ajar. Taking a breath, Lucy knocked lightly, but even that was enough to cause the door to open a few inches further before Elise even had time to answer.

The senior didn't look at Lucy when she walked in, although Lucy had most certainly looked at her. Lucy didn't think the pen and clipboard had ever felt so far from her before. Once she'd reached her destination, she performed everything so robotically that she had to check the paper one more time to make sure she had written her own name, and not one of the insane thoughts flying through her mind.

And, just like before, it wasn't until Lucy made a move to leave that Elise spoke for the first time.

"Lucy..." Elise's voice was uncertain and small.

Timid, even.

Hours seemed to pass as Lucy locked eyes with the senior, mouth pressed into a thin line.

I'm waiting.

Elise drew in a sharp breath, looked away from the redhead, and said, "Lucy, there are...quite a few things I'd like to say. And I understand if you don't want to hear me out."

Lucy crossed her arms and said, "By all means, continue."

The senior paused for a moment before beginning again, "I'd like to start by...thanking you for staying on Sunday, even though I told you to leave. You had no reason to stay and work, but you did, and I appreciate it, even though I didn't deserve your help after I had talked to you like that. And I would also like to thank you for giving me the information about Matt. Because as it turns out...you were right. We—well, Kai and I—found this," Elise placed an object on the desk—a plastic bag that contained one full and one empty syringe—both topped with the green cap that Lucy had identified from earlier, "in his bag yesterday. This matter is to be dealt with seriously, and he will be punished accordingly."

Elise paused again, still not looking up at Lucy. And Lucy thought that maybe she was finished, but then she continued talking, "And...I want to apologize, Lucy. It was wrong of me to just assume that it was you. I know that you would never purposely put a horse in danger. I know that now, and I knew it then. And I know it's no excuse, but you were absolutely right—I was angry. I was upset. I wanted someone to blame. And that person was, wrongfully so, you. We may have had clashing opinions, but it was wrong of me to hold that against you. And you have every reason not to forgive me, but I'm sorry."

Well, the part about Matt was something she'd already known, but it took all of Lucy's effort to keep the surprise she felt from showing on her face.

Elise had *never* apologized to Lucy before.

With the way the senior had handled the situation, of *course* it had warranted an apology. But still...

"Well, you're right about one thing—it was definitely wrong of you to jump to conclusions like that. But the most important thing is that no one's hurt. Legacy is fine. So...it's okay. I'm willing to put this behind us. Leave the past in the past," Lucy said, uncrossing her arms.

Elise's blue eyes found their way to Lucy's own with an incredulous expression, as if she didn't believe the words that Lucy had said. To reinforce the fact that, yes, Lucy had (gladly and with *much* relief) accepted the apology, she gave Elise a small smile.

And Lucy turned then, slipping through the door without completely closing it behind her, because she didn't want the senior to see how relieved she was. She felt like she could almost cry all over again—but from happiness—and *that* was certainly something that she didn't want Elise to witness. At least, not something that she wanted the senior to witness at this very moment.

But it didn't change the fact that Lucy couldn't have been any happier with the way the last few minutes had gone. Because not only had Elise seen that it hadn't been Lucy's fault, but the senior had pointedly admitted that she had been wrong. She had *asked* Lucy for forgiveness. And somehow, that meant more to Lucy than anything else.

The forecast of snow had definitely proven itself true by the time Lucy had finished. And, oddly enough, both Elise and Legacy were nowhere to be seen.

Seriously? Why would she go out in a storm like this? Lucy wondered.

She had just been about to call Harley to pick her up, but for some reason, she felt weird leaving before she knew that the two of them were back safely. The storm was only supposed to get worse...

You don't even know where she went. She could be anywhere. Their property is huge, Lucy reminded herself. *And she can take care of herself.*

Lucy was instantly conflicted, but decided that going to look couldn't hurt. Legacy was a training project, after all. What if she'd gotten freaked out by the sudden storm?

Making up her mind, Lucy put her phone back in her pocket, and headed to the tack room to grab Dee's bridle, along with her helmet that she had conveniently left in her bag. A voice in the back of her head told her that this wasn't her barn, or her horse—it wasn't her place to take a horse out, alone, in the dark, without permission.

But at the same time, her mind was clouded with thoughts of Elise. And Lord only knew when she thought of the senior first, it could lead her to do many things without thinking before she acted.

Not wanting to waste any time, Lucy didn't bother running back upstairs for a saddle, but she did head to the supply room for a flashlight, because Lucy knew that she wouldn't be able to see without one in the storm. Then she bridled the chestnut mare, who didn't seem to care that Lucy was taking her out even though it was well past dinnertime.

It really is cold out here, Lucy thought, zipping her jacket all the way as she walked Dee outside. Although there was no mounting block in sight, there was one lone hay bale that had been separated from the others in the hay barn, no doubt because something was wrong with it, and it provided Lucy with enough of a height boost to get in the saddle. Turning Dee back towards the barn, the redhead surveyed her surroundings.

The flood lights from the barn allowed Lucy to see out around the pastures, and the snow, while it had been falling for a while, was light, and so Lucy could still see the vague indentations of hoof prints that must have been none other than Legacy's, headed off in the direction of the woods.

Lucy had never been on that part of the property, but nonetheless, she turned Dee in the direction of the trees, the mare taking surefooted steps in the snow beneath her. When they came to the woods, Lucy turned the flashlight on, Dee's ears flicking backwards uncertainly at first. But when the mare's surroundings became slightly more illuminated, and less dark and intimidating, Dee settled down. And although she was inclined to stay more alert than the mare who had settled down so easily, even Lucy had to relax slightly the further they traveled. Because she found that, surprisingly, the ride was actually quite peaceful.

While Lucy wasn't a fan of the dark, or the woods—and especially both of these things in the middle of the winter—she enjoyed watching the small snowflakes fall. She liked how they would land on Dee's mane, peppering the mare's vivid copper color with little splotches of white. She loved how, within the beam of light from the flashlight, the snowflakes seemed to dance as they floated to the ground.

And in a way, it was mesmerizing.

Lucy really hadn't known how beautiful winter truly was.

She had always regarded the season as a time of bitter cold and harsh winds, and had resented the fact that it was the sole reason that she had to be cooped up riding inside for months at a time.

But here she was, riding out in the snow...It really was an experience comparable to no other.

It didn't take Lucy much longer to find the senior. While the hoof prints had practically all vanished with the constant new coating of snow, the path in the woods was straight and direct, spilling out into a clearing where the trees parted.

And that was where she found Elise and Legacy.

Lucy realized that she didn't need to keep the flashlight on, because although it was dark, the moon was still slightly visible behind the clouds, and the snow around them gave off its own kind of glow. Silently clicking the flashlight off (a sound only addressed by the swiveling of Dee's right ear) Lucy took in the sight of the senior, sitting tall atop the Arabian mare and looking out at what could only be a small lake that was now completely frozen over.

And if Lucy had thought that winter was beautiful...then Elise was, indeed, the epitome of winter itself.

The senior's white polo shirt blended so well with the snow around them, and she wore no jacket. Because...the cold had never bothered her. Elise's pale skin seemed to glow, and snowflakes glistened in that platinum blonde braid. From the distance, Legacy's flea-bitten coat looked pure white as she stood tall and elegant.

And there was no doubt in Lucy's mind, as she took in the sight before her, that Elise herself truly was as regal and graceful as Legacy's namesake.

When Lucy was finally able to draw her eyes away from the sight, she figured that she should most likely make her presence known. But then a movement that she caught ever so slightly out of the corner of her eye stopped her from saying anything.

While Elise had remained perfectly still the entire time Lucy had been there, she watched as the senior, in very uncharacteristic display of emotion, leaned all the way forward in the saddle, arms encircling Legacy's neck, face pressed against the snow-covered mane of the Arabian mare. And Legacy didn't seem to mind at all; she merely turned her head briefly in Elise's direction, gave a small huff that to Lucy sounded quite content, and then faced forward once more, unmoving until Elise was once again sitting up.

No longer willing to verbally announce her presence, Lucy settled for just walking Dee over to Elise and Legacy, positive that the senior would hear her approaching. And it took Dee twenty steps exactly until the two of them were side by side. The horses touched noses, greeting one another. But Elise's gaze remained on the frozen lake in front of her.

Lucy's gaze, while first focused on Elise, also found its way to that frozen lake. A perfect sheet of ice, with only a thin dusting of snow when compared to everything else around them, was framed between Dee's copper ears. The mare's breaths were visible in the cold, each one making it seem like a fog was hanging over the lake. And Lucy thought she could sit there all night, with the senior beside her.

But it was Elise's soft voice that eventually broke the silence, "You know, you're right about everything."

Although Lucy tried to think of what the senior was referring to, she couldn't decide what exactly 'everything' entailed, "What do you mean?"

"I mean just that," Elise said simply, "Everything. You're right about the way I ride. About the bit. About the training. You're right about...everything."

Elise's straightforward confession startled Lucy slightly, and she wasn't quite certain how to respond. She paused for a moment before saying, "Well, I just like to think of it

as...borrowing freedom. These horses, they're incredible animals. They could crush us in a heartbeat if they wanted to.
But something inside them—something so incredibly self-
less—makes them want to try to listen to what we ask them
to do. And if they don't understand, or they get frustrated
and do the wrong thing it's okay. Because they're not perfect.
We're not perfect. And letting us work with them in the way
we do...it's a privilege, not a right."

Following Lucy's words, the only sound around them
was that of the horses' quiet breaths.

And then Elise turned to look at her, "That was kind of
beautiful."

Lucy was positive that her face flushed slightly, "Really?"

Elise nodded, giving Lucy a small smile, "Yeah."

Lucy didn't know how to reply after that, but before she
could figure out how to, her phone rang, disturbing the for-
merly peaceful moment.

"It's Harley," Lucy stated, slightly frustrated that he'd
chosen this time to call, "Give me a minute."

Lucy sighed and answered the call with words that she
hoped weren't tinged with too much annoyance, "Hey,
Harley."

*'Lucy, I've been worried about you. You didn't even call,
and I didn't know whether to just come get you or wait or what.
Are you done yet?'*

"Well..." Lucy trailed off, glancing at the senior out of the
corner of her eye. She saw that Elise had turned away from
her, most likely to make it seem as though she was giving
Lucy some semblance of privacy even though there was no
way that Elise couldn't at least hear Lucy's end of the con-

versation. And knowing this, Lucy chose her words carefully, answering her friend with a vague, "Not yet."

'I'm a little confused.'

Lucy only smiled even though she knew he couldn't see it, "I'll talk to you later."

'But—'

"Later, okay?"

Lucy heard a sigh before Harley said, *'Fine, later. Just don't make me get you at midnight, please.'*

"I won't," Lucy said with a laugh, and then she hung up. Turning back to Elise she said, "So...are you ready to head back?"

Elise only nodded.

But when Lucy tried to turn on the flashlight, it flickered for a moment before going out completely.

"Ugh," Lucy groaned, tapping the flashlight against her palm in the hopes that it would bring the batteries back to life. But all it succeeded in doing was startling Dee. "Sorry, girl," Lucy gave the mare a pat before pocketing the flashlight once more. Then she turned to Elise and said, "I guess we're stuck without light...or wait, I'll use my phone. That'll work," Lucy held up her phone, but it didn't give off much light at all.

"It's all right," Elise said, "We'll be fine."

Oddly reassured by the senior's words (although it was Elise's home, after all. She definitely had to know where she was going), Lucy felt better about heading back into the dark woods even if her phone was only giving off enough light to see only about a foot in front of her.

Their ride was silent, even though while they had been talking by the lake, the wind had definitely picked up and the snow was falling more heavily. And although less often when she was around the senior, Lucy found that she herself was the one to break the silence, with the most random (yet relevant) exclamation of, "Tree!"

"What?"

"There's a tree. Across the path," Lucy said, holding the phone out closer to Elise so that the senior could see further, and when Elise's eyes widened slightly, she knew that Elise had seen what she had.

"That wasn't there before," Elise sighed, "It must have come down from the wind."

"I'm jumping it," Lucy said.

"What? You're crazy."

"It's only got to be about a foot and a half high," Lucy said.

"You can't see anything in front of you, there's snow everywhere, and you don't even have a saddle," Elise argued.

"Hey, I'm not telling you to jump it, too. You can walk around it."

"And that, I am going to do," Elise said, "But I think I'll wait until the coast is clear."

Lucy only took that as her invitation to go first.

Yes, she was a little wary of the fact that she really couldn't see in front of her. But she had jumped without a saddle before, and she trusted Dee despite the spunky personality she could sometimes have. Lucy was confident in the fact that, because Dee had been quiet and responsive the entire ride, the mare would be more than willing to listen to her directions.

Lucy repositioned Dee a little further from the tree so that she had enough space to gain momentum. Then she asked Dee to trot, and trusted the mare to find her own distance. And when Lucy felt Dee take off, she kept her position forward. She managed to stay balanced over the jump, but had to lean slightly on Dee's neck to reposition herself once the mare landed, as Dee had taken a larger jump than Lucy had expected. She let Dee canter a few steps, since that was how she had landed, but brought the mare back down to a walk before they ended up too far away.

"You're crazy," Elise repeated once more as she maneuvered Legacy around the tree, bending in and out of the various trees that lined the right side of the path without ending up too far in the thicker part of the woods.

Lucy only shrugged in response, even though she knew Elise couldn't see it. But she didn't really know what else to say to that, so the rest of the five minute ride remained as quiet as it had begun.

When they arrived back at the barn, they dried the horses as well as they could before putting their blankets on, working in each horse's respective stall. But Lucy ran into Elise once more when she brought Dee's bridle up to the tack room. And Lucy probably would have missed the senior's soft spoken question had she not been so close to her.

"Why'd you come look for me?"

The tone of the question wasn't angry or facetious; simply genuine.

Lucy shrugged, "You were gone for a while. And it was getting late. And dark. And the storm was supposed to get worse, which clearly it did."

And if Lucy had thought that the previous question was quiet, Elise's next question was barely even audible, "Why are you even being so nice to me? I was awful to you, and yet you went completely out of your way to find me."

"Well," Lucy carefully deliberated her words before she said them, "I guess you could say I've given it some thought, and...I've decided what's worth worrying about."

Elise's blue eyes shifted from the ground to Lucy's own, realization passing through them almost instantaneously.

Whether the senior knew *all* of the implications that Lucy associated with her declaration, the redhead wasn't certain. But now Elise at least knew that their friendship meant more to Lucy than Lucy had ever let her believe before.

Chapter Fourteen

J ust like with their previous argument, Lucy found that, with little time, things went back to normal.

And it seemed that although the fight pushed them further from one another during the course of their misunderstanding, they now almost ended up closer to each other than they had been before as far as conversations and small talk went—which was *perfectly* fine with Lucy.

Elise would talk to Lucy more during Lucy's shift, and Lucy noticed that Elise would ride more in Lucy's presence as well. And Lucy didn't know where the Pelham bit had gone, but it was no longer in the tack room. Elise didn't use it with Legacy again. This didn't mean that Legacy no longer fought, though. Elise's work with the Arabian mare, while improving, never exactly ended any differently than in a game of tug-of-war. It had simply become more of a matter of getting the mare to behave for longer amounts of time *before* putting up a fight, which, as it were, wasn't that simple at all.

No matter what she felt though, Lucy knew by now that it wasn't her place to intervene. Lucy was the only reason that Elise was now working with the horse in the snaffle, so that was good enough for her. Even if the senior hadn't yet attempted to alter the way that she was riding, relying less on corrective aids was something Lucy considered to be a step in the right direction.

But on this particular day, a week and a half after the argument, Elise had Lance out on the crossties instead of Legacy.

"Giving Legacy a break?" Lucy asked as she worked her way down the stalls.

Elise shrugged, her response not quite as straightforward as Lucy would have expected, "Sort of."

"Okay," Lucy said, choosing not to question it, "But doesn't it get overbearing though? You know, having to work with two horses at once?"

"Well, I'm not exactly *working* with him yet," Elise said.

"What do you mean?" Lucy asked, confused.

"The only time he's been ridden here was when you rode him."

At the senior's words, Lucy wondered if maybe there was a reason for that. She distinctly remembered Elise saying that she wanted to watch someone else ride the horse before she did—that she needed to see the way he moved. And in a way, it made sense. But Lucy had a feeling that there was more to it than just that.

"Oh," Lucy said, "So are you just hacking him then?"

"Not exactly. I mean, I've got to start with him sometime, right? My parents are coming back from wherever they are now—Cloudside Rim, I think?—sometime after winter break starts. So ideally I should have made some progress with him already. But it is what it is."

"All the exercise he's gotten is turnout, right?" Lucy asked.

"And some work on the lunge line," Elise added, "to make up for the fact that he can't exactly be a part of the lesson program. Hopefully he's got some manners now, but I guess we'll just have to find out."

"Well, have fun with him," Lucy joked as she moved on to the next stall. And though she was already halfway down the aisle, she heard Elise's answer loud and clear: "Fun is *quite* an understatement."

And an understatement it was, as Lucy spent most of her time watching the senior ride. Because once she had figured out how to (for once) keep her mouth shut, watching Elise ride had recently become a habit. And even better yet, Elise no longer seemed to mind.

Lucy could tell from the very beginning when Lance pinned his ears and walked in circles around the mounting block instead of staying put that the entire ride was certainly going to be one hectic experience. The horse was certainly in no mood to work.

It seemed that the mounting block itself was what spurred Lance's response; Lucy figured that he must have picked up this habit from wherever Elise's parents had gotten him. Lucy could practically see the thoughts going through the devious horse's mind: the mounting block meant someone getting on and someone getting on meant work. And work, Lucy was positively certain, was something that Lance wanted to avoid at all costs. But Elise outsmarted the warmblood gelding by leading Lance away from the mounting block and just getting on from the ground.

This action impressed Lucy, as getting on from the ground was a skill she had yet to master, and the distance from the ground to the stirrup was in no way short. But it surprised Lance, who had been standing still, probably thinking he'd been the one to outsmart Elise and get out of working. And even before Elise had her other foot in the stirrup, Lance just started to walk off on his own. The sight nearly made Lucy laugh, but Elise, of course, was able to adjust her position as if nothing had ever happened. And she made Lance halt, which ended up turning into the gelding attempting to sidestep every which way in order to evade staying in one place for an extended period of time.

Seeing how uncooperative Lance was being from the beginning, part of Lucy wondered why Elise's parents would have even considered the headstrong gelding to be a dressage prospect.

But that's probably because you know nothing about dressage, Lucy reminded herself.

Once Elise had gotten Lance to stay in place for just about a minute—probably as long as the gelding would allow for—she continued to walk him around the arena. And Lucy could tell that Elise was already preparing for the worst, holding the reins tightly, with a stature that looked almost...defensive.

Lance didn't need *any* encouragement to get moving. Lucy hadn't even seen the senior's leg move at all when Lance burst into an erratic trot. Forget collected—the gelding had a mind of his own. He ignored any pressure that Elise put on the reins (of course, it didn't help that it was *constant* pressure), and acted against it by jerking his head up and flying onward twice more around the arena before finally coming back down to the walk.

The second time Elise asked Lance for a change of gait, he completely skipped the trot, diving forward into the canter. Lucy remembered from the time that she had ridden Lance that his *collected* canter had actually been comfortable. But when Lance got faster—then Lucy had had to really put her riding skills to the test. The faster Lance got, the more she'd had to fight for every muscle in her body to stay in one place, attempting to avoid what had inevitably happened: falling off.

But unlike Lucy's experience with the crazy gelding, there was no doubt about the fact that Elise really was an excellent rider as far as hanging on for the unexpected. Because what Lucy *hadn't* seen coming was for Lance—seemingly the king of taking off—to finally give into the tugging on the reins. But naturally, being the king of mischief, he decided to do so in the most disrespectful way.

Instead of transitioning from the canter to the trot, Lance decided to skid to a complete stop, ducking to the side of the arena as if he were refusing a jump. And Elise, who had most certainly not been expecting that, was thrown forward slightly onto the gelding's neck. Once Elise had fixed her position, she use her leg to urge the horse onward again. Even though the intention had been for the horse to stop, he couldn't get away with stopping short. But, being stubborn as usual, Lance remained firmly planted in place. So after a larger kick that earned no response, Elise tapped Lance with the riding crop that she was carrying. But instead of moving forward, Lance kicked out with one of his back legs,

and then promptly walked backwards. His chain of respons-
es was the complete opposite of what he'd been asked to do.

Lucy knew, as she was sure Elise herself knew, that Lance
couldn't be allowed to get away with his behavior. But one
more tap from the crop—harder this time—was enough to
get Lance moving forward again.

Lucy had to assume that he was used to getting away
with his bad behavior, and that he wasn't used to getting reprimanded for it. But the most basic foundation of training
was respect; if the horse had no respect for the rider, progress
would be minimal and very difficult to achieve.

Continuing along with his disrespectful nature though,
Lance skidded to a stop in the next corner of the arena. This
time, Lucy knew that Elise had prepared for it by the way she
seemed to brace her body slightly before they'd even gotten
close to the corner. And because Elise hadn't been unseated
in any way, she was able to attempt to correct the problem
immediately, again with the crop. But this time the gelding's
reaction was immediate. Lance shot off like a bullet, going
right from a walk to a canter than was nearly on the verge of
a gallop. But not before giving another one of his signature
large bucks, sending Elise forward once more with enough
force to cause the senior to lose not just one but *both* of her
stirrups. Which she now had to manage without as Lance
barreled onward once more.

But as much of a fiasco as it seemed (what with Lance's
head pointed to the sky, the stirrup irons flapping wildly
by his sides, and the continuous increase of speed), Lucy
was really in awe of how Elise was able to stay on. While
the stirrups jolted about aimlessly, Elise's legs remained firm

and unmoving. She leaned as far back in the saddle as she could, having to work both against Lance to get him to slow down but also *with* Lance so that she wouldn't end up on the ground. What Lucy didn't agree with was how much Elise was holding Lance's head. Lucy was positive that if the senior had worked the horse on a looser rein from the beginning, Lance wouldn't have been as awful. But nothing changed the fact that Lucy was impressed by how well Elise had stuck it out. Not *once* did the senior seem as if she was going to lose her balance. And when she finally succeeded in getting the gelding back down to a springy trot that seemed as if it would turn into another canter at any given moment, she didn't even bother trying to get her stirrups back.

Instead, she focused on circling Lance to get him back under control. What Lucy thought was even smarter was the fact that, instead of sitting the trot—as this was part of the cue to canter—Elise returned to posting. And as Lucy watched the senior rise with the rhythm of Lance's gradually slowing trot, legs never once slipping back, heels immaculately positioned downward, upper body firm and maintaining control, she couldn't help but find herself drawn to the sight.

But, soon enough, Elise was able to bring Lance down to the walk as the circle grew tighter and tighter, only leaving room for Lance to slow down.

"Well, I think we've had enough *fun* for one day," Elise said, her words filling the empty arena. And with that, she took the reins in one hand and swung down from the tall horse, who only balked and pinned his ears when Elise tried to lead him forward. Giving a firmer tug on the reins, Elise said, "You're ten times worse than Legacy. Come *on*."

But no amount of coaxing could get the gelding to walk out of the arena.

Lucy only sighed, shaking her head, not exactly sure how Elise was going to get *anywhere* with a horse that awful.

Especially if she keeps holding him back, Lucy thought.

If Elise had let the horse get the energy out of his system in the beginning instead of holding him back every time he got faster, maybe then he would have been more willing to listen. And while Elise probably knew that, Lucy also knew that the senior was in no way willing to give up that much control.

Lucy sighed. She needed to stop thinking about things like this. Because even though she believed it could work...

It's not my place to intervene.

So turning her attention away from the standoff between the blonde and the stubborn horse, Lucy continued sweeping. And all went well for the first few seconds of the simple task but, of course, being her clumsy self, she didn't see that there was a water bottle sitting abandoned on the edge of the railing. And she didn't realize, with all of the layers of clothing that she was wearing, that her elbow had come into contact with it until she heard a small scrape from the bottom of the plastic against the wood of the ledge.

And she turned just in time to watch the water bottle fall down.

Down.

Down.

Until it landed with a small *crunch* in the arena below.

And that small noise was enough to send Lance *reeling*.

Lucy visibly cringed when she watched Lance's eyes grow wide, his two front legs prancing as if he were threatening to lift them entirely off the ground. He snorted angrily and threw his head upwards, nearly causing the reins to slip out of Elise's hands.

"*Whoa*, Lance," Elise said, her tone firm.

It took Lance a few seconds—most likely to decide whether or not he wanted to bolt—before he settled for lunging forward at a springy walk, in a direction that was most certainly *away* from the life-threatening water bottle.

But at least it was in a direction that just so happened to lead out of the arena.

And once Elise had managed to get Lance back on the crossties, Lucy, mentally berating herself for her stupidity and clumsiness, rushed back downstairs to remove the water bottle from the arena.

"Sorry about that," Lucy said, after she had thrown out the water bottle and gone to find the senior.

"Don't apologize," Elise said, "If it weren't for you, I don't think I'd have even gotten him out of the arena."

Lucy laughed, "Lance really is something."

"Something crazy."

"And stubborn," Lucy added.

Elise rolled her eyes, "Insane."

And then somehow, it turned into a battle to see who could exhaust all the possibilities of adjectives to describe Lance first.

"Wild," Lucy shot back.

"Uncontrollable."

"Headstrong."

"Adamant."

"Difficult."

"Arrogant."

"Unreasonable."

"Obstinate."

Lucy stuck out her tongue, "Using big words is *not* fair."

"That's a very flattering look for you," Elise laughed.

Oh, that *laugh*...It was making it very difficult for Lucy to keep up her feigned annoyance, and for once, she didn't know what else to say.

"But if you can't think of anything else then...it looks like I win," Elise said very matter-of-factly as she fastened the last buckles of Lance's blanket.

"I can *so* think of something else," Lucy narrowed her eyes.

"All right, then. Let's see you try," Elise challenged.

Lucy desperately tried to picture the dictionary, or pull some scholarly word from the far recesses of her mind. But...nothing was coming to her. And before she could open her mouth to accept defeat, she felt something warm against her neck, which caused her heart rate to momentarily soar in shock.

Upon careful consideration of the situation, Lucy found that it definitely *wasn't* Elise, who was by Lance's stall getting the gelding's lead rope.

But of course, my brain would definitely jump to that idea, wouldn't it, Lucy thought in embarrassment.

Once she got over her hyperactive thoughts, she realized that what she had felt—and what she was *still* feeling—was Lance's head, resting slightly on her shoulder.

Lucy hadn't realized how close she had gotten in proximity to the large horse. And while she was slightly confused by Lance's sudden display of affection, she didn't dare move, for fear of startling him.

The moment lasted for barely five seconds longer, but it was long enough for Elise to have turned around and caught the sight—meeting Lucy's confused '*I don't know how this happened*' look with slightly widened eyes. And it was only when Lance had once again picked his head up that Lucy spoke again, her voice soft, "Misunderstood."

"What?"

"My word," Lucy clarified, "He's...misunderstood."

Elise thought about it for a minute, before slowly nodding, all thoughts of competition set aside, "Yeah," she said, eyes meeting Lucy's own, "some things are. And...it takes someone special to see through all of that."

And as Lucy held the gaze of the senior, her heart seemed to soar once more ever so slightly. Because something told Lucy that Elise's words held meaning for more than just the horse standing next to her.

"THE LIMIT OF ONE OVER zero from the right is...infinity," Lucy spoke aloud a week later as she attempted to complete her work at the barn and simultaneously review for her pre-calculus exam. Almost all equations had limits, meaning a specific number that the graph approached as the values got either larger or smaller. In Lucy's cause, she had to memorize the standard, commonly known limits. And considering how well this little review was going...she had no hopes of doing quite as well as she would have liked. But she continued on anyway, knowing that it would benefit her in the long run to see what she remembered, "The limit of one over zero from the left is...infinity...no, it's *negative* infinity—"

"Calculus?"

Lucy heard the question followed by a soft laugh.

Turning to find Elise walking out of Legacy's stall, Lucy told her, "Pre-calc, actually."

"I didn't think they got into limits in pre-calc," Elise said, placing Legacy's halter back on the stall door.

"Yeah, well, apparently the professors have this new perspective called 'hey, let's torture our students'," Lucy rolled her eyes, "And so now I've got a huge exam tomorrow. It's our last one. It's worth about fifteen percent of our grade, or something crazy like that. And I barely understand limits at all. I'm trying to memorize everything that we're supposed to, but it's hard when I don't even understand the concepts behind everything."

"Well..." Elise started. She paused for a moment and then said, "I could help you if you want."

"Really?" Lucy exclaimed, "That'd be great! And here I was thinking that I was going to fail this exam!"

"Hey, I didn't promise that I'd remember *everything*," Elise said.

You're the smartest person that I know. Of course you'll remember everything, Lucy thought. But all she said was, "I'll take all the help I can get."

"I just need to finish up with a few things first. And you need to finish sweeping."

"Right!" Lucy said, "I'll be finished soon. I just need to go upstairs, and then I'll be done."

And Lucy didn't think she'd ever swept so quickly in her life.

It's a good thing you have your books today, Lucy thought as she grabbed her backpack from the lounge before she headed back down stairs. She put the broom away, and went to sign out in the office.

"Would you be opposed to going up to the house to work on this? I don't think there's enough room on this desk with all of the papers I have here," Elise said.

Opposed? Lucy thought, fighting her grin, "No. Not at all."

Lucy waited for Elise to finish whatever it was she was doing at the computer, and then the two of them walked silently up to the house. When they stepped inside, Elise said, "The kitchen would probably be the easiest place to work."

Lucy only nodded, heading into the gigantic kitchen and placing her bag down on the floor next to one of the chairs.

"I guess I should ask you if you want something to eat?" Elise said, "I'm...not really used to having anyone over."

"Well, I didn't eat anything before I came for work. But I don't want you to go through the trouble of getting anything. I'm already taking up your time."

"You're not taking up my time," Elise said, "I offered. It's not like I'd be doing anything but paperwork. Or studying for my own exams. Just work and schoolwork on top of it. Got to keep that GPA up."

And although it was a seemingly simple statement, there was something about the senior's voice that sounded more distant and lonely than the words themselves.

"Okay," Lucy said, not wanting to make Elise upset, "What do you have?"

Elise shot a confused look at the redhead, "What, my GPA?"

"No, no, not at all!" Lucy said, her tone rushed. Elise *really* must have gone somewhere else when she'd said those words, and now Lucy had to make up for accidentally spurring the touchy topic as a point of conversation, even if it had all transpired over a misinterpretation, "I was talking about the food. Like what you had to eat! Not that I wouldn't want to know your GPA—or wait, no, that came out wrong! I don't need to know your GPA. Most people don't want to talk about that. Not that yours isn't high or anything. I'm sure it's *insanely* high. Like, a 4.0—"

"Lucy," Elise interrupted the redhead's rambling, "It's fine. It's my fault—I just..." Elise trailed off here, and Lucy thought that she was just going to stop talking altogether, but was rather surprised when the senior continued, "Whenever I...think about work and grades and school, even for the tiniest moment, I get hung up on it. *Really* hung up on it. I can't help but think how I've worked so hard *all the time*—to be this...this good, obedient little girl that my parents wanted to grow up to be the perfect spitting image of what they saw me as in order to run the riding school. And sometimes I can't stand that I'm still trying to be that perfect. I work so hard to get those grades, and to make sure that every little thing runs smoothly in the barn and with the equestrian team and with the clients. And I do everything for them and do they ever stop and think about what I want?" Elise closed her eyes, as if the words that came from her mouth physically hurt her, "It just...reminds me so much that this isn't the life that I want."

While Lucy knew that the life her parents had chosen for her was a decision that Elise had been forced into unwillingly, she was still surprised to hear such a forward admission of the senior's feelings.

In fact, it was a rarity.

And for once, Lucy didn't know what to say; didn't know how to comfort Elise, although she wanted to desperately.

"But never mind all of that," Elise spoke again before Lucy even had the chance, "I've already accepted it. I've decided that it's for the horses, anyway, not for my parents. What was it that you wanted to eat?"

And so there Elise went, pushing Lucy away before she even had the *chance* to help. But as much as it pained Lucy to see Elise's beautiful eyes clouded with pain and worry, she knew that if she tried to talk about it with the senior, they'd just go backwards again. So bottling her own emotions and thoughts of comfort, Lucy answered, "I like sandwiches. And anything and everything involving chocolate."

At this, Elise actually smiled, "I should have guessed about the chocolate. You mentioned it before. And you were the one who put it in my coffee, after all."

"You remember that?" Lucy thought back to that day when she had barely known Elise at all. There was no way that *Lucy* had forgotten about it.

"Any coffee I've had since has yet to taste that amazing," Elise said.

"I guess you should come in more often when I'm working then," Lucy told the blonde, knowing very well that it would just be another excuse for Lucy to be able to see Elise even more.

"Maybe I will," Elise said.

A few minutes later, Elise set a plate down in front of Lucy, and then sat down in the seat next to her. Noticing that there was only one sandwich, Lucy asked, "Aren't you going to have anything?"

"Well considering the fact that I already ate dinner, I think I'm going to wait for the chocolate. Which comes *after* you have mastered the concept of limits," Elise said.

"That's so not fair!" Lucy exclaimed, "I'm hopeless at math!"

"You won't be if we actually get to work."

Sighing over dramatically, Lucy pulled out her books, and handed Elise the homework she'd been using as a review, "I get how to *solve* for limits. But I don't understand how to find them on a graph. Like...in the second example. The limit as 'x' approaches zero from the right, with the one over 'x' equation. I know from memorization that the limit is infinity."

"But you want to know how to find it on a graph," Elise said.

"Right."

Elise took the pencil that Lucy had also taken out, flipped the piece of paper over, and began sketching the graph that Lucy couldn't even remember how to draw herself.

"So when you look at the graph, what can you tell me about it?" Elise asked.

"Uh..." Lucy looked at the graph, but all she could think about was how precisely it had been drawn. Nothing mathematical stood out to her at all. There were two curves, one on the right and one on the left. And all Lucy could come up with was: "It looks like the letter 'L' and its mirror image...diagonally."

Elise laughed slightly before saying, "Okay. That wasn't exactly what I had in mind. But...if that's what you'd like to consider them, which one of these so called 'L's do you think applies to the statement of 'x' approaching zero from the right?"

Lucy stared at the graph for a few more moments before guessing, "The one on the right?"

"Correct," Elise said, "Now what you want to look at is *what* the line of the graph is doing as it gets closer to zero."

"It's going upwards," Lucy said, "The 'y' values are getting larger."

"Indefinitely," Elise added.

"Wait a minute..." Lucy said, as realization hit her, "I think I get it. Because they're constantly getting larger, the limit is infinity."

"Exactly," Elise said, "So what if I asked you, just by looking at the graph, what the limit is as 'x' approaches zero from the left. Forget what you had to memorize; I want you to explain *how* what you memorized is true."

"Okay," Lucy said, "So this time I'm looking at the left part of the graph, right?"

"Right."

"And so this time as 'x' approaches zero...the line is going downwards, which means that 'y' values are getting smaller. Indefinitely. Which makes the limit negative infinity."

Elise smiled, "See, you're getting the hang of it now."

"I guess I am," Lucy said, amazed at how much more clear the concept was becoming.

"So then, what would happen if I asked you what the limit is as 'x' approaches zero?"

Lucy considered the question. And then continued to think about it.

For a long time.

They had *definitely* gone over this in class, but Lucy didn't remember a single moment of discussing it.

"I don't know," Lucy said eventually, staring at the line of the graph that went up indefinitely, and the line of the graph that went down indefinitely, "I don't know if it's infinity, or if it's negative infinity."

"And that's because it's neither," Elise said. Picking up the pencil again, she drew over each line that bordered the y-axis, effectively making them stand out more than the rest of the graph, "If the limit as 'x' approaches zero from the right goes up to infinity, and the limit as 'x' approaches zero from the left goes down to negative infinity, then the side limits conflict. Which means that the limit as 'x' approaches zero, *just* zero, doesn't exist."

"Hold on. So you're telling me that the limit doesn't exist at zero? Even though we just found two of them?"

"Well...your problem is that you're not exactly thinking about the concept of a limit the right way. You see it as a value at a point on the graph, am I right?"

Lucy couldn't even comprehend what the senior was talking about, and she didn't have a better way to say it, "I have no idea what you're talking about anymore."

Elise paused for a moment, and then suggested, "Why don't we compare it to something you're familiar with. Let's say you're riding a horse. And you're in the arena and you're riding on the rail, bending around the turn. You want to steer as close to the rail as possible, so that you don't cut the corner. But your horse never actually *touches* the rail."

Lucy nodded.

"So it's the same for a limit. The graph can never actually *touch* the number it's approaching. That would be impossible. So it just gets as close to it as it possibly can. Does it make more sense now?"

"Kind of," Lucy said, "I think so."

"Are you sure?" Elise asked.

Lucy nodded, "Yes. It's not what the graph is doing *at* zero. It's what it's doing when it gets *close* to zero. And because the graph is doing two opposite things on either side of zero, it doesn't match so the limit can't exist."

"Well, if you're satisfied with that, then I think you've earned your chocolate," Elise smiled.

"Chocolate makes learning things worth it," Lucy joked. Though silently she added, *well, that and you. Sitting here with me. Talking with me.*

Elise only laughed, and came back from the refrigerator with two slices of chocolate cake. And with it being *cake*, Lucy's was gone in a matter of minutes. But she stayed until Elise was finished, and since it was late and already dark, Elise drove Lucy back to campus.

"Thanks for your help," Lucy said, before she shut the car door, "I don't quite know what I would have done otherwise."

"No problem," Elise said, "I...enjoyed the company."

Lucy smiled, "Then I guess we'll just have to do this again."

"With the math and all?" Elise teased.

"Preferably *not* with the math," Lucy laughed.

"We'll see," Elise answered. But even amid the dim light of the car, from where Lucy was standing outside of it she could see all of the features of Elise's face shift slightly as the senior smiled.

And then entire walk back to her dorm room, Lucy couldn't manage to keep another smile of her own from spreading across her face.

"Well *someone* worked late," Kendra said when Lucy opened the door.

"Actually, Elise was helping me with pre-calc," Lucy said, "So if you need any pointers, let me know."

"I *told* you that you should ask her. Glad you finally took my advice," Kendra joked, "But as for me, I'm planning on just dealing with whatever comes tomorrow."

"Meaning you're not studying?"

"I looked over my notes. And I'll look over them again tomorrow but...yeah I'm not studying."

Lucy shook her head in amazement, "You're crazy."

Because sure, maybe Lucy wasn't always a perfect student. But at least she chose to make an effort even when it seemed like there was no hope.

And because you were studying you got to spend more time with Elise, Lucy reminded herself.

Just thinking about the evening she'd had with Elise made her smile again—a ridiculous little smile that somehow escaped her roommate's attention unscathed and safe from teasing. And once more it remained plastered onto face until...

A thought struck her.

A thought so insane and crazy and uncanny, yet so perfectly accurate that Lucy couldn't believe she hadn't thought of it sooner.

Elise was the definition of a limit.

It didn't matter how hard Lucy tried; how *long* Lucy tried.

They could move three steps backward and two steps forward, or two steps backward and three steps forward...no matter what, it seemed as though she couldn't get completely through to Elise

There was never a close enough point *at* which Lucy could be in relation to Elise.

There was always a distance—a distance at which Lucy had to stay.

But *God* did she want to break that limit.

And I'm not going to stop trying, Lucy vowed, *I don't care how long it takes. I don't care if it's considered impossible.*

I'm not going to give up.

Chapter Fifteen

"*Yes*!" Lucy exclaimed, unable to contain her excitement and ultimately doing a little dance within the confinement of her seat when the professor handed back her pre-calculus exam. It had taken him *forever* to grade it—a whole week; Lucy had been counting. And now as she stared down at the 98% marked at the top of her paper, she realized that everything she had done in preparation had been worth it.

And of course, having Elise explain everything was beneficial in multiple ways, Lucy reminded herself. Because who knew studying could be...well...fun? It was almost unheard of. But when Lucy was around the senior, at times it seemed like almost anything was possible.

On the other hand though, from the seat next to her, Kendra let out a small groan. Turning her attention to her roommate, Lucy was almost afraid to ask what the verdict was. So she settled for, "I'm guessing it didn't go quite as planned?"

"Unless you'd consider a 72 great, then no," Kendra answered. But her tone was light and she was smiling anyway, so it didn't seem as though the grade bothered her too much, "But I still have the final to bring it back up."

"I don't even want to *think* about a final," Lucy said with a laugh, even though she knew that it would be quickly approaching. Winter break was right around the corner, which meant that finals were even closer.

Lucy's roommate only shrugged, "Me either. But I realized over the course of doing so poorly on this exam and almost failing my last biology exam that slacking off at the end of the semester *maybe* isn't the smartest thing to do. Even if I spent the whole first part of the semester working hard. Actually, *especially* if I spent the whole beginning of the semester working my butt off because now all that hard work is going to go right down the—"

Kendra was cut off by the professor's voice, ringing loud and clear among the fairly large pre-calculus class: "And make sure to check online for the final review guide. I plan on posting it tonight, and I want you all to have problems one through twenty completed for next class."

This comment earned a subtle, yet collective groan from the students—Lucy's roommate included. But Lucy only laughed to herself, knowing all too well from the torture of trying to memorize *every* possible date and detail from her history class that they were all lucky that they even had a review guide to study from at all.

THAT NIGHT, LUCY HAD one of her last riding lessons of the semester. Even though there wouldn't be any more competitions until closer to the middle of the spring semester when they would return from break, Rattenber still felt that the team members needed to "keep in shape before putting on those extra pounds during the holidays". Lucy had laughed and Belle had rolled her eyes, and Owen—being Owen and the kind of person who wouldn't want to insult even the most annoying of insects—nodded his head like he agreed very much with Rattenber's assumptions.

But now, however, there was no joking of eating too much or getting out of shape. Tonight seemed to be drill after drill after drill of insanely strenuous exercises—so much so that Lucy swore she'd only ridden with stirrups for about five minutes of the entire lesson. And it didn't help that Knight decided to jump every little crossrail as if it were two feet instead of not even a foot. Of all nights to not be assigned to ride Dee...

Lucy made a mental note to ask Elise why the mare wasn't in their lesson tonight if she got the chance to see her. It was a rarity now (even though Elise told her time and time again that it was good for Lucy to ride different horses since that was the basis of the competitions) that Lucy would go even two lessons without getting the chance to ride Dee. But Lucy honestly couldn't remember the last time she'd had a lesson with her favorite chestnut mare. And while spunky and more willing to do what *she* wanted to do rather than what she was asked to do, Dee was certainly a smoother ride than Knight.

"But I think," Lucy said as she leaned down to give Knight a pat for his good behavior during the lesson, "That is something that we'll deal with *after* you're back in your stall."

Lucy put the reins in on hand and slid down from the saddle, wincing as soon as her feet hit the ground, "Though on second thought, maybe it's something I'll have to deal with after I've regained feeling in my legs."

Rattenber had already left the arena, so when Lucy's comment was voiced louder than she'd intended for it to come out, she was met with a response from Owen, who most likely felt that it was now okay to complain because their instructor was out of earshot: "You can't feel your legs? I can't feel *my* legs! It's probably been since last year that I had a lesson that difficult!"

"Better get used to it," Belle laughed. Being a junior, she knew all about the team and what the 'newbies' were in for, "Rattenber only gets more strict by the spring semester when he realizes that all we can think about is summer."

"Oh, but I love summer!" Owen exclaimed, his exited tone nearly making his horse jump, "All things warm, and the beach, and—"

"Nice going," Lucy laughed, "Now you've gotten him back on one of his summer rants."

She knew how much Owen loved summer. Well, maybe it was more like the entire *school* knew how much he loved summer with how much he talked about it. He was in the drama club as well as on the equestrian team (although how he managed both activities and classes, Lucy wasn't sure), and rumor had it that for the club's performance at the end of the year, he'd be singing his own song that he'd written about none other than summer.

"The damage has been done," Bell stated gravely as Owen continued on and on about his favorite season.

Lucy only laughed again, knowing how ridiculous her teammates could get at the end of a long lesson. If anyone were to ever witness their craziness, they'd probably be more apt to label the three of them as part of a middle school team rather than as part of a college team. But even still, Lucy couldn't resist continuing along with the joke, "The horror! We'll be trapped in summer until the end of time!"

"Or until a certain someone turns off the lights in the arena and your summer world is plunged into darkness."

All three teammates frozen in place. Belle looked to the ground. Owen—in mid-description of a palm tree by the ocean—even stopped talking without finishing his thought. And Lucy's almost uncontrollable laughter was replaced by nothing but a burning that she felt make its way first to her face, and then all the way down her neck.

Of all the people to overhear that, it had to be *Elise*?

"Um, yeah, about that..." Lucy mumbled, "We were just leaving."

Belle made a dash for the door the fastest, her sprightly little pony all too eager to follow, and, never one to be embarrassed, Owen gave an exuberant wave before following in her footsteps. Which left Lucy in the middle of the arena with a confused looking Knight ,who was no doubt wondering why his friends were allowed to head back and eat their dinner while he was still stuck in the arena.

And of course, there was Elise, who was leaning against the wall with her arms crossed, her focus on Lucy with a look that was borderline amused. But no matter what Lucy had been anticipating the senior would say to her, none of her thoughts came anywhere remotely close to the question she was actually met with, "So what do you think would be better, an eternal summer or an eternal winter?"

"Which one do *you* think would be better?" Lucy asked, still not quite over her embarrassment and finding it much easier to ask the questions instead of being ridiculed (albeit jokingly) for her answers.

"I asked you first," Elise said very matter-of-factly.

"Fine then. *I'd* like an eternal *spring*," Lucy said in the same tone of voice, daring the senior to challenge her.

"Spring wasn't an option," Elise answered, "You're avoiding the question."

"And you didn't answer when I asked you, so I believe that makes us even," Lucy declared.

Elise held the redhead's gaze for a moment longer, a hint of a smile still tugging at the corner of her mouth, before saying, "Just bring Knight inside so I can shut the lights in here. He's done more than his share of work."

Not entirely sure what to make of their not-so-serious interaction, Lucy only answered, "Okay," before leading Knight out of the arena. And by the time she had the gelding in his stall, both Owen and Belle were long gone. So it startled Lucy—for the second time that night—when she heard a voice from what she had previously thought was an empty aisle.

"Want some help?"

"That would...actually be great," Lucy admitted, turning to find the senior who had already let herself into Knight's stall.

Elise—much more quickly than Lucy ever could in the exhausted state she was in—had Knight's tack off and back upstairs before Lucy even had a chance to finish brushing the gelding off. And there was a particular order of brushes for grooming a horse: the first was the curry comb, the second was the hard brush, and the third was the soft brush. Lucy was still using the curry comb by the time Elise was back downstairs. And so joining Lucy once more in the gelding's stall, Elise worked on brushing one side of Knight, while Lucy stayed on her own side. Then, unsure of what to say, or how to fill the silence, Lucy settled for taking the opportunity to ask about Dee.

"All horses need breaks every now and then, which I'm sure you probably know. So there's nothing wrong with her," Elise explained, "She'll be back in your lessons by the time we're back from winter break. But hey," Elise said, already changing the subject, "How'd you do on that pre-calc exam?"

"Actually pretty well, thanks to you," Lucy answered proudly.

"You caught on more quickly than you gave yourself credit for," Elise answered, "All it took was fifteen minutes and the promise of chocolate cake."

At this, Lucy laughed, "Where there's chocolate cake, there's a way."

"I believe the saying goes 'if there's a will, there's a way'," Elise corrected.

Lucy narrowed her eyes jokingly, "Same difference."

The two seemed to fall into a peaceful silence after that, Lucy noticing that neither of them had even reached for a different brush in the time they'd been talking. And as ridiculous as it might sound, Lucy reveled in that small fact. Because couldn't it mean that Elise wanted to stay here and spend time with Lucy just as much as Lucy wanted to spend time with the senior?

It was Knight, though, who eventually disrupted the quiet, lowering his head from his feed bucket once he'd finished the last of his grain, and moving towards the corner of his stall, where there was a fresh pile of hay waiting to be diminished.

As he remained preoccupied with more food, it didn't take long after that to finish grooming Knight and get his blanket on; the gelding was situated happily in his stall in a matter of minutes. And Elise's offer of a ride back up to campus was one that no longer really even needed to be asked aloud.

"You know," Elise said as she pulled the car up to the curb, "I don't think I'd mind if the only season we ever got around here was winter."

"Well yeah, that's because no matter the weather you just wear the same polo shirts. Not all of us are immune to temperatures below freezing," Lucy laughed.

"Spring's not perfect either. Why deal with the rain when you could have snow instead?"

"Snow is pretty, but it's impractical," Lucy said as she opened the door, "It gets in the way."

"Maybe," Elise answered, "But only if you let it."

THOUGH ELISE'S WORDS about snow and winter seemed to resonate with her for a few days after she'd heard them, Lucy had to remind herself that sometimes, Elise surprised her with these seemingly optimistic words of wisdom. And while there was an obvious truth in the statement, maybe what mattered most was not so much what the words meant, but the fact that Elise had, once again, been willing to share something so heartfelt with Lucy. And she was lost once more thinking about the progress she'd made with the senior when she was startled out of her thoughts by Harley.

"So I'm sorry, did you say that you knew about this already?"

The two of them were walking side by side on their way back from another team meeting. Kendra was trailing along with them since she had, surprisingly, come to the meeting as well. Most likely, Flynn had given her some sort of special permission since she wasn't part of the team, but she refused to admit it.

"Know what?" Lucy asked, completely oblivious to what was going on at the moment having been lost in her own thoughts.

"About the team party?"

"Uh...I may or may not have mentioned that Elise told me about it. Why?" Lucy was slightly confused as to why Harley was asking. They had just talked about it in the meeting, after all. It was going to be held the Friday before break, on the Akiyama property, of course. And, being her crazy self, Lucy could only grin at the thought.

"I'm leaving early for break," Harley said, "If I had known..."

"Wait, what?" Lucy whipped her head around to meet his gaze with wide eyes, "You didn't tell me this."

"Sorry," Harley said, shoving his hands in his pockets, "I didn't think it would be a big deal. My parents decided that they wanted to take a trip since this is the first year our break is so long. And they booked the flight for that Friday morning since I don't have any finals."

"*Why?*" Lucy groaned.

"Sorry," Harley apologized again.

Lucy sighed, and then, half joking and half serious, she complained, "Who am I going to go with! And how in the world am I going to get there!"

And she instantly regretted saying it.

Because Harley immediately suggested, "Ask Elise."

And while Lucy hadn't yet told her roommate *everything* that she had told her best friend, she was almost positive that Kendra had come to her own conclusions. Kendra's face broke out into a large grin, "That would be so perfect, Lucy!"

Oh, yes. Kendra had *definitely* come to her own conclusions.

Lucy had the urge to hide her face behind her hands, but all she managed to mumble was, "Elise said she never goes to them."

"Just ask," Harley said, "The worst she can say is no."

"I *know* she's going to say no," Lucy said, "I mean what am I supposed to do, just walk into the office on Sunday night and say, 'Hey, Elise, want to go to the party with me even though you pointedly said you never go to them?' No. Then I'll just sound inconsiderate."

Kendra laughed, "Who said anything about being inconsiderate? You're just being friendly."

But the way her roommate mouthed the word 'friendly' again, mainly to Harley, while adding air quotes around the word, caused Lucy's face to burn slightly, "Okay, first things first—we'd be going as *friends*. And second, I haven't even asked her yet!"

This only caused Kendra to laugh harder, "Defending it only makes what you're refusing to say more true."

Lucy shot Harley a look that clearly said—*help me!*—but he only said, "She has a point there."

"You two are impossible," Lucy muttered.

"I'm going to ask Elise for you if you don't," Kendra declared.

Lucy sighed, knowing very well that her roommate would, "Okay. *Fine.* I'll think about it."

But somewhere inside, she already knew what she was going to do. Because it was one thing to deny the comments of her friends...and another thing to deny what she knew she felt in her heart.

LUCY'S FRIDAY MORNING shift at the coffee shop was almost over.

Just ten more minutes, and then I can head back and sleep, Lucy sighed as she watched the singular clock in the small coffee shop tick above the door. She thought back to two weeks ago when she'd looked at her schedule to find that she'd actually been given a day off for no reason at all. *It's a shame that day wasn't today so I could have stayed curled up in bed...wait...hold that thought...never mind!*

All feelings of tiredness suddenly flew out the window when Lucy spotted a familiar platinum blonde braid at the end of the line of people that now had four customers instead of three.

Lucy's boring, annoying morning just got a hundred times better, and she felt herself smiling instantly at the fact that Elise had actually taken the invitation to come to the coffee shop more often during Lucy's shift. And this time, Lucy was more than happy when she was the one to take the senior's order.

"So the same as last time?" Lucy asked.

"Same as last time," Elise confirmed with a smile.

And after Elise had paid, Lucy set to work, making sure to *intentionally* add the chocolate to the iced coffee this time.

"Thanks," Elise said, before taking her coffee from Lucy's outstretched hand and heading over to one of the tables.

And of course, when Lucy's shift was over—literally only ten minutes later—she found herself hurrying to sign out so that she could rush over to the table where Elise was sitting and plop herself down in the chair opposite of the senior. Elise's eyes snapped immediately upwards from her book when she noticed Lucy sit down across from her, but if she was surprised at all by the redhead's spontaneous action, she didn't show it.

"Hey," Lucy said (although a little belatedly for the current situation), "My shift is over. So...mind if I join you?"

"Not at all," Elise said, closing her book that Lucy could now see was physics related.

"Hey, don't you have class on Friday mornings anyway?" Lucy asked, her question prompted by the book's cover.

Then jokingly she added, "Don't tell me you skipped just to see me."

Elise rolled her eyes, "Really, Lucy, does that sound like something I'd do?"

Lucy shrugged, "You never know."

Elise chose to say nothing more about skipping classes, instead explaining, "My second class was cancelled. My last one doesn't start for half an hour."

"That's physics, right?"

Elise only nodded, leaving Lucy with nothing else to say.

As silence fell across their secluded corner table, Lucy began to wonder if she should take this opportunity to ask Elise about the party. She had originally planned on asking the senior on Sunday after her shift at the barn, but she had been worrying about it in the back of her mind ever since she had talked about it with Harley and Kendra. Not to mention that the sooner she got a definite answer from Elise, the sooner Kendra would stop threatening to intervene.

The party was a week away. Exactly.

Was it too early to ask?

And what if the answer was 'no' and everything just got more awkward?

"Hey," Elise's words brought Lucy out of her thoughts, "You okay there?"

Lucy blinked once and said, "Oh, yeah. I'm fine. I was just...thinking."

Elise looked at her expectantly.

Wrong thing to say, Lucy. Wrong thing to say.

"It's nothing," Lucy said, trying to forget the whole thing.

"Clearly something's bothering you," Elise said, and it if weren't for her nervousness at what exactly *was* bothering her, Lucy would have found the senior's concern much more endearing.

Lucy sighed.

It was now or never.

"Well, I wouldn't say *bothering* me, exactly," Lucy said. She paused, taking a breath, but knew that if she didn't get it out now, she might never have the nerve to ask, "I know you said that you don't go to the team parties. But I was wondering...if maybe you'd go with me?"

But as soon as she registered the fact that the blonde's eyes were wide, Lucy immediately launched into another (rambling) explanation, "I mean, as friends of course! And you don't have to go. I know it's probably silly of me to ask, because you said that you don't. I don't want to make you do something you're not comfortable doing," Lucy took another breath before finishing lamely, "And really even if you don't want to stay, all I need is a ride because Harley is going home early."

Elise seemed to take a moment to let the redhead's rushed explanation sink in before she finally said anything. And in a tone that sounded slightly amused she asked, "So you're telling me you want me to drive all the way to campus to pick you up, just to drive you back to my house?"

"That was part of the request," Lucy mumbled, "It's only five minutes."

Once more, Elise didn't answer immediately—instead, seeming to deliberate Lucy's request in its entirety. And Lucy's heart seemed to race faster with every second that ticked by. Because, sure, she had told Elise that they would be going as just friends. But...what would it really be to Lucy if the senior said—

"Yes."

Now it was Lucy's turn to be shocked, "What?" she asked, more out of astonishment than anything else.

"I said yes," Elise repeated, "I'll...go with you. It might be a nice change."

"Really!?" Lucy exclaimed, a part of her denying what she'd actually heard.

"Well, remember, half of the reason is because you need a ride," Elise said, and although Lucy couldn't tell if the senior was joking or not, for the moment, she was too elated to care. And after another minute, during which Lucy had to fight to contain another ever-growing smile, Elise said, "And now as much as I'd like to stay, I really do need to get back to campus."

"Oh, right. You have a class," Lucy said, managing to come to her senses, "But my shift's over so I'm heading back, too."

"You can come then if you want," Elise offered as she put her book away, "You know, since we're headed to the same place."

"That'd be great," Lucy said, "Harley dropped me off this morning, so I'm sure he'll be happy about the fact that he won't have to come all the way back for me. I'll just send him a text."

When Elise got up, Lucy followed. But as her fingers flew quickly over the screen to send Harley a message, she wasn't looking where she was going. And of course, just for spite, she walked right into Elise when the senior stopped to open the door, colliding into the blonde's backpack.

"Sorry," Lucy said.

Elise only sighed, not even bothering to turn around, "I don't understand how you've been around horses this long without landing yourself in a hospital."

"Well, you know," Lucy started, Elise's sarcastic comment reminding her of something that had actually happened, "There was this one time, it was probably the second year I was riding, and I didn't realize that there was a hose on the ground in the barn. And of course, because I'm me, I tripped over it. And I was leading this horse—he was huge, like a Clydesdale-draft cross or something like that, and he spooked at *everything*, and so when he noticed that I almost went down, he freaked out. But instead of just spooking and shifting to the side like *most* horses, he had to be even more dramatic and kick. And one of his lovely hooves hit me right in the leg. And I *almost* ended up in the hospital after that one. Almost."

"I can imagine that would hurt," Elise said, her tone serious, although the redhead could tell that she was trying to hold back a laugh.

"It's okay," Lucy said, climbing into the car once they had reached it, "You can laugh at me."

"It's not funny. It could have been a lot worse."

"Yeah, yeah, I know. But really. A *hose* of all things. That's probably the most common tripping hazard in the barn—something that you'd think I'd pay a little more attention to, but *no*..." Lucy rolled her eyes.

But for the rest of the ride, Lucy found herself telling Elise all of the embarrassing stories she had from her old barn—from tripping over the hose, to knocking over an entire rack of saddles, to getting stuck in the mud while leading a horse and inevitably also falling into it—each embarrassing scenario eventually earning Lucy a gradually larger laugh from the senior the crazier, yet less dangerous, the stories became.

And Lucy found that she didn't mind sharing all of these memories (in which she sounded like a complete idiot) with Elise. Even though they were stories that Lucy normally avoided talking about, each one just seemed to slip more easily from her mouth than the next. And she wasn't exactly sure what had prompted her to even begin telling all of these stories at all. But if all it took was to share embarrassing moment after embarrassing moment...

Hearing Elise's laugh definitely made everything worth it.

Chapter Sixteen

Come Wednesday, Lucy found that she couldn't decide if she was more nervous or excited for the big event at the end of the week. Because the fact that she was going to the party with *Elise*...

But it's not a date, Lucy reminded herself. *Not a date.*

And by showing up for her chemistry lab, she also found that she had quite a difficult time focusing on acid and base reactions when said blonde was her lab partner. Because while finals were now over, there was still one 'final' lab that the class was required to complete. It wasn't graded as a final, which Lucy had been more than thrilled to hear (although with Elise as a lab partner, there was no doubt that they could ace anything the professor threw at them). Instead, it was simply the last lab scheduled that happened to fall during the week of finals.

Initially, when Lucy had seen it on the syllabus, she had been more upset about the fact that she'd wanted all the time she could possibly get to study for her actual finals. But when she realized that the finals for her other classes would be over and done with before that Wednesday even rolled around, what was once a worry just turned into a smaller annoyance of having to wake up at eight a.m. for one class. And, all in all, Lucy found that she couldn't really deem *anything* an annoyance when it meant she had an excuse to both see and talk to Elise. And this lab provided her with the opportunity to do just that.

Well...that and get lost in her thoughts about the party that was now only two days away. Hence her lack of concentration. Because while Lucy was off in her own little world...

"Lucy. Hello?"

Lucy finally found it within her to focus her attention on the blonde in front of her. How many times had Elise said her name in the past minute?

"Hi...hi, me?" Lucy asked, still bringing herself back to reality.

"Yeah. It's an expression. Like 'hello, earth to Lucy'. Spacing out now is not going to get this lab finished."

"But we didn't even *start* it yet," Lucy complained.

"I started it," Elise said pointedly, but Lucy could tell that she wasn't mad. Just quite possibly amused.

"Okay, okay," Lucy sighed, "What do you want me to do?"

"Can I trust you with the acid?"

"Uh...maybe?" Lucy stated tentatively, knowing very well that it might not exactly be a great idea. But when Elise pointed towards the container labeled 'HCl'—the hydrochloric acid—she knew that she couldn't just say that she didn't want to be the one to work with it. She followed Elise's finger all the way to an empty lab station where all of the materials had been set out in one common area so that nothing ended up misplaced.

"We need five milliliters of that," Elise said, "Go measure it out, and then we need it over here when you're finished."

Lucy only nodded.

This is so not a good idea...

But while thoughts of warnings and worry clouded her mind, her hands seemed to move on their own. And this, Lucy knew, was what got her into all of her clumsy situations in the first place—limbs moving on their own with no direction as her mind did anything but think rationally. But...

Focus, Lucy. If you focus, maybe you can actually do this without destroying anything.

Sighing, Lucy carried the graduated cylinder that was already in her hand over to the other lab table. She picked up the bottle of hydrochloric acid, and very carefully poured it into the graduated cylinder. She held her breath the entire time, and didn't let it out until she had placed the bottle back down on the counter without any spills. And when she realized that she had accomplished this, she let a grin break out on her face. What had she been worrying about? That had been a piece of cake!

She picked the graduated cylinder up off of the counter, and began to head back to her own lab station, eager to show Elise what she'd accomplished—no matter how small or simple the task. But when she looked up at the senior, who was now half way across the room, Lucy just so happened to be met with the perfect view of Elise's usual polo shirt and jeans wardrobe ensemble. And from there, of course, Lucy's mind inadvertently jumped to none other than thoughts of the party.

Because polo shirts were *all* Elise usually wore. Yet could it be that, under certain circumstances outside of the usual, during other events besides school and everyday barn life (*...let's just say...a party, perhaps?*) Elise might just wear something...*other* than a polo shirt and jeans? Like maybe...

A dress?

Just the thought was enough to make Lucy stop in her tracks, her mind wandering almost instantly to that very scenario. But, as per her hand's ability to gain a mind of its own while her actual mind was consumed by thoughts she wasn't quite ready to give up, it was none other than the sound of shattering glass that could ground her once more.

It was a sound that effectively brought her back to reality much more quickly than anything else could have. And it was also a sound that drew the attention of the *entire* class. Including Elise's attention. And—

Oh, shit.

The *professor's* attention.

So while Lucy stood there with her face burning as bright at her hair, the professor decided not to make a huge scene out of it by cleaning it up in less than a minute and telling her that it wasn't a big deal. It was only a graduated cylinder—not a *buret*, as he had pointedly added. Because a buret was no inexpensive piece of equipment; graduated cylinders were easily replaceable.

But pride, Lucy thought as she dared to sneak a glance at a laughing Elise, *is not.*

"It's okay," Elise reassured her when another graduated cylinder with the proper amount of HCl (measured by the senior this time, of course) was safely at their lab station.

"Not really," Lucy mumbled, her embarrassment refusing to let go.

"Well, I commend you for trying anyway," Elise said, attempting to hide another laugh.

Lucy let out an overly dramatic exasperated sigh, "You knew that was going to happen, didn't you?"

"No...but I guess I never should have trusted the girl who trips over hoses to carry something breakable," Elise joked.

"Yeah, well..." Lucy trailed off, "I really have nothing to say to that because it's absolutely true."

Elise only rolled her eyes, "If you want the chance to redeem yourself though I *might* let you pour the HCl into the buret. That should be fairly simple considering it only involves one countertop and no walking."

"You take your chances," Lucy answered.

"No. You take *your* chances," Elise said pointedly, holding out the graduated cylinder.

Lucy sighed. She still had the tiniest sliver of doubt in the back of her mind that some unpredicted, unprecedented *something* could cause even this mediocre task to go awry. But only because it was Elise holding that graduated cylinder so expectantly, Lucy took the glass instrument with the dreaded HCl, and somehow managed to get the chemical into the buret without breaking anything else.

"Pride regained," Lucy laughed as she placed the graduated cylinder back down on the counter.

And from there, the rest of the experiment seemed to go rather smoothly. They completed all of the required steps, and noted all the measurements and numbers before working on the last set of lab questions they'd been given to hand in at the end of class.

"Wait," Elise said suddenly, putting her pencil down in the middle of writing out a complex equation that Lucy was actually able to follow *and* contribute to this time, "I need your number."

"What?" Lucy asked, confused, "I just told you. We added 7.3 milliliters of HCl—"

"No," Elise cut the redhead off with a laugh, "Not the number I told you to remember. I already have that written down. I meant your *phone* number."

"Wait, what?" Lucy asked, "Why?"

"Because if I'm picking you up on Friday night I'm going to need a way of reaching you," Elise said, as if it were the most obvious answer in the word.

Lucy's mouth formed a tiny 'o' shape, but she never really gave a response as Elise pulled out her phone and placed it on the table in front of Lucy. Tentatively, the redhead picked it up, fearing for a moment that she might drop it, too, getting lost in the thoughts of how she was *finally* going to have Elise's number. It was a thought that had passed her mind multiple times, yet it was one that she never really seemed to have acted upon. Because sure, she had the number of the phone down at the barn that she'd call if she would ever be running late to work, or if she would have to miss a day of work. But having Elise's *actual* number...was definitely something that could make Lucy's day.

As soon as Lucy was finished, she handed the phone in its ice blue case back to Elise, who promptly typed something that resulted in the screen of Lucy's phone lighting up only seconds later.

Lucy read the words twice, before exclaiming, "'It's a good thing barn work doesn't involve chemical reactions'!? That's a little harsh, don't you think?"

"But it's true and you know it," Elise said very matter-of-factly.

Lucy only rolled her eyes, knowing that Elise was joking, "Let's just finish these questions. I'm on a roll here."

"I've never seen you so excited for chemistry," Elise laughed, "But I like it."

Guess I'll keep it up then, Lucy thought as she moved closer to the paper (and Elise) to read the next question, *because I like* you.

WHAT AM I GOING TO *wear*!?" Lucy wailed, staring at her mess of a closet with a distressed look on her face.

"I told you not to wait until the last minute," Kendra chided, throwing in a sigh that made her roommate seem not unlike Lucy's own mother in that very moment.

"Do I look like someone who gets things done ahead of time?" Lucy grumbled.

"Well, no," Kendra said, "But that's beside the point. I need to go meet Flynn in about an hour, but I can help you pick something out I guess."

And Kendra did indeed have to go meet Flynn.

Because it was Friday night, the night of the party. And Kendra had been invited by Flynn.

Lucy had been extremely excited for her roommate when she had heard the news. But of course, it also meant that Lucy was going to be left by herself to get ready. And getting ready for parties was something that Lucy wasn't used to. She didn't exactly *enjoy* getting ready, either. She preferred to just throw something together and show up, hoping for the best. But now, of course, since she was going with Elise (*not a date, Lucy, not a date*) she realized that her procrastination may just end up being detrimental.

"Do you know what time she's coming to pick you up?" Kendra asked.

"She gave me her number, so I assumed she'd text me. The party starts at eight, right?"

Kendra nodded, "Yeah."

That was in...two hours.

Lucy groaned. It would normally be plenty of time, but now she wasn't so sure.

"Don't worry," Kendra said, her tone positive, "With my help, we can accomplish anything."

"Someone's a bit conceited," Lucy joked, "Because with your help we usually end up taking twice as long to accomplish anything."

"That's with *schoolwork*," Kendra said pointedly, rolling her eyes, "But come on, we're wasting time, and by the look of your closet, your lack of organization skills will definitely make our job ten times harder."

At this, Lucy only laughed. She couldn't argue with that.

DESPITE LUCY'S SMALL amount of skepticism, by the time Kendra had to leave, Lucy was nearly finished.

With her roommate's help, she had decided on a purple short sleeve shirt that was off the shoulder and had a simple pattern around the hem and sleeves that had always reminded Lucy of rosemaling—Kendra insisted that it brought out her eyes. When Lucy had told her that that didn't matter, her roommate only laughed. But once she'd gotten past Kendra's relentless teasing, she'd managed to piece together the rest of what she thought was an adequate enough outfit by pairing the shirt with dark jeans and black flats.

Lucy had also considered wearing a dress, but she knew by now that it was definitely a casual party. And as much as the thought disappointed her, she didn't really think that Elise would be wearing a dress (like her previous impromptu thoughts had suggested in the middle of chem lab).

Not that it matters, Lucy reminded herself.

"I'll see you at the party then," Kendra said, grabbing her bag and heading out the door.

Lucy waved after her roommate, "Thanks again for your help."

"Not a problem," Kendra answered with a smile.

And while Lucy waited the next half an hour in anticipation, it was the buzz from the phone that she was anxiously fussing with that caused her heart to beat just a little bit faster.

Hey, I'm here. In the main parking lot.

The text made her smile instantaneously. Because...

Yeah, Elise definitely seems like the kind of person who texts in complete sentences.

Lucy's fingers flew across her phone in her eagerness to get out the door:

I'm on my way

Placing her phone in her pocket she looked once more in the mirror, tucking a stray strand of red hair behind her ear in the process. She wasn't used to leaving it down, but Elise had said before that she should wear it down more often.

And so that, I fully intend on doing, Lucy thought as she walked across campus.

Much to Lucy's surprise, it had decided to stop snowing that night, and so the sidewalk was clear as she made her way to the parking lot. Elise's silver car wasn't hard to see either. The senior had parked in the front of the lot, and kept the headlights on.

"Hey," Lucy said, after she had gotten in the car and shut the door behind her.

"Hi," Elise returned the greeting, waiting for Lucy to have her seatbelt *completely* on before putting the car in reverse.

Okay. So now what do I say to her? Lucy momentarily panicked. *It's not a date. But what if this is just awkward? Because I'm awkward...wait, let's not go there again. We've already established this. I'm awkward, and she's gorgeous.*

Filling the silence normally would have been so simple for Lucy, had it been anyone else in the seat next to her. But it instead it was Elise who broke through Lucy's thoughts, and the quiet between them, "So I know I already told you that I don't usually go to these parties, but..." Unexpectedly, Elise actually trailed off without finishing her sentence. And although the senior's eyes were focused on the road, Lucy could tell even without looking at Elise that something was bothering her.

"But what?" Lucy asked, prompting Elise to finish.

Elise only shook her head, in an attempt to dismiss her prior thought, "Never mind. It doesn't really matter."

"It does matter," Lucy insisted, "What's wrong?"

Elise sighed. But after a few seconds of silence, the senior admitted, "I haven't really been to any party. Ever."

"That's okay," Lucy said, hoping her words sounded reassuring, "I've never been to a college party before."

"So you're telling me neither of us have any clue what to expect?"

Lucy shrugged, although she wasn't sure that Elise could see it, "Harley always says to just roll with it. So that's what I plan on doing."

"That's easy for someone with socialization skills."

"Hey, don't say it like that!" Lucy protested, "You know almost all of the people who are going to be there."

In the amount of time that it had taken Lucy to finish her statement, they had arrived at the farm and Elise had parked the car. It always amazed Lucy how quickly they could get there when the means of transportation was anything but her bike or her own two feet. But...that wasn't something to focus on at the moment. Instead, she turned her attention back towards Elise, waiting for the senior's response.

"I know," Elise shrugged, addressing Lucy's reasoning, "But it's not like I ever talk to them."

"Hey," Lucy said. And something in the tone of her voice—probably the seriousness that she'd subconsciously assumed in her efforts to get the senior to *really* listen to her—caused the senior to look up and into Lucy's eyes instead of down at the steering wheel, "I'm going to be right here with you, all right?"

Elise held the redhead's gaze for a moment longer before nodding slowly, "Okay."

But after that, it seemed that this sudden, rather odd display of emotion from the senior made Lucy unsure of what to do next. She bit her lower lip, not knowing what else to say. But a moment later, Elise turned her head, taking the keys out of the ignition and deciding, "Let's head in. Before I change my mind and turn around."

And just like that, the moment—or whatever it had been—passed.

"Oh, no. I'm not letting you change your mind!" Lucy exclaimed, "You're going to this party if I have to drag you there!"

"Really, Lucy, that won't be necessary," Elise laughed as she got out of the car. But when she shut the door behind her and walked around the back of the car to meet Lucy...Lucy's brain momentarily stopped functioning.

Forget walking. All her brain could manage to do was come up with the phrase: *well damn*.

Because Elise was wearing a dress.

A freaking *dress*.

Lucy hadn't realized in the car because she'd been too anxious over what to say, and then too preoccupied with trying to reassure Elise. But now, that dress—and the gorgeous girl wearing it—was in plain sight.

It had two thin straps, although one was hidden behind that perfect platinum blonde braid, and came just to the top of the senior's knees. Elise was also wearing a pair of silver flats, but Lucy's eyes only lingered on those for a brief moment. Because that dress...it really was something. It was so simple—a solid royal blue. But the way it brought out the senior's eyes, and how it seemed to accentuate Elise in all of the right places...

"Lucy."

"Hm?" Lucy said, vaguely aware that she had just been spoken to.

Elise, clearly trying to hold back laugh, pointed over Lucy's shoulder, "The house is that way. Which would require you to turn around. And walk."

"Walk. Right," Lucy said, face heating at the senior's words.

Without further instruction, Lucy spun on her heels, with Elise following after her. And they walked in silence up to the house, although Lucy had been almost entirely positive that Elise was going to tease her about everything that had just transpired. When the senior didn't, Lucy just chalked it up to the fact that Elise was probably still nervous about the party. And that was only okay with Lucy in the sense that she didn't want to make a fool out of herself a second time. Because really, could she be any more obvious? They were supposed to be here as friends. Just. Friends.

But it seemed that it was going to take her brain a lot of convincing to even *remember* that.

All thoughts of her awkwardness, however, were long gone when get finally got inside the house. The place was complete chaos already, and Lucy felt the senior seem to almost stiffen beside her. Team members were laughing, shouting, and dancing. Music was blaring, and red cups were already visible in nearly everyone's hands.

"Well, I daresay I expected this from Flynn. But certainly not Maria or Sydney," Elise sighed, clearly rethinking her parents' trusting of the team captains to 'maintain order'.

Lucy nudged Elise's shoulder with her own, "Oh, lighten up. We're here, so you're going to have some fun, okay?"

And Lucy had been about to add to that statement when suddenly and without any warning, Flynn ran across the room from where he had been standing with Kendra and a few other teammates. Thoughts no doubt racing will all of the different things that the extremely enthusiastic junior could do to either of them at that very moment, Elise started, "Whatever you have in mind, I don't think—"

But before she could even finish her statement, with a wide grin and a mischievous look in his eyes, Flynn took his free hand (the one without the cup) and dragged Elise into the middle of the living room, despite the senior's continued protests. Once the two of them were the center of attention, Flynn exclaimed, "Elise's home!"

And the whole room erupted into a series of excited whoops and cheers.

Clearly, Flynn had already had plenty to drink, and while he stood in the center of the room holding Elise's hand in the air like she'd just won a gold medal, the senior looked like she wanted to die of embarrassment. Lucy had to fight to keep back the torrent of laughs that were threatening to spill out of her mouth, instead biting her lip to hold them in as she marched over to where Flynn was.

"Sorry, Flynn," Lucy said, pulling a now rather grateful looking Elise away from the center of the room, "We can make a dramatic entrance all by ourselves, thank you."

Flynn threw his hands in the air, "What? No, of *course* you need me to—"

At this point, Lucy was drowning out what the junior was saying, more amused than annoyed. She turned to Kendra and said, "Seriously, keep your boyfriend under control."

Kendra gave her an incredulous look, eyes wide, "What!? We're not...I mean, we're just..."

"Yeah, sure," Lucy grinned.

Payback was *wonderful*.

Ignoring the vast array of looks she got from her other teammates, Lucy led Elise into the kitchen where there were slightly less people, still not daring to laugh about the entire situation in front of the senior. And when she turned to face Elise, she could see that beneath the light dusting of freckles that she had, her face was still a deep shade of red.

"And this is what you consider to be *fun*?" Elise asked, but one corner of her mouth was turned upwards slightly, so Lucy knew that the senior wasn't entirely upset.

"Hey, it's no big deal. And see, they like you. You have nothing to worry about. So...just let go for one night and have some real fun. It'll be better when you get to talk to everyone, you know, let people in for a little bit. Let them get to know you. You'll thank me later," Lucy said, with a blatant certainty present in her voice.

"Will I?" Elise's response still held a hint of doubt.

"Of course," Lucy grinned, "Now let's find some food. I'm *starving*."

"It's my house, Lucy. If you want food I can just get you whatever you want," Elise pointed out with a laugh, her uncertainty dissolving a little more with each word.

"Well *yeah*, but they ordered pizza," Lucy turned as she talked, giving Elise no choice but to follow, "And I know you definitely don't want anyone else going through your refrigerator when they find out that I have special privileges."

"Who said anything about special privileges?" Elise shot back.

"No one," Lucy said simply. But then with a devious smile that earned her a joking glare from the senior she added, "But I *do* believe that it was very much implied."

TWO HOURS LATER, HOWEVER, Elise certainly *was* doubting the redhead's statement, while Lucy couldn't even remember what it was that she had said.

"Come dance with us," Lucy pleaded for the tenth time, after downing one of her God-knew-how-many drinks.

"I don't dance," Elise said pointedly, as the redhead sat down next to her on the sofa.

Elise had been sitting there for most of the night, and Lucy was growing increasingly more frustrated with the fact that she wouldn't participate in *anything*.

"So you won't drink with us, and you won't dance with us. You're no fun," Lucy pouted.

Elise sighed, merely repeating the answer she'd given the first time, "I don't dance, Lucy."

"You dance with horses."

"What?"

"You dance with horses," Lucy repeated. Because while she'd clearly had a lot to drink, she was surprised by the fact that she was still fairly responsive to questions. She'd been drunk only two times prior in her life (tonight was definitely going to be the third), and so knowing what she remembered of her non-sober state, this was a record for retaining some amount of sanity

"No, I heard what you said. But what in the world do you *mean*?" Elise clarified.

"Oh," Lucy said, "Dressage. Horse dancing. You dance with horses."

It made *perfect* sense.

In Lucy's mind.

"Okay," Elise said slowly, "I think I get it. But really, that's not even true."

"Of course it's true," Lucy argued.

Elise bit her lip, as if holding back a laugh, "Yeah, and you'd say that about absolutely *anything* at the moment."

"So why isn't it true, then?" Lucy challenged, although a distant voice in the back of her mind reminded her that it really *wasn't* entirely true, what with the way Elise kept such a strong hold on the reins no matter what.

"Because..." Elise paused before continuing again in a much lower voice, so quietly that Lucy could barely hear it over the raging music, "I really can't. Especially with Lance.

All he does is fight me. I'll never be able to work with him. Especially when I can barely work with Legacy."

Lucy contemplated the senior's statement for all of three seconds before an idea came to her. An idea that she also contemplated for all of three seconds (if not less). She barely knew what she was doing—all she knew that was she'd definitely had too much to drink. Yet her new idea sounded absolutely *wonderful*. So in a rush of putting her cup down and flying up from the sofa, she exclaimed, "Come on!"

And then she grabbed Elise's hand, and dragged her away from the party and out of the house.

"Lucy, where are we going?" Elise asked, but she didn't pull back or protest; she simply followed Lucy, who didn't let go of her hand until they had reached the barn.

Ignoring the blonde's small groan, Lucy burst into the barn with just as much enthusiasm than she'd had in the house, despite all of the out-of-place elements that her mind was explicitly ignoring. Which began with the obvious fact that Lucy wasn't wearing boots. In fact, she was barely wearing anything suitable to ride in at all. But she ran right to Lance's stall, haltering the tall black horse and leading him out without a lead rope before Elise could tell her otherwise.

Of course, knowing that this horse was insane and crazy, a lead rope *probably* would have been a good idea. But Lucy, not thinking clearly at all, just barely managed to get the gelding to the arena, Elise silently following.

And it was only when Lucy walked Lance over to the mounting block that Elise spoke again.

"You're not even wearing a helmet."

"Pshh," Lucy tossed her hand to the side, "I'm going to show you how this horse needs to be handled."

And...that was definitely *very* forward of her.

Even for having one too many drinks.

Holding the horse still, Lucy swung onto his back and walked him forward, her hands gripping the thick black mane at the base of the gelding's neck. She couldn't even believe that Elise was letting her do this; letting her *talk* to her like this. Because sure, Lucy had hinted at it before. And sure, Elise herself had admitted that Lucy was right. But still...

"*This* is how he needs to be worked. And *this* is how you need to ride. Not yanking and pulling back every time a horse does something wrong—*any* horse, whether it's Legacy or not. Especially with Lance. Do you see how he's not fighting me? How calm he is now? You need to *let him go*."

Lucy couldn't believe that such coherent, sincere sentences were coming from her mouth.

But they had been bottled up inside of her for so long, they just *had* to come out.

And Elise—Elise said *nothing*.

She only folded her arms, one of her hands playing with the tip of her perfect braid. And her beautiful blue eyes that read nothing but amazement at Lucy's actions, framed by slightly raised eyebrows, followed Lucy all the way around the arena.

Without really giving it much thought—although Lucy really hadn't given a thought to *anything* during these past five minutes—she asked Lance to trot. But in doing so, she instantly realized that, out of all of the not-so-smart decisions she had made this evening, this was probably among the worst of them. Because what she had forgotten was that this horse was the definition of uncomfortable and *bouncy*. And without the stability and balance of a quiet rider, an inexperienced and devious horse like Lance was definitely going to take the opportunity to break into speed and gallop away.

"Lucy, so help me— If you fall off of that horse *again*—"

Too late, Lucy thought, as she felt herself slipping to the side.

Had Lucy had a clear mind and been able to see straight, she may have been able to mange to stay on and get Lance back under control.

But her mind was spinning, and all she saw was Elise.

Elise.

Elise.

Coming closer and closer as Lance barreled forward.

And usually, the words that went through Lucy's mind when she fell were thoughts of 'oh crap', or any other phrase capable enough of replacing it.

But instead, she thought something else, and the word came out of her mouth instead of staying inside.

"Catch!" she cried, when she could hold on no longer.

And she slipped completely sideways, right in front of Elise, who immediately put her arms out to try to steady Lucy's fall. But she could only manage to catch Lucy by the shoulders, as Lucy had succeeded in falling forward onto Lance's neck before falling *off* of the horse. And neither of them were prepared for the impact that Lucy would have. So even though Elise tried to remain standing—and hold

Lucy upright in the process—the two of them were suddenly falling backwards, right into the sand of the arena.

It took Lucy all of two seconds to realize that she was sitting practically on Elise's lap, looking down at the blonde senior who had now propped herself up on her elbows, staring right back at Lucy with an expression her eyes that Lucy had never seen in them before.

And Lucy was way too disoriented to attempt to figure out what in the world it was.

But she wasn't disoriented enough to realize that she probably shouldn't remain quite exactly where she was sitting, as much as she would have liked to stay there for a few seconds longer.

So instead, she awkwardly rolled over, put her legs all the way out, and crossed them over one another. She leaned back on her elbows so that her head reached just above Elise's shoulder, mirroring the senior's posture, yet remaining close enough so that their legs still touched.

"That was like a crazy trust exercise," Lucy mused aloud.

But Elise said nothing in return.

Instead, the senior's attention seemed to have already shifted to something else; transfixed on one thing.

Lance.

The gelding was prancing around the far side of the arena, seemingly without a care in the world.

He held his head tall, parading around the long end of the arena at a trot, and then breaking into a canter once he turned. He passed the outside door of the arena, where the moon shone in and cast a single ray of light, and when his three-beat pattern carried him magnificently past it, the light danced as it was contorted for a split second by each of Lance's pitch black legs.

And then Lance was dancing all on his own.

Truly dancing, keeping his neck arched and carrying himself majestically through the same pattern.

And for a brief moment, Lucy realized that if Lance changed directions, or grew tired of circling, he might run them right over.

But Lucy wasn't going to break this moment...because Lance was beautiful.

This amazing creature, so wild at heart, and crazy, and distant, and shut out, was...*beautiful*, letting his spirit run free.

Almost as beautiful as the person sitting next to her.

Remembering where she was, Lucy vowed that she wouldn't let this opportunity go; she was going to take a chance—to become closer to Elise than she ever had been before.

And so, heart pounding, Lucy moved her head ever so slightly, and rested it against Elise's shoulder.

At first it grew rigid, beneath Lucy's head, and then it just seemed to relax. Elise seemed to relax; to let her guard down—let out a breath than Lucy didn't even realize that the senior had been holding.

No.

Elise was nothing like that magnificent horse.

She was beautifuller.

Well, not *fuller*, but more beautiful.

Beautiful-*er*.

Was that even a word?

Lucy felt that shoulder shift then, suddenly, as she heard a small laugh from somewhere slightly above her line of sight, "Only if you want it to be."

And Lucy didn't exactly know what Elise was referring to with her sudden comment, but she didn't want to ruin the moment by asking. So she just sat there, reveling in the presence that was Elise; the odd and pleasantly surprising *warmth* that was Elise, so much different from her normal icy composure.

The beauty that was Elise, letting Lucy in like she never had before.

Chapter Seventeen

When Lucy woke up, she was greeted with the sight of the back of a sofa.

And a horribly blinding light.

Squinting against the brightness, she wondered why she heard horses whinnying.

Maybe she was still dreaming. Yes, that had to be it. She had been dreaming that she was at the barn, and had ridden Lance without a saddle for some reason. Without a bridle, too. And was Elise there? Maybe she was...

"Good afternoon, Lucy."

...or maybe this wasn't a dream.

Lucy rolled over, but as soon as she shifted her position, a rather awful feeling settled in her stomach. It took all of her efforts to hold back a groan as she took in her surroundings—the upstairs lounge at none other than Akiyama Riding Academy. And Elise, who was currently standing by the side of the sofa.

"It's about time you got up," Elise said.

"Ugh, what time is it? How long was I asleep?" Lucy asked.

"It's one. PM. And as far as how *long* you were asleep, I could only manage to carry you up here by midnight."

"Wait, really?" Lucy asked.

"Yes," Elise confirmed.

"No, like, you had to *carry* me up here?" Lucy clarified, face already burning.

"Well, if you want to be technical about it, no. But I consider having to hold you up and keep you standing close enough to carrying you."

"Oh," Lucy's face was crimson now, she was sure of it, "And how much of a fool did I make of myself last night? Honest, I really didn't plan on drinking. Was I annoying? Oh, who am I kidding, I *know* I was a pain. But please, please tell me I didn't do anything too stupid?"

Elise sighed, "Well, you spent the entire night trying to get me to dance. And drink. And then you tell me if you consider getting on a maniac project horse bareback and bridle-less *without a helmet*, to be a stupid idea?"

Well, now that Elise mentioned it, it did seem a little more familiar than just a dream...

"Um," Lucy grinned sheepishly, "It seemed like a good idea at the time."

"Not to mention the fact that you kept blabbering away about who knew what all the time I was trying to *catch* Lance, which only succeeded in making him all antsy and nervous. And trying to get him back in his stall while simultaneously trying to keep you from letting the rest of the horses loose because you wanted to go ride out on some quest to find your sister—who I'm fairly certain doesn't even *exist*—wasn't exactly a task I'd call easy," Elise continued, mouth now pressed into a thin line and arms crossed.

Now *that* part Lucy couldn't remember at all.

"Yeah, no, I don't have a sister," Lucy offered meekly, "So I honestly have no explanation for that one."

While Elise stood there shaking her head disapprovingly (yes, Lucy felt quite like a reprimanded and ashamed child at the moment), the redhead desperately tried to remember the events where her mind when blank. But her hazy memory left off after...

"Oh, right. And before all of that I fell. And I...uh...landed on you. And then...then I don't really remember anything else."

"Well, you're right. That definitely happened," Elise said.

And Lucy didn't know quite how to respond after that.

She was still on the sofa, the senior standing above her. And although the features of Elise face showed that she was most definitely upset about what had happened, all Lucy saw were two beautiful blue eyes that she could get lost in all afternoon.

Stupid thoughts. Stop staring at her and start apologizing.

Lucy sighed, "I'm sorry. I screwed it up, I guess. No, I don't guess. I *know* I screwed it up. I'm a complete mess."

"Hey," Elise said, her voice softening as she dropped her arms to her sides, "You don't have to apologize for anything. I was just...worried, that's all."

The senior's comment caused Lucy to hesitate momentarily before saying, "You were?"

"Well, it's not every day that I get to watch an intoxicated person attempt to ride an insane horse," Elise shrugged, looking down at the floor rather than at Lucy, "And it...*you*...scared me."

"Oh," Lucy said, feeling ten times more horrible about what had happened than she had before, "Well, then I'm definitely still sorry."

"I already said you don't have to be sorry," Elise told her, "And besides, there's something else I need to say to you, anyway."

"Which is?" Lucy questioned.

"Thanks."

Lucy looked at Elise for a moment, attempting to understand what the senior meant. But she couldn't think of anything, "Okay, I'm confused."

Elise sighed, "I know you probably don't remember. But one of the first things you said to me last night was that I should let go for a night. And you said it would be better when I let people in for a little bit. That I'd thank you later."

"So then...you did?" Lucy asked.

Elise drew in a breath, but smiled slightly before she said, "Yeah. Kind of."

"And...was it better?" Lucy asked hesitantly.

Elise seemed to contemplate the question for a moment. But she nodded her head as she spoke, sounding completely confident, although Lucy still couldn't put her finger on what had happened to make the senior answer that way, "Yes. Yes, it definitely was."

LUCY FOUND HERSELF in the main parking lot of the college campus only half an hour later. Elise had driven her back to campus after Lucy had finally found the strength to walk again (which of course was after a necessary trip to the nearest bathroom, a borrowed change of clothes, and a makeshift meal that Elise insisted she had to at least *attempt* to swallow before going anywhere else).

And yet, sitting there in the car with the senior, in a silence that was actually more peaceful than uncomfortable, the events of the morning and the few that she could remember from the night before slowly melted away. Because instead, they were suddenly replaced with the realization that this was most likely the last time she was going to see the senior before they came back from winter break. Which meant no more chem lab—she'd certainly gone out with a bang (or a crash, really) with that one.

The only time Lucy would get to see Elise in the spring semester would be for wrk, or whenever else she'd be at the barn for her lessons.

Holding back the disappointed sigh that almost escaped, Lucy instead attempted to sound a little more cheery, "Well..." she said finally, "Thanks for the ride. And...thanks for going to the party with me. Even though I totally understand if you don't want to go to a party with me ever again. I know *I* wouldn't want to go to a party with me ever again if that was the case—"

Elise cut Lucy off with a laugh, "Okay, this experience may have ruined me for ever going to a party again. *But*...if the opportunity ever arises and you *promise* to not go as crazy, I might make an exception."

Lucy's whole face lit up, pure elation replacing any of her previous disappointment about the spring semester, "Really!?"

"I said *might*," Elise reminded her.

"Good enough for me," Lucy grinned.

The two were silent again after that, neither exactly sure of what to say next. Or, at least, *Lucy* didn't know what to say next. But instead of having to come up with something, Elise surprised her by speaking first, "So I guess I'll...see you after winter break?"

Lucy nodded, "Yeah. A whole month of lots of sleep, no work, and no school."

And no Elise.

"Thursdays and Sundays will definitely be much less eventful around here," Elise offered Lucy a small smile.

Was that the senior's way of saying she was going to...miss Lucy's company?

Lucy merely gave a small shrug, "Is Kai filling in for me?"

Elise nodded, "Yeah."

"Just make sure he gives Dee some extra attention," Lucy instructed, thinking of the little chestnut mare who she was definitely going to miss as well.

"Kai's got enough to worry about as it is," Elise said, "But I wouldn't mind."

Lucy smiled. Although in the moment it may have seemed silly, it really did mean a lot to her, "Thanks."

A few more awkward seconds passed in which Lucy didn't know what she should be doing or saying. Should she just open the door and get out? Say a quick goodbye and leave? Maybe she would have if Elise had had her attention on anything else. Normally, when things got awkward between the two of them Elise's gaze would shift toward her hands; out the window; *anywhere* besides Lucy. But Elise just seemed to be staring at her—not quite in the way that Lucy had many times before—but, Lucy hoped, maybe in a slightly similar way.

"I didn't really get the chance to tell you last night, but you looked nice," Elise paused then, one hand flying to the end of her braid in a rather unusual display of nervousness, "Sorry. That's an awkward thing to say, I guess. Because you *still* look nice. I mean, you always look nice. But..." Elise trailed off, ducking her head, "God, I sound like you now."

Lucy bit her lip to keep from laughing. Elise was adorable when she was rambling—and even better yet, when she was rambling about Lucy.

"Thank you," Lucy said finally, but then continued, "You looked nice too."

Not to mention the fact that I already told her she was freaking gorgeous that one day whether I meant to or not, and that she's caught me staring more times than I can count.

At Lucy's comment, Elise's face seemed to flush slightly, although Lucy regarded that as something that she *herself* would have done. It seemed as though, for an entire minute, they had switched places. But the moment passed when Elise regained her composure, echoed Lucy's thank you, and followed it with something along the lines of the fact that she had to get back to the house and make sure that everything had been cleaned up and put back in order.

"Okay," Lucy said, as she got out of the car, "I'll see you after break then."

Elise gave a small wave before turning out of the parking lot, and Lucy didn't start walking back to her dorm room until the silver car was out of sight.

Well, that was quite *an eventful night. And morning,* Lucy though as she headed for her building.

It hadn't been a date...but it had definitely felt like one. Especially with the giddy feeling she now had. And despite the fact that she *knew* she had nearly made a complete disaster of the night.

When Lucy walked into her room, all springy steps and smiling, Kendra only laughed, "Was your date *that* much fun?"

"Not a date," Lucy said, her voice a little too cheery.

Kendra rolled her eyes, "Well when the two of you *disappeared—*"

Lucy spun on her heels, quick to defend the *certain* implications of Kendra's statement, "We were *at the barn.* Nothing happened."

This only made Kendra laugh harder, "I was just joking. Sheesh. Where's Harley to calm you down when you need him? And really, what in the world were you doing at the *barn?*"

At this, Lucy sat down on her bed with a sigh, "Long story."

"Oh, please. Do tell," Kendra ordered, plopping herself down next to Lucy.

"I may or may not have had a *little* too much to drink," Lucy said.

"Well, I was there for *that.* But continue."

"And I thought it would be a great idea to go down to the barn and try to show Elise how Lance—this project horse—needed to be worked," Lucy said, "Which...may or may not have ended with me falling off of the horse."

"I can see that you make brilliant decisions while under the influence," Kendra grinned jokingly.

"Oh, shut up," Lucy said, "It was only the third time."

"*Only* the third?" Kendra laughed.

"Yes."

"What, falling off a horse, or being drunk?"

Lucy glared, even though she knew her roommate was still only teasing her, "I think you know the answer to that question. But look, it doesn't matter anymore. What matters now is that I need to finish packing. My parents are coming to get me tomorrow, and while you're completely ready to leave, my side of the room looks like a tornado went through it."

Kendra sighed, "Okay, fine. I'll help you."

"Did someone say they need help?"

Both girls turned their heads at the same time, to find none other than Owen standing in the open doorway. Their fellow freshman certainly had a habit of sticking his nose in other people's business—intentionally or not, though Lucy wholeheartedly believed that he had only the best intentions in mind. And an open door was far from a deterrence for Owen. It was merely an invitation to enter with a only small announcement of arrival.

"Uh, not exactly—" Lucy started.

But Kendra, taking one look at the mess of Lucy's side of the room, cut Lucy off and said, "If you're free, we'd *love* some help."

Lucy rolled her eyes. She actually didn't mind Owen helping, but really, did Kendra not trust that the two of them could finish this together? Did Kendra really think her side of the room was *that* much of a mess that it would take three people to finish the task?

But when Lucy turned around to assess the cluttered desk, her tiny closet with most of the clothing half on and half off of hangers, the large pile of clothes in a heap by her bed that she'd set aside to fold a few nights ago, and who knew what else *under* her bed, she realized that maybe...they couldn't finish in time with only the two of them working at it.

"What do you need me to do?" Owen asked.

"I say we start by folding clothes," Lucy decided.

"Agreed," Kendra said.

"But really," Lucy warned jokingly, "I hope you know what you're signing up for here. I claim no responsibility if you get swallowed by a pile of clothing or trip over a shoe."

Kendra only rolled her eyes, and Owen laughed. But with three people helping and three very different voices to make it all the more interesting, Lucy had a feeling that cleaning this mess wouldn't be too horrible after all.

TWO HOURS, FOUR PACKED boxes, and a very *odd* conversation later, the three were sitting on the floor, much too tired from cleaning (and also, most likely, the party and all of its still subtly present side effects) to move another muscle.

"What even *is* the meaning of pre-calc, anyway?" Kendra laughed, "I mean, yes, we suffered through it this semester. But in the long run, is it even going to *do* anything for me?"

"Well, it might. Or it might not," Owen said, "But maybe...that's just the meaning of life."

"What?" both Lucy and Kendra said together, looking at their fellow freshman sideways.

"Just what I said, maybe that's the meaning of life," Owen repeated, looking very content with his answer.

"Do you always talk in riddles like this?" Kendra asked.

"Yeah, why?" Owen asked.

"And people just accept it without questioning it?" Lucy asked.

"Yeah, why?"

"And they understand without getting *frustrated* by it!?" Kendra exclaimed, but she was laughing. And so was Owen.

"Yeah, why?"

Owen could act like such a child sometimes, but it struck the two girls funny. Or at least, Lucy thought it was funny. And she also thought that it was so peculiar that, even though Owen sometimes acted much younger than his age, he seemed to know things—important *moral* things—that not a single college student would normally take into consideration.

"Why!?" Owen repeated again, "Why all the questions?"

"Because we have no idea where that came from!" Kendra laughed.

"What, the meaning of life?" Owen asked.

Lucy and Kendra nodded their heads in unison.

"And what it has to do with pre-calc," Lucy added.

"Oh," Owen said cheerily, unbothered by their blatant confusion and seeming to genuinely want to explain himself and help them understand, "They relate because maybe obscure things matter even more than we realize. Maybe even the simplest things that we find useless—or that we take for granted—will end up giving our lives meaning by becoming more important to us than we ever could have imagined."

"Huh," Lucy said, taking Owen's words into consideration. Because these ideas, or musings, or *whatever* they were...actually had Lucy quite intrigued. And they didn't just apply only to the terrible pre-calculus class they had all suffered through—Owen was only using the one example to get to the bigger picture. So maybe what he was saying really was true. Because she had never thought about it like that before.

"Okay then, philosopher," Kendra crossed her arms jokingly, "If you're so good at this, then do you have a theory for the meaning of *everything*?"

Owen shrugged, "I don't know. Pick a topic—I'm willing to try."

Kendra's look of pure thought told Lucy that her roommate was actually interested in coming up with a challenge, "What's the meaning of love. What *is* love?"

Lucy watched as Owen contemplated the question for a moment. And the response that he came up with was one that neither Lucy nor Kendra ever would have guessed, "Love is...putting someone else's needs before your own."

And no matter how long Lucy thought about Owen's statement, she couldn't really figure out what it meant.

At least, not when she'd only first heard it.

But she couldn't figure out what it meant before Owen abruptly stood and said he was late for a last minute meeting.

And she couldn't figure out what it meant before she fell asleep.

She couldn't figure out what it meant before breakfast the next morning, or before Kendra left at noon, or even before she had all of the boxes in the back of her family's old SUV.

And she *still* couldn't figure out what it meant until an hour later—in the middle of the ride home.

Love is...putting someone else's needs before your own.

Like maybe how...Elise had agreed to go to the party with Lucy even though she was clearly terrified of going. Like how Elise had *actually* tried to catch Lucy when she had fallen off of Lance, even if it ended with both of them landing in the dirt. Like how Elise had spent the *entire* night—and morning—making sure that Lucy was okay, when she could have just sent Lucy back off to her dorm room.

So then did that mean...did Elise...love her?

No.

There was no way *that* was true. Because love was...a whole other, larger entity itself, right? More than just a crush, or saying that she *liked* someone. And there was no way that Elise felt the same about Lucy as Lucy felt about Elise.

But...Elise *cared* about her. That much Lucy was certain of. Especially now that the senior had admitted that what had happened the night of the party had worried her more than it had annoyed her.

And remembering all of this, the seemingly distant events from two nights ago, the events had had previously seemed so foggy, somehow became more vivid.

Like that one comment...what was it again? It was on the tip of her tongue. Right there in the back of her mind, but slightly out of reach...

Only if you want it to be.

There.

That's what it was.

Lucy had compared Elise to Lance. She had thought—and definitely *said* without realizing it—that Elise was 'beautifuller'.

Because it wasn't a word.

Only if you want it to be.

Lucy could only smile thinking about that. Sure, she hadn't meant to say it. But still—it was no wonder that Elise had been flustered in the car yesterday morning. She must have definitely remembered that. And now it was Lucy's face that was flushing.

She had only said it because Elise had let her in...

Oh.

Realization hit Lucy suddenly. *Now* she understood what Elise had said to her yesterday—how the senior had thanked her, said that she had let go and let people in.

Kind of.

Kind of, meaning that it wasn't just *anyone* that Elise had let in. It was *Lucy* who Elise had let closer; closer than Lucy had ever been to the senior before. Letting Lucy sit there, next to Elise, with her head on the senior's shoulder.

And if she continued to analyze the conversation they'd had earlier, she remembered that she had asked Elise if it had been better. If it had been better to let go, and let her in instead of keeping her at a distance—if it had been better to close the gap between them, even if it was only for the smallest of moments. And Elise had answered...

Yes, it definitely was.

Don't miss out!

Visit the website below and you can sign up to receive emails whenever Hannah Conrad publishes a new book. There's no charge and no obligation.

https://books2read.com/r/B-A-PDRK-MVPLB

BOOKS 2 READ

Connecting independent readers to independent writers.

Did you love *The Perfect Distance*? Then you should read *The Journal of Irene Summerset*[1] by Hannah Conrad!

[2]

Darci and Benni are about to embark on an adventure of a lifetime when they find themselves investigating the mysterious disappearance of Professor Summerset.

Darci and Benni's summer program experience is about to teach them more than they had bargained for when a professor at the university mysteriously disappears. Upon finding Professor Summerset's journal, they are thrust into a world beyond anything they could have imagined – an eighth continent known as Akiyama. However, Darcy and

---

1. https://books2read.com/u/bMX6Ak

2. https://books2read.com/u/bMX6Ak

Benni's search for the missing professor will prove harder than they could have ever imagined. In this secret land, wonders and dangers alike will meet them at every turn and they have only the professor's journal to aid them. In a society that calls the rest of the world forbidden, the friends will need to trust each other even more as they navigate through this place of magic with talking animals, wizards, magical horses, a mysterious ruler and a dangerous organization. They must rely on each other, find the professor and hope that the journal will be enough to lead them back home.

Also by Hannah Conrad

Akiyama Quest
The Journal of Irene Summerset

Apprentice of the Night Empress
The Orphan
The Apprentice

Black Ribbon
Black Ribbon

Magical Girls
Magical Girls
Magical Resolve
Magical Healing

New Tokyo Superheroes
Superhero, Cinderella

Sherlock Holmes Fantasia
The Mystery of the Red Rose

The Demon Prince
Demon Blood and Angel Feathers
Magic Schools and Secret Powers

The Perfect Distance
The Perfect Distance
Legacy

The Wilds
Into the Skies
Children of the Wilds

Standalone
The Ravens

A Book of Fantastic Tales
The Legend of Lady Robin Hood
An Assassin and Her Unicorn
Sherlock Holmes, Vampire
Moon Magic
When the Pretty Horses
A Study in Souling

About the Author

Hannah Conrad has been been passionately writing and reading her entire life. Early on, she became enthralled by fantasy novels as well as by horses. She desires to write the kind of books she would want to read. Hannah specializes in portal fantasy and fantasy books involving horses. Her main series take place in the Akiyama Quest verse.

About the Publisher

Dimension Seal Studios is a new, multimedia studio that aims to bring new and engaging stories into the world of entertainment. The studio was founded in 2019 by Hannah Conrad and Walker McMullin.

With an emphasis on film, television, and literature, Dimension Seal Studios creates fresh and entertaining stories in a variety of genres. Our stories encompass a wide variety of genres and we have something for everyone. Check out Dimension Seal Studios' works and meet your new favorite characters!